Joanna had climbed to [...] she could survey the idyllic countryside. She drank in the lush green of the meadows and woodlands below, and the sheep that dotted the land in ever-changing patterns.

Then, out of nowhere, Sir Lucas appeared.

His gaze settled on her with disturbing intensity. "You are alone."

"Indeed, sir. I have experienced not a speck of difficulty," she said, then added under her breath, "until this moment."

His lazy grin ought to have prepared her, but it didn't. His hands caught her head, and she knew the taste and feel of his lips against hers. It was shocking. Even more shocking. she found herself melting against his lean body, fitting her soft curves into his firm length. Quivers ran through her as she wondered at the trembling that flowed over her.

And now Joanna realized her solitude had trapped her, and there was no escaping advances she ached to meet. . . .

The Abandoned Rake

by

Emily Hendrickson

A SIGNET BOOK

SIGNET
Published by the Penguin Group
Penguin Books USA Inc., 375 Hudson Street,
New York, New York 10014, U.S.A.
Penguin Books Ltd, 27 Wrights Lane,
London W8 5TZ, England
Penguin Books Australia Ltd, Ringwood,
Victoria, Australia
Penguin Books Canada Ltd, 10 Alcorn Avenue,
Toronto, Ontario, Canada M4V 3B2
Penguin Books (N.Z.) Ltd, 182–190 Wairau Road,
Auckland 10, New Zealand

Penguin Books Ltd, Registered Offices:
Harmondsworth, Middlesex, England

First published by Signet, an imprint of Dutton Signet,
a division of Penguin Books USA Inc.

First Printing, June, 1995
10 9 8 7 6 5 4 3 2 1

 REGISTERED TRADEMARK—MARCA REGISTRADA

Printed in the United States of America

Chapter One

"I confess I had not thought freedom to be so onerous," Joanna Winterton said with a sigh to her remarkably cheerful Aunt Caroline. Joanna stood by the window, fingering the festoon shades that had been lowered to near eye-level. She turned away from the enticements offered by the world without and faced her aunt with a heartfelt sigh.

"Anyone would think that a young woman who—it must be agreed by all—is passably pretty and possessed of lovely manners would not entertain such blue-deviled thoughts." Aunt Caroline paused in the act of inserting a needle into her piece of embroidery and gave her beloved niece a thoughtful stare.

"Passably pretty, indeed," Joanna said, grinning at her aunt's choice of words, her blue eyes sparkling with amusement. "You know how black makes me look a veritable quiz."

"Well, I think it was quite odious of your betrothed to go aloft right in the middle of the Season. What a nasty war, to kill our fine young men without regard to their families and futures." Aunt Caroline emphasized her feelings with a sad shake of her head.

"I doubt if Napoleon gave that a thought in his ambitious schemes," Joanna said with a wry look at her sometimes absurd aunt. "And I suspect that Mr. Underhill went dashing into battle without the least expectation that he might be killed."

"It is not as though you entertained the least fondness for Mr. Underhill. And in the first place," Aunt Caroline continued while stabbing her needle into the air, "I think it was utterly frightful of your father to insist on honoring that silly agreement made while you were still in the cradle. To demand you marry Robert Underhill! You had not seen him in ages and I daresay not liked what you heard about him—all that racketing about in a most scandalous manner. He was *not* the man for you, my dear."

Joanna bestowed a wry smile on her aunt while smoothing down the soft black of her gown. "I feel an utter fraud, wearing black for someone I scarce knew and liked not at all. I feel so dreadful. Such respect I am given! Such consideration! Society treats me with enormous compassion. How scandalized they would be to know how I truly feel."

"I believe we had best attend some function—lest they believe you have sunk into a decline," her aunt said with a wise nod.

Joanna gave an inelegant snort, then turned a shrewd gaze on her aunt. "When and where?"

"This evening!" her aunt cried with childlike delight. "I accepted Lady Jersey's kind invitation to her little party."

"Which will not be the least *little*, and you know it. I suppose I can endure it, if only to get out of this house and mingle with others for a time. I declare, if I receive one more consoling pat on the hand and another round of soothing words to the effect that my life is not over, I shall have mild hysterics."

Joanna drifted across the room to take a seat by her aunt, inspecting the delicate needlework with an expert eye.

"Perhaps you might wear your silver-gray figured muslin with black gloves?" her aunt suggested mildly while holding up a piece of yarn for Joanna's approval. When her niece nodded at the choice, Caroline threaded her needle and began to work anew.

"Tomorrow," Joanna promised, returning to the matter of the color of her gown. "I had best be garbed as a would-be widow this evening. I look forward to a little entertainment and perhaps a bit of gossip, since I most likely should not dance." She paused a moment, then idly inquired, "Do you think Sir Lucas Montfort will be there with his timid little bride-to-be? I should like to see them together. I have heard all manner of things about the pair."

Easily diverted, Aunt Caroline chuckled. "If ever there was a mismatch, that is it. The premier London rake with a country mouse? It will never do. He needs someone with spirit to match his own, not a dab of a girl who will shrink in terror when he so much as looks at her, never mind what she will do once in bed."

"Aunt Caroline! The things you say," Joanna said, choking back her laughter.

"Well, and so it is true," Aunt Caroline said in defense of her words. "Would you like to go to their wedding with me? For I shall not believe he actually weds the chit unless I see it with my own eyes."

Joanna thought about the lean, clever, and wildly handsome man she had met on several occasions and gave a delicious shiver. His thick thatch of silver-blond hair fascinated her almost as much as his dark, luminous eyes—such an unusual combination and so very attractive. He had a wicked tongue and a reputation to match, yet she suspected there was not a woman alive who did not find him desirable and appealing. He was spoiled, of course, and much too accustomed to having his own way. And his intended bride, Drusilla Thorne, had to be the *most* insipid of the girls making their come-outs this season. She was docile and obedient, however—no doubt a requirement for a rake's sit-at-home wife.

"I believe I shall join you," Joanna said. "I feel much the same. I cannot but think they will be one of those couples who marry, breed an heir, then go their separate ways." Joanna paused, looking at her aunt. "Does it shock you that I speak of breeding?"

"You have never been in the common way, my dear. I suppose that is my fault, for it has been such a delight to have the rearing of you that I have treated you more as an equal than a child. How happy I am that your father allowed me the joy of bringing you up when your mother died. It is not every man who will turn over a child to his dead wife's sister to raise, particularly a maiden lady with no expectations of marriage."

"Which serves to illustrate how stupid men are, to ignore you because of a trifling limp and miss that shrewd and agreeable wit you possess." Joanna placed a fond hand over her aunt's and exchanged a perceptive look. "I believe we make an excellent pair, the two of us. This evening we can gaze upon Sir Lucas and his intended, Miss Thorne, with amusement and perhaps a shred of pity. I wonder if Miss Thorne's parents have arranged this marriage for her? 'Twould be a likely thing."

"Most likely indeed." Aunt Caroline glanced across the room at the longcase clock, then put her embroidery into the workbasket at her side. "Time to prepare for dinner, then on to Lady Jersey's little party."

She rose and shook out her skirts while giving her beloved niece an assessing look. "I should like you to make a splash this evening. Mind you, nothing dramatic, but it would be lovely should a nice gentleman see you, take note, and perhaps pursue his interest. You will encourage such a regard should it happen? I'd not wish you to end up your life alone and lonely." Then she shook her head and added, "Not that I have been lonely, what with you around. But you might not be so fortunate as I."

Thinking that she was the one who had been fortunate, Joanna followed her aunt from the room.

Following a modest but tasty dinner, the two set out for the Jersey party in high spirits. Joanna had worn her best black gown, the one with tiers of black lace on the skirt and across her shoulders, with the added touch of a blush pink rose on her bodice. Aunt Caroline had dressed herself in a delicate rose sarcenet with a single flounce at the bottom of the skirt and a simple lace collar at the neckline that managed to look both demure and fashionable.

Joanna curtsied to Lady Jersey and her earl, then followed her aunt into the vast ballroom after accepting her program from the master of ceremonies. She studied the two pages that listed the order of the dances and provided a space where a gentleman might scratch his name, and was not alert to those before her.

A gentleman backed into her path and she bumped into him. An upward glance revealed his identity even before he turned around. No one else in London possessed such a mane of silvery hair.

"Sir Lucas," she said politely, hating her sudden breathlessness when he turned to face her—for he was far too close for any unmarried woman's peace of mind, "I do beg your pardon for not avoiding you."

"You do it very well," he replied after a sweeping glance at her black gown and eyeing the blush pink rose nestled at the very center of her low neckline. "I believe you have managed to completely avoid me this entire Season. What a pity, Miss Winterton." He raised his brows after bestowing that easy smile on her, the sort that must cause any number of female hearts to flutter madly. It certainly had an effect on hers.

Joanna was not surprised that he knew her name, for she was quite certain she had been gossiped about for some weeks. She *was* surprised that he put her name with her face, however. "It was not deliberate, I assure you," she countered, then wondered how she dared to exchange such words with this man.

"You shall prove it by granting me a dance. Surely your *mourning* must be over by now," he said with a trace of mockery. "After all, you were not wed to the man." He raked her with a cynical gaze, one that set her back up.

"Odious creature," she said quietly. "You would have me cause a minor scandal?"

"Shall we try it and see what ensues? Or are you too faint-hearted to dance with me?" His look challenged her even more than his words.

Since this was precisely how she felt at the moment, Joanna firmed her lips, then said, "Thank you for the so gracious invitation to dance. How could I possibly refuse?" She checked her program and took note of the country dances. "Shall we say the third dance?"

She dipped a sweeping curtsy, then hurried after her aunt, wondering what in the world had possessed her to accept that ... that *rake's* demand that she dance with him. It had to be those eyes, she decided. They dared her, taunted her, even as they teased. Were there ever such eyes as his? She extracted her ivory fan from the black-beaded reticule on her wrist and opened it. The Jersey ballroom had suddenly become very warm.

"And what was that little contretemps about, my dear?" Aunt Caroline inquired mildly. She had most likely not bothered to return to her niece's side because she felt Joanna capable of handling anything that came her way. It was well Aunt Caroline did not know how Joanna had trembled at his look, the inflection in his voice.

"I bumped into him—although it was his fault, for he would back into my path without looking. And when I apologized for not avoiding him, he demanded that I grant him a dance. *And* he had taken note of my black garb," Joanna concluded in a huff, fanning herself with great vigor.

"And you will dance with him?"

"Indeed." Joanna closed her fan with a snap. "I granted him one dance—I could not permit him to think I am afraid of him. Poor Miss Thorne, to be required to deal with that man on a daily basis."

"Indeed," Aunt Caroline murmured as she turned slightly to gaze at the man who had managed to turn her niece into a perfectly splendid bundle of nerves.

The third dance arrived all too soon to suit Joanna. She had half-hoped that Sir Lucas would forget his request, but her hopes were dashed when he purposefully crossed the room to bow before her aunt, then Joanna.

"You will permit your niece to dance?" he inquired with the assurance of one who is never denied.

"Indeed, Sir Lucas. I trust that her reputation is such that it will stand the connection, however momentary," Aunt Caroline said with what was, for her, great daring. "I shall do my best to squelch any talk about impropriety, you may be certain. It is high time that Joanna be permitted to leave her state of imposed mourning."

"Quite so," he replied with a glimmer of amusement in those clever brown eyes.

Joanna permitted him to lead her out onto the floor, joining the line of young ladies with her emotions well in control. She raised her gaze from the polished floor to find him watching her closely. His was a disconcerting gaze, for it revealed nothing of his inner thoughts, but seemed to seek hers.

She curtsied, then began the simple steps, advancing, retreating, allowing him to twirl her about in elegant rhythm. Even through her gloves, she sensed a firmness in his clasp, a strength, if you would, she had certainly not found in Mr. Underhill.

While the steps of the dance were familiar, the sensations she experienced were not. Every time her gaze clashed with his, she felt an odd stirring within her. She finally decided that it must be something she'd eaten at dinner, although nothing had been unusual—then.

When she glanced about the room she could detect no hostile looks nor censure in the eyes of the dowagers. Aunt Caroline must have been busy suggesting it was time for Joanna to resume life, perhaps even offering the notion that Sir Lucas was nobly assisting in the cause. He was considered safe now that he was a betrothed man. And a man less likely to be safe, Joanna could not imagine.

He stared down into her eyes when the pattern of the dance required them to draw close, hands raised gracefully up high. "I shan't eat you, you know."

"I would not permit it, sirrah," she quietly countered. "I am no meek and mild miss." Their steps retreated and she reclaimed her hand even as she wondered what in the world had possessed her to utter such sentiments. If his considering expression was anything to go by, she might be required to prove her rash statement. Horrors!

Fortunately, the dance concluded shortly after that and, after sweeping her best curtsy to him, she turned away in hopes of escaping to her aunt's side.

She found her elbow firmly clasped and Sir Lucas at her side, escorting her—as was only proper, she reminded her fluttering nerves.

"You are an uncommon girl, Miss Winterton. Mr. Underhill is to be greatly pitied." Sir Lucas appeared oblivious to the curious looks from the gentlemen, the avid stares of the dowagers, and the timid glances from the girls making their come-outs.

"He is no longer among us," Joanna managed to say, puzzled at his remark and uncomfortable at being the co-object of so much speculation. She had endured quite enough of that this Season.

"Precisely what I meant, poor chap. I wonder who shall

have the pleasure of your company in future? Surely you do not consider your life over because that wastrel has gone aloft. Consider yourself well rid of him."

"I had heard you possessed a wicked tongue. I was unaware that description included speaking ill of the dead." Joanna glanced about her, wondering how to extricate herself without saying something truly nasty to this odious creature, even if he was correct in his summation of Robert Underhill's character. "I shan't detain you for I see Miss Thorne has entered the room. This has been . . . most interesting, Sir Lucas."

She curtsied again and whirled about to find herself but a few steps from her aunt.

A surreptitious glance served to reveal Sir Lucas attending his bride-to-be with proper deference.

"Well, that seemed innocent enough," Aunt Caroline said mildly. "You appear annoyed at something. Surely he did not dare to say a word out of line?"

"He said I was well rid of Mr. Underhill," Joanna muttered in a soft aside.

"Did he, now?" Aunt Caroline turned a thoughtful gaze upon the handsome gentleman and continued, "I had not thought him so perceptive."

"Aunt Caroline," Joanna said in scandalized accents. Then she nodded. "I could not tell him how right he was in his assessment, of course, but Sir Lucas did surprise me."

"Indeed," Aunt Caroline said, then guided Joanna along to where several dowagers sat, dissecting the character and dress of the people about them. "At least my friends understand your situation. They agree with me that you did no wrong in performing that quite acceptable country dance with Sir Lucas. Indeed, it was frightfully thoughtful of the man to take pity on your plight."

Joanna choked back words to the effect that she did not desire any gentleman's pity, least of all Sir Lucas Montfort's.

She consented to dance a second time with a polite young man who had not known Mr. Underhill and treated Joanna like she was arising from deep mourning for a husband.

Following an experience that she found rather lowering, Joanna persuaded Aunt Caroline that the hour was late and they both needed their sleep. Aunt Caroline was very easy to lead.

The following days brought no great improvement. Her aunt's stratagem had failed. Again Joanna found herself the object of pity and consolation. And she felt such a fraud.

When she went into gray and lavender gowns, the dowagers praised her for her courage to fashion a new life and future for herself. It seemed she could do no wrong in their eyes. She attributed most of her standing to her good aunt's character. Having a viscount for a father who also had pots of money most likely did not hurt, either.

She had observed that people who were well to grass could behave slightly more scandalously than poorer folk. Not that she was scandalous, not in the least. She wished she *might* do something to create a stir. Life was so boring that she thought she might suffocate under the sympathy of all the dowagers and those perky young girls making their come-outs this Season.

They most likely appreciated the withdrawal of one who might be only passingly pretty but possessed a sizable dowry. Joanna had no illusions about her position, and even welcomed the trickle of fortune hunters who began to frequent her aunt's drawing room these days.

They were all of a muchness, these men. They dressed well and had lovely manners, but she could sense a desperation concealed beneath their polished exteriors. Most likely they would never seek marriage unless driven. A little mousing about by Aunt Caroline brought their true straits to light. They all were perilously close to bankruptcy and debtor's prison.

"Captain Fortesque, how charming to see you again," Joanna murmured as yet another of these gentlemen sought her attention.

The captain was no different from all the others, showering Joanna with pretty compliments, offering a modest posy, and staying to tea, as Aunt Caroline always offered a substantial one. She felt she performed a kindness in feeding the poor young men.

A half-pay officer was not a good prospect for marriage,

even if he was as dashing and handsome as may be. Yes, an heiress had a difficult time of it, Joanna decided while she watched the young captain consume the bountiful tea spread before him.

Should an impressionable heiress meet up with the gallant captain, he would most likely carry the day—and the heiress off to Scotland as well. The notion amused her.

"Surely you plan to marry at some future time, Miss Winterton," the captain implored before taking another bite of his watercress sandwich.

"Perhaps," Joanna said vaguely. " I would not be pushed into marriage as some, like Miss Drusilla Thorne."

"Yes," interposed Aunt Caroline, "one would think an heiress could have the choosing of a husband instead of having Sir Lucas thrust at her. Must be utterly terrified, poor dear," Aunt Caroline concluded with a pious and most saintly sigh.

"I had not realized Miss Thorne was not eager to wed a man who must be admitted as being most handsome. An heiress as well, you say?" The captain finished the dainty sandwich, then took another, polishing off the last of the substantial tea while deep in reflection.

"Indeed, Captain Fortesque," Aunt Caroline said earnestly, "Miss Thorne is quite an heiress, being her father's only child. She is to inherit not only a sizable income but also a vast estate, for her thrifty and intelligent parent has done extremely well with his investments."

"Really?" the intrigued captain replied. He made his farewells shortly thereafter, whereupon Joanna collapsed in laughter against the pillows behind her on the sofa.

"Really, indeed. You *are* a naughty one, setting the captain to speculate on a girl who is another's intended. That is truly placing the cat among the pigeons."

"If she is the widgeon I suspect, the coming weeks could be interesting," was Aunt Caroline's bland reply.

And they were, from that standpoint. There was no lessening of sympathy toward Joanna. If anything, the dowagers fussed over her even more. Lady Jersey—who, after all, was not that much older than Joanna—offered more than most.

Joanna finally decided that if she returned the family betrothal ring, that might aid in stopping the flow of condolences.

So the ring, carefully wrapped and accompanied by a thoughtfully worded letter, was dispatched to the Underhill home. Joanna had decided to take the position that the ring—being a family heirloom—did not belong to her, and that she felt it ought to be returned to the Underhills.

The first one to notice her ringless state was none other than Sir Lucas. At the Hatherton's annual party, he insisted in his assured manner that she favor him with another country dance. The slight lump beneath her glove was gone. He held her hand firmly in his, then turned to give her an assessing look.

"So you break the last of the bonds. Good. Ring was too small for you—not that it did not fit, but the stone and setting was too dainty for one who has long, elegant fingers like yours. You deserve a ring that is magnificent."

"How kind of you to think so," she managed to say when they came together again in the dance. "I shall remember to tell my future husband should I ever reach that happy state."

"You *will* consider marriage? You must," he said in that maddeningly confident manner uniquely his.

"Oh, no doubt I will find some squire intent upon improving his fortunes one of these days. I have no taste for half-pay captains, you see," she said when she chanced to catch sight of the delicate Miss Thorne chatting with Captain Fortesque. Rather, it should be noted Miss Thorne listened raptly to the words spilling forth from the dashing captain. She did not appear the least frightened of him.

"Perhaps you had best look to your own future marriage, sir," Joanna said with a glance toward Miss Thorne.

That infuriatingly male smile directed at her made Joanna long to give Sir Lucas a rousing set-down.

"Miss Thorne will do as bid. Whereas you, my dear Miss Winterton, I sense in you a spirit of independence altogether unseemly in a female. I suspect you have been given far too much leeway over the years. Your aunt is a dear lady, if misguided and indulgent."

"True," a very angry Joanna snapped when able to speak.

"She is also a very loving and kind lady. I feel quite blessed to have had her serve as my mother these past years."

Appearing somewhat chastened at her reproving speech, not to mention her glare, Sir Lucas subsided. He did give her a number of speculative looks, however.

Joanna was still annoyed when the dance was over. Since good manners did not permit her stalking off in high dudgeon, she permitted Sir Lucas to escort her back to her aunt.

"Good evening, sirrah," she said quietly, while clenching her fan tightly in her hand, longing to whack him across the noggin with it. "I look forward to attending your wedding. Your biddable bride will no doubt do you great credit."

Sir Lucas cast her a puzzled look before bowing, then striding off to where Miss Thorne still conversed with the captain.

"Ohhhh, that man!" Joanna whispered tersely behind her fan to her aunt.

"What did he do now, dear?" Aunt Caroline asked mildly.

"I am too independent, he declares. He thought you had given me too much leeway when rearing me. The man is a nodcock. Truly he is," she said, when her aunt chuckled. "I doubt if there is a more infuriating man on the face of this earth. Poor Miss Thorne."

"But she is not, is she?" Aunt Caroline observed. "Poor, that is. I wonder if she has been advised on the dangers of a half-pay officer who may be handsome but is penniless."

"As you cautioned me?" Joanna joined her aunt in watching a pale Drusilla Thorne. She danced with Sir Lucas, but cast curious glances at someone across the room. Joanna could not see who it was but had her suspicions.

"Quite so," Aunt Caroline said.

"Well, no woman could have possibly been a better mother than you," Joanna said in a fierce undertone. "And I hope Sir Lucas reaps the humbling he so richly deserves."

After this uncomfortable encounter Joanna danced with several quite eligible young men who, without exception, treated her as they might a fragile and ailing younger sister.

"This is so frustrating," Joanna murmured to her aunt. "I do not think I can tolerate it any longer. I am seriously considering a pleasant journey. I should like to go to some area I've not been before. You would come with me, would you not?" Joanna begged her, ignoring those who sauntered past them.

"Of course I would," Aunt Caroline said with a perceptive frown. "And I begin to share your concern. Perhaps if you are away for a time, then return wearing fashionable gowns in pretty colors, they will forget you were ever betrothed. It shall be ancient history."

"I shall begin planning our trip on the morrow," Joanna exclaimed with delight.

"Going away, Miss Winterton?" Sir Lucas said with a bow, surprising Joanna with his sudden appearance. "Are you planning a visit to a fashionable spa, Miss Staunton? London can become a dreary place at times."

"I agree," Aunt Caroline said. "We look forward to a change. And I expect that soon you will be taking off on a leisurely wedding trip."

"Not a long one," he said. "I have much business to attend to at my estate come summer."

"How practical," Joanna murmured. "Your bride will have a chance to become acquainted with her new home and her new husband at the same time."

Sir Lucas shot her an unfathomable look, then bowed over her aunt's hand before making his way out the front door.

"He does have a way of popping up at the oddest moments," Joanna complained quietly, deliberately turning from that doorway. She had no wish to watch him depart.

"In that case, his wife had best be on her good behavior at all times," Aunt Caroline said with a smile.

The following day, Joanna was eagerly studying various maps and consulting books on travel in England that she had ordered delivered from the bookseller's.

"We will have Papa's most comfortable coach, and I will insist on a ground-floor bedroom so you need not worry about stairs," Joanna declared to her aunt.

"Before we leave I want to attend that wedding. You promised to go with me."

"And when is it?" Joanna said, as though she didn't know.

"Tomorrow."

* * *

And the next day found the two ladies slipping into the back of the church, quietly taking seats and hoping to remain unobserved. There were not a great many people attending. The building was quiet save for the faint murmur of those in the pews.

Then a door opened and Sir Lucas strode forth wearing handsome attire quite suitable for a groom of the first stare of fashion—gray pantaloons over which he wore a deep gray coat and a corbeau waistcoat delicately embroidered with gold thread. Of the bride there was no sign.

They waited in utter silence as the minutes ticked by. The minister conferred with Sir Lucas, who in turn conferred with his best man, Lord Hatherton. A faint murmur rose from the guests when a footman appeared in the vestry door with a white missive in hand.

The minister read it, then handed it to Sir Lucas. He clenched his jaw, turned pale, and immediately left the church by way of the vestry.

"There will be no marriage," the minister declared, failing to reveal anything else.

"What has happened?" Joanna demanded of her amazed aunt.

"A nine days' wonder, that's what."

Chapter Two

"Jilted! The premier rake of London jilted?" Joanna's hand crept up to her mouth as she contemplated the awful repercussions of such an act. "Good gracious! It would seem that Drusilla Thorne is not as timid as believed," she concluded, exchanging a wry look with Aunt Caroline.

Then she gathered up her reticule and the soft shawl that had warded off the chill in the unheated church and rose from the hard pew. Aunt Caroline rose as well, casting speculative looks at the vestry door all the while.

"How could that silly widgeon ruin her life in such a manner?" Aunt Caroline said softly, while they slipped from the church out into the breezy June day.

"I cannot suppose she ruined Sir Lucas's life, but I feel certain she did not improve it," Joanna said with a shake of her head. "What do you suppose happened?"

"Time will tell. I should dearly like to know what was in the message brought by the Thorne footman," the older woman said, bustling Joanna from the church portico and down the steps to the walkway. "That foolish girl most likely ran off with some half-pay officer or the like. Someone who did not frighten her half to death and who cozened her into running away with him with sweet and gentle talk."

Aunt Caroline climbed into the carriage that had waited for them around the corner of the church, and then, when Joanna had settled beside her, resumed her reflections on the matter.

"At least Sir Lucas is able to take himself off to the Continent should he so please."

"I can sympathize with him in a way," Joanna said reflectively. "Poor man—to be subjected to the unctuous commiseration offered by Society. Or mayhap he will suffer through titters of amusement and sly nudges wherever he goes. He *must* wish to leave London. I know I do. As a matter of fact, the sooner we go—you and I—the better."

"Then we shall pack our trunks and be off. Have you decided where we will go?" Aunt Caroline inquired complacently.

"How good you are, to be so indulgent. Most others would be insisting on joining in the decision."

"Well, it does not really matter to me. I only wish to see you happy. I am content wherever I am." Aunt Caroline peered from the window, then signaled the driver to halt.

"Whatever?" Joanna asked with a frown.

"I wish more yarn and such if we are going away for a time. Goodness knows what is to be found in some remote place. I know you well enough to be certain you will not choose an ordinary location."

"I have decided," Joanna said cautiously while leaving the carriage, "that a trip to the Lake District would be beneficial to us both. Lovely scenery, fresh air and sunshine, and quite removed from anyone we know in London. The area has become a favorite with those who wish for a change of scenery, but none of the *ton* are likely to be found there now. It seems ideal. Is that agreeable with you?" She studied her aunt's face when she joined Joanna on the walkway.

"Entirely, dear girl," Aunt Caroline said with a pleased expression. "I have never been there, my family thinking it far too strenuous a place for a fragile female such as myself."

"Fragile, bosh," Joanna said in denial. "You are the hardiest woman I know. I would wager you could climb mountains if you so chose."

"I should like that—I think," Aunt Caroline replied with a certain amount of hesitation. "I hope you will do the walking you so enjoy. How lovely to be going to a district where walking is all the thing. You will not be out of place in the least. Do you require new shoes? Something exceedingly sturdy, no doubt?"

"Indeed, not to mention a goodly supply of stockings. I do

detest mending stockings, for invariably there are lumps no matter how careful I try to be, and they are so uncomfortable."

"I agree," Aunt Caroline said. And following the visit to Ackermann's Repository where she found precisely what she desired, she directed the driver to take them to Clark and Debenham's, considered by most to be the premier hosier in London.

In a traveling coach that was not going traveling after all, Sir Lucas Montfort grimly stared out of the window. When the coach pulled up before his town house, he climbed from the vehicle in icy silence, then strode into his London home like a storm cloud blowing off the North Sea.

Only his butler greeted him, and that was with his usual discreet murmur. No one else was in sight—which was just as well, Lucas reflected. He was in no mood for explanations to anyone.

Once in the privacy of his library he paced the Turkey carpet, thinking furiously. "Blast the chit," he muttered. "Why could she not have tossed the mitten *before* the last moment? Jilted! Fancy that, jilted." He paused to stare at his father's portrait and gave a mirthless laugh.

"You would have appreciated the irony of this, sir. And advised me what I must do now," Lucas said with deep regret. He missed his father, for they had been very close, far more so than most fathers and sons. Lucas cast a glance across the room to the portrait where his mother serenely gazed upon the world, then back to where his father gazed with similar serenity—and a twinkle almost hidden deep within his dark eyes. "Here I provide the latest *on dit*, and I find I have no wish for Society to make sport of me in their usual cruel manner. Shall I flee like a coward? Take refuge at my country estate? Heaven knows I can find much to occupy my time there." The neglect while he was overseas had not been completely erased.

Lucas silently admitted that the decampment of Miss Drusilla Thorne had affected him more than he could believe. His pride, most likely, was the root of it all. His blasted Montfort pride. It was a family trait he had not overcome.

"I am taking a trip," he informed the portraits. "I shall go where I am not expected, where no one is likely to find me, for they believe I shall go to the Continent." Lucas rubbed his chin for a minute or two, then continued. "Instead, I will go north to the Lake District. Tramping across the fells, climbing the hills, perhaps a quiet time spent fishing, will be good for my soul. Tranquillity, that is what I seek. And a pox on all women!" The latter remark was uttered in momentary pique, not something expected to last a long time. Lucas enjoyed the ladies far too much for that.

He cast a last lingering look at the portraits, then strode from the library and marched up the stairs to his bedroom, where he found his valet.

"Emery, I am going to the Lake District—without my expected bride. Take what is necessary for a leisurely sojourn. Hiking, fishing, that sort of thing."

With his unflappable nature, Emery did as bid, allowing only one or two curious glances at his employer as that gentleman audibly altered his plans.

Aunt Caroline was the one who made arrangements for their accommodations while in the Lake District. A land agent leased them a cottage for the remainder of the summer for the princely sum of three pounds.

"Outrageous," Aunt Caroline grumbled when relating the matter to Joanna. "Some person in the village of Grasmere thinks to fleece the summer residents."

"He most likely needs the money, dear aunt, else he would not be renting his home." Joanna surveyed the stack of trunks, boxes, and portmanteaus required for the trip and sighed.

Aunt Caroline sighed as well. "I felt it necessary to bring all the essentials with us. One never knows what those heathens will have in a house—or not have."

Joanna chuckled. "I doubt they are heathen, precisely. Perhaps they are merely less inclined to luxury?"

They left London early on a hazy June morning, one that promised to bring a reasonably warm and sunny day. A few clouds were scattered across the sky, but not the sort to threaten rain.

Joanna cast a musing look out of the window, then turned to her aunt, who was nestled among a pile of pillows.

"I wonder where Sir Lucas is by now? To my knowledge he has not been seen since that disastrous wedding that did not take place. Poor man." She exchanged a knowing look with her aunt.

"I hope that silly twit of a girl is happy with Captain Fortesque. To think I felt sorry for him and plied him with tea and cakes," Aunt Caroline said, followed by a disdainful sniff.

"I imagine that made it all the more difficult for Sir Lucas. Fancy Miss Thorne jilting a handsome, wealthy knight for a mere half-pay officer. They must live on her inheritance, unless he fritters it away." And both women knew that was all too likely, given what they had heard of the captain's nature.

Sir Lucas Montfort left the confines of his traveling coach to survey the little village of Grasmere. Lush greenery sparkled with the remnants of a morning rain, a fresh breeze whipped in from the not too distant lake, and June flowers nodded in the dappled light of sun cast through spreading trees. He could hear the soft bleating of sheep in the distance. Peace, quiet, and not one member of London Society in sight.

A surprising number of people bustled up and down the main street of the village, intent upon errands. There were no doubt a goodly number of tourists like himself. He wondered if there was another poor soul who sought refuge from the malicious tongues of London Society. He nodded to his coachman and groom, then strolled toward the Prince of Wales Hotel, where he would stay until he might find the right lodging—one secluded and comfortable, not necessarily in that order.

Once in the confines of a neat and pleasant room, he studied the view from his window while recalling the past weeks. His principal emotion was one of annoyance. To be sure, he also knew anger at the little chit who had decamped rather than wed him. But he had felt no attachment to her. She had not touched his heart, other than offering the solution to his decision to wed. He hoped she would not regret her hasty flit to

Gretna Green with Captain Fortesque. It had irked Lucas when he found out her choice of husband. Fortesque of all men!

It was good to be away from the snickers and titters of the gossips, the sly commiseration of the *ton*. Going north proved easier than dashing off to the Continent, even if it was available for travel now.

No, he intended to settle in for the remainder of the summer, perhaps indulge in a light flirtation with a likely tourist. He was in the mood for dalliance, nothing more. It might soothe his wounded senses. Not that he felt he needed to restore his status in Society, mind you. He felt secure in his position, for it was always the woman who was blamed in a situation like this. And he had to admit that she seemed the fool for fleeing from one who had wealth that was far from modest.

So it was with a serene mood that Lucas left his new abode for a saunter along the one street of the village, which also led toward Rydal Water, and beyond that, Ambleside. Emery had been slightly incensed that Lucas chose to walk. But that was what one did here, although Emery did not appear to accept that news too well.

Lucas knew that the poet Wordsworth and family lived somewhere in the vicinity. The writer Thomas De Quincey had reportedly also taken lodgings in the locale, as had the poet Coleridge. Lucas intended to avoid all these poets and writers, not being in the mood to ponder over the mysteries of life as seemed their wont.

No, he thought, breathing in deeply of the fresh, country-scented air, he wanted a casual, simple life while here. He wondered if Emery had thought to pack his fishing gear. If not, there most likely would be a shop in Ambleside that could provide all the necessary equipment.

And so it was the day after he arrived in Grasmere—sans fishing gear—that he found excellent equipment in precisely such a shop, complete with flies suitable for catching trout and pike. He also picked up a copy of a guide to the Lake District, thinking it might prove helpful should he desire to see a particular sight. In the main, he intended to wander where his feet took him, and did not plan to begin a methodical survey of the area.

It was while Lucas was off on the first of his wanderings that another traveling coach from London pulled into the village of Grasmere. After a pause to inquire directions, the coachman rolled along to a neat house near the far end of town, one with a tiny garden spilling over with flowers and herbs.

Joanna was first from the coach, surveying the small house with the hope that it would be more comfortable than it looked. While it might be quaint, it did not follow that also meant ease.

"Oh, my," Aunt Caroline exclaimed as she also exited the traveling coach, "such a display of flowers. I can forgive a great deal for that." She shook out her skirts, then turned to give orders to the coachman and groom regarding particular parcels.

Since Joanna wished more than anything to please her generous and forbearing aunt, this settled things for her. She set aside her misgivings and pushed open the little gate to walk up the brief path to the front door. Once inside, she found the spacious sitting room as neat as a pin with tolerable chairs and a pleasant fireplace that looked as though it might not smoke. Next was an agreeable dining room. A glance through to the back revealed a tidy kitchen equipped with enough pots and dishes for their needs. Off to one side were two bedrooms, as specified by Aunt Caroline. One possessed a dear little cherry bed with starched white curtains at the windows that overlooked a garden of summer posies. Stairs rose to where servants might reside.

"Aunt Caroline, come see your room."

While her aunt cried out with delight at her cozy chamber, Joanna claimed the adjacent one as her own.

From the window she could see green hills rising from the village, lines of stone walls drunkenly marching up and down and across the fields with total disregard for the steepness. After days spent lurching north from London, she yearned to explore the abundant paths to be found.

Her eyes narrowed as she watched a man walk down the

path toward the village. There was something vaguely familiar about the set of his shoulders, the way he strode along the track. Then a gust of wind snatched at his hat, sending it cartwheeling down the hill. Joanna stiffened a moment, then chuckled.

"And what is so amusing, love?" Aunt Caroline said, joining Joanna at the window.

"I had thought we would escape London Society here in the wilds. It seems someone else had the same idea."

"Who?"

"Our jilted knight, none other than Sir Lucas Montfort, lately of London. There is no mistaking that thatch of silvery hair, nor that arrogant stride of his. Even you have remarked on it, dear aunt."

"And so I have, 'tis true. Why," Caroline said with a vexed air, "did he have to select Grasmere of all places on earth?"

"Most likely for the same reason we did. He desired peace and serenity and no one to twit him about being jilted. Do you suppose we may be able to avoid him?" And as the words tumbled from her lips, Joanna recalled that Sir Lucas had complained that she had managed to avoid him for most of the year in London. Were that the case, she should surely be able to avoid him in the wilds of the Lake District. There were acres and acres of land to explore, paths in every which direction, not to mention boating excursions and fishing—for Joanna loved to go fishing.

As though echoing her train of thought, Aunt Caroline said, "There are regattas, and you enjoy fishing, and I read there are caves to explore, not to mention all those paths over the hills and across the fells. You need not cross his path—if that is what you wish."

"I cannot abide the man, for all I pity him. He makes me a trifle uncomfortable with that knowing grin and those wicked looks. Oh, I do wish he were elsewhere." Joanna tried to calm a fluttery feeling that had crept over her.

She turned from the window and set about assisting her maid, Susan, to unpack the trunks. She could hear Aunt Caroline nattering away at Bodkin, her maid. All they needed now was to locate a cook, and then they could consider themselves settled in—more or less.

Over at the Prince of Wales Hotel, Tom Coachman and Jim, the groom, inquired about stabling the horses and keeping the coach. A curious Emery, having time on his hands, struck up a conversation with Jim, who was a superior sort of groom. Emery asked a goodly number of questions. Jim replied loquaciously.

Lucas stamped into the hotel, then strode across to climb the stairs to his rooms. He was met at the door by a sober-faced Emery.

"What is it now, Emery?" Lucas said, wondering why it was that the perfect fall of his cravat was sufficiently important for him to retain such a somber chap.

"New arrivals in Grasmere, sir." Emery said, while removing a coat from his master that appeared to have spent some time on the ground serving as a pillow.

The inflection in his valet's voice brought Lucas to a halt before his dresser. He really would have to find a more suitable place of his own. Although there was a comfortable chair set close to the fireplace, and he supposed the room was adequate for a week's stay, he wished for more space. As well, at night he could hear the creaking of other beds not to mention the hall floorboards when trod upon.

"Londoners, sir. Miss Caroline Staunton and her niece, Miss Winterton, have just arrived for the remainder of the summer. They have rented a house at the far end of the village."

"The devil you say!" Lucas exclaimed. He wondered if those two had attended his abruptly terminated wedding as Miss Staunton had said they would. No matter. It was likely they would have heard the juicy tale of the jilted gentleman, given the love of gossip in Town. And Lucas had thought he might escape the little world he knew.

"Blast! Well, we had best hunt for a house to let, preferably at the opposite end of the village. Or perhaps in Ambleside, if such is available." Lucas began to change for dinner, all the while cursing the fate that had brought the pretty Miss Winterton to Grasmere.

Was she still in mourning for her departed betrothed? The dratted man did not deserve such devotion, the way he had chased every available lightskirt and gambled far beyond his means. Perhaps she also sought peace and tranquillity—in her case, to soothe a broken heart, if such was possible. Lucas didn't believe in broken hearts. But if she desired repose, Lucas would be only too happy to oblige on his part. He would keep as much distance as possible.

Unless . . . and he paused while chancing a glance out of the window, unless she might be open to a bit of dalliance? Then he grinned at his reflection in the looking glass. The cool Miss Winterton and dalliance? Not likely.

He went down to dinner with a lighter heart, certain he would not encounter Miss Winterton or her charming, if somewhat unusual, aunt while ruralizing.

Emery had again gone off to see about renting a house while Lucas ate his dinner. There was a flurry of activity midway through his meal, and he almost groaned when he saw the two women who hesitantly entered the room where the simple but good meals were served at the Prince of Wales.

Well, he decided, he would ignore them if possible. Surely if he concentrated on his food, he could manage to avoid their gaze. He wanted no spurious sympathy or coy glances from any unmarried women, no matter what their age.

However, he was spared any conversation from them. He wondered at that. Surely any unmarried girl would be prodded into making some gesture toward a man in his position. Miss Winterton and her aunt were of a different cut, it seemed.

Lucas, to his utter amazement, found himself stopping by their little corner table—quite out of his way—to say hello. "Good evening Miss Staunton, Miss Winterton. I must admit it is a surprise to discover you here. It is a rather remote location, particularly in the height of the Season."

"We are equally surprised to see you, Sir Lucas," Aunt Caroline replied, giving him a serene look. "We hope to find peace and tranquillity here. Joanna is much inclined to walking, and perhaps a bit of fishing. She wishes to return for the next Season with the past well behind her."

"Aunt Caroline," Joanna said quietly, "I sincerely doubt if

Sir Lucas is the least bit interested in our reasons for leaving London or our plans while here. We shall take care to respect your desire for privacy should that be your wish," Joanna concluded.

Although that was precisely what he had wished, Lucas found himself wanting to share their cool and collected company. All of a sudden, being alone with naught but the taciturn Emery for conversation lost its appeal.

"As to that, we are far from strangers. If you find you need help with fishing, do not hesitate to call on me, Miss Winterton." Lucas smiled, then excused himself, wondering if the rain had affected his head. For, as his father had often said, green grass required abundant rain, and it was very green around here.

Joanna watched Sir Lucas leave the little dining room. "Why do I have the feeling that he really does not want our company, but is considering it as a reserve in the event he becomes bored?"

"That may be," Aunt Caroline said with a nod. "However, dear girl, it will do no harm if we keep on polite terms with him. It would be unseemly to do more than that."

"Aunt!" Joanna declared, choking on a bit of custard. "I do hope you do not mean what I think you do."

Aunt Caroline smiled placidly.

The following days brought a bit of sunshine and no sign of Sir Lucas. Joanna breathed a sigh of relief and decided that she would explore the surrounding countryside.

"Joanna, my dear girl, are you really haring off across the trails in that scandalous skirt?" Aunt Caroline cried when she saw Joanna garbed in the divided skirt topped by a modest spenser.

"It is quite decent, you know," Joanna said in her own defense. "Most of the time it looks like a regular dress. I shan't be likely to see anyone we know. And what if I do?" she queried, the image of Sir Lucas popping into her mind of a sudden.

"Well," Aunt Caroline said in a very considering way.

"Oh, fiddle," Joanna said with a grin, then took herself off across the intervening space toward the path up the hill after seeing that her dear aunt would be cheerfully occupied while she was gone. They had found a cook, and Aunt Caroline intended to test her on the finer points of cooking.

There had been some talk about having Susan tramp along with Joanna when she went off on her rambles. Joanna soon convinced her aunt that Susan would be far better off remaining to help at the little house. Indeed, Susan had her hands full just keeping Joanna's clothing in good repair, what with brambles and rain taking their toll.

It was a glorious day and Joanna felt a burst of joy at the sense of freedom that she rarely experienced. Not that she was inclined to rebellion. She knew full well how foolish it would be to challenge the established customs of society. Miss Thorpe had done so, and Joanna doubted if she would be the happier for it.

She lengthened her pace until she climbed at a goodly speed. It enabled her to cover the ground quite fast, and before she knew it she had reached a high point in the path from which she could survey much of the countryside. Off to one side, rocks cropped out from the earth in sharp contrast to the lush green of the meadows and woodlands below. She paused to catch her breath, sitting down to rest against a large rock. Walking up this path had been harder than expected, but quite exhilarating.

Herdwick sheep dotted the land below in ever-changing patterns, faint bleats rising every now and again with a wisp of wind. She wondered if they really were descended from sheep washed ashore after the wreck of a Spanish galleon, as she had been told by a wide-eyed Susan. It was a romantic notion, one she quite fancied.

The fells rose behind her, spreading across the hilltops in what she supposed some might consider a bleak manner. Joanna found it oddly beautiful in a stark way, even inspiring.

She was startled when a hand clamped on one of the rocks, followed by a silvery head and another hand, after which came the rest of the man.

He saw her at once when he clambered over the last of the

stones, dropping down on the earth to catch his breath. He stared at her without uttering a word.

"Hello," Joanna ventured. "Do you do this sort of thing often? Popping up out of nowhere to alarm one almost out of one's wits?"

"Frequently," came the dry rejoinder. "I make it a practice to pop up out of nowhere at least once a day."

"Absurd man," Joanna said with a grin, feeling suddenly at ease with the man she had so studiously avoided while in London.

His gaze settled on her with a disturbing intensity that instantly put her on guard again. "You are alone."

"Indeed, sir. I have experienced not a speck of difficulty—until this moment," she added under her breath.

He seemed not to notice. Tilting his head, he inspected her at greater length until Joanna quite lost patience with the man. She rose from her uncomfortable spot, deciding at once to seek lower ground.

He rose as well, apparently having caught his breath and restored his energy.

Before Joanna could make good her escape from his disturbing presence, he had captured her hand, pulling her to a halt. "Sir?" she asked firmly, trying to ignore the fluttering of her heart.

His lazy grin ought to have prepared her, but it didn't. His other hand caught her head and suddenly she knew the taste and feel of his lips against hers. It was shocking, this first kiss, for her betrothed had not bothered to attempt such a familiarity. And this kiss was far too enticing for her own good. She found herself melting against his lean body, fitting her soft curves into his firm length.

Little quivers ran through her and she wondered at the trembling that flowed over her. Then she came to her senses and pushed at him, after which he released her. A trifle. And not very far.

"Sirrah, let me go. I would return to the village." She gestured to the foot of the hill, where bits and pieces of the town could be glimpsed through the trees. She did not look in that direction, for his gaze held hers captive.

One of his hands tugged at a brown curl that peeped from beneath her straw hat. "I rather liked that kiss," he said in a husky voice that charmed her far too much. "Do not tell me that you did not, for I'd not believe it."

"Odious, impossible man," Joanna said, giving him a shove with one hand, enough to put him off balance so that he had to release her to regain it. "Do not believe it, then." She took that time to begin her clamber down the hill, calling over her shoulder at him, "Good day, sir." And she disappeared around an outcropping of stone and was gone from view in an instant.

Lucas sank down on the ground, leaning against the same stone Miss Winterton had used as a prop. "Well now, would you ever?" he asked the clouds gathering overhead. "The cool Miss Winterton has a most delightful—and warmly responsive—kiss."

Chapter Three

"That utterly horrid man!" Joanna fumed as she hastily slid around a bend in the path. She refused to think about her reaction to Sir Lucas. Never would she have believed she could be so abandoned as to respond to a kiss as she had. Not only was *his* behavior shocking, *her* response was even worse.

Considering how long it had taken her to reach her high point on the hill, it was amazing how fast she came down the hill. And, she reflected, she had to come down in more ways than one. It would never do for Aunt Caroline to see her in such a state.

"He is a *most* impossible creature," Joanna declared to a sheep as she sailed past. The animal gave her a curious look, but otherwise ignored her. "Would that Sir Lucas had taken your cue and ignored me as well. Oh, this will make things so difficult with him residing in the same little village. With any luck at all, he will take himself off to another spot and leave us to a bit of peace. For," she stoutly vowed, "I have no intention of leaving!"

She did desire peace, she assured herself. That exhilarating kiss was far too upsetting to her tranquillity. But she did wonder, slowing her pace as she reached the lower part of the path to the village, what a kiss from her late betrothed might have been like. Somehow she imagined that it could not equal that of the experienced Sir Lucas.

She announced to a tall elm tree, "Well, now I know why he is called a rake. He is without conscience." But, she admitted to herself, she ought not have been alone. Susan ought to have gone with her to prevent just such an occurrence—but there was the rub. She could not envision little Susan climbing hills.

A lively terrier dashed across the path, chasing after an errant cat and giving Joanna an idea.

"Well," Aunt Caroline said when Joanna burst into the front room of the cottage, "time was when you would enter a room like a young lady, not a hoyden."

"I need a dog," Joanna said baldly. Then, realizing how she sounded, she temporized, "I just saw the dearest little terrier, and thought it would be wonderful to have one like him for company when I go on my walks or perhaps fishing," she trailed off vaguely while avoiding her aunt's piercing gaze. For one who could be as absentminded as the worst, Aunt Caroline was dreadfully perceptive at times.

"Indeed," her aunt observed mildly. "And did you have a nice time on your walk? I must say, you look rather wild. Is there a wind up higher? It is quite peaceful here, nestled among the trees as we are."

"Oh, yes," Joanna cried, grateful for the offered straw. "There is a breeze. And then I could not resist running down the last part of the hill, for it felt so delicious. Do you know, there must be several hundreds of sheep around here. They dot the valley from one end to the other—and that is another good reason for a dog," she added carefully. "One never knows when one of those stupid sheep will take a notion to chase one."

"Were you chased by a sheep?" Aunt Caroline asked with alarm.

"No," Joanna assured her, thinking that Sir Lucas was not the least like those docile creatures she had viewed. But perhaps a ram? One with a harem, most assuredly. Then, rebuking herself for her wayward thoughts, she set about changing her garb so she might go hunting for a dog—a nice, fierce little dog who would protect her from unwanted advances.

Lucas lounged against the stone, watching Miss Winterton appear and disappear around various turns and bends in the path until she reached the flat and the village. She ran that last bit, flying over the ground like a dark-haired angel, and vanishing into the trees.

He had not been wise in his actions. But, oh, she had been

such a surprisingly delicious armful—he simply had not been able to resist her. And although he had expected her to be stiff and unyielding, she had been soft and warmly responsive for a few moments until her sanity returned.

Lucas shifted away from the stone, easing back on the grass to contemplate the sky above. The few gathering clouds skittered across the sky like newborn lambs, frolicking before a rising wind.

She had smelled of lilacs, although their season was long past. And she was nicely formed, just the right height, and all in all precisely what he needed to take his mind off his troubles. That those troubles were fading rapidly did not impinge upon his awareness. He had not thought of Miss Thorne's defection in hours, not for the past two days, as matter of fact, had he realized it.

"What a pity the pretty Miss Winterton is not available for dalliance," he said aloud, followed by a regretful sigh.

He sat up, propping himself with his hands behind him. But he could apologize, gain her forgiveness, and then pursue her with all the skill at his command, which—he admitted—was considerable. A crafty smile lit his face, to be replaced by a rueful acknowledgment that she was of the gentry, most gently bred, and more a candidate for a wife than a mistress.

"But she offers a diversion." His self-respect nudged him to follow through with his interest in the girl. He would flirt with her, maybe entice her to fall in love with him. It would perhaps soothe that wounded pride that still smarted a trifle whenever he recalled Drusilla Thorne.

He rose from his resting spot, brushed off his sturdy breeches, clapped his hat back on his head, then took the same path down the hill that Miss Winterton had taken so precipitously not long ago.

Yes, he would apologize, charm her aunt, and in so doing pave the way for a bit of fun. He whistled all the way back to the Prince of Wales. Here he found Emery awaiting him with the news that a suitable cottage had been located, one with a sizable bedroom, a tidy sitting room, and a kitchen where a first-rate cook could prepare his meals with dispatch.

Not bothering to change his clothes, Lucas set off along the main street to find his new residence. Once there, he paused. Miss Winterton and her aunt must rent the little cottage across the lane. If he was not mistaken, that was her aunt puttering about in the garden alongside the house. How very convenient.

It did not take long to decide the house would do for the summer. He sent Emery back for his belongings, indicating he would be along directly to settle his accounts with the manager of the hotel.

With Emery striding along toward the Prince of Wales, Lucas strolled across the way to lean on the little fence that surrounded the yard. "Good day, ma'am. How nice to see you again."

Aunt Caroline looked up in confusion, then her face cleared and she smiled sunnily at Lucas.

"Good day to you as well. I had not thought to see you." Her look was inquiring, but she said no more.

"As matter of fact, we shall be neighbors. I intend to lease that stone cottage across the way from you." He gestured to the picturesque building set amid a wild mixture of herbs and flowers.

"Oh, dear, I fear you will not like the place. I understand that these stone cottages are dreadfully damp when it rains. I insisted that we have a plaster exterior for that very reason. It remains to be seen how well our chimney draws."

Pride would not allow him to admit that he had heard something of the same and forgotten all about it. "I doubt it will be a problem, but I do thank you for your concern." He bowed and then went on his way, intent upon making his change from the hotel with all speed. Now that he had spoken with the aunt, he sensed his way would be all the easier with the niece.

Aunt Caroline gazed after Sir Lucas's retreating figure with a faint frown. Several minutes later when Joanna joined her to check the condition of the herb garden, Caroline said, "Sir Lucas is to lease the little stone house across the way from us. Poor man. It rains quite often here, and I fear he will suffer greatly from the damp. Our cook tells me that the chimney does not draw well, either. We had best be prepared to expect him on the next windy, rainy day."

"How frightful." Joanna cast a horrified look at the innocent house that had not done the least to offend her.

"He might turn out to be a dab hand at cards, you know. Evenings can be a trifle dull hereabouts without parties or other festive occasions."

"I heard there is to be a regatta before long," Joanna said, hoping to change the topic. "It will be over on Windermere where the lake is broader and deeper. Does that not sound delightful? I should like to watch a regatta, I believe."

Easily led to a different matter, Aunt Caroline beamed a smile and nodded, her bonnet lurching precariously on her head. "Oh, indeed, I should like that as well. I wonder if Sir Lucas sails." She thought a moment, then added, "He probably would not admit it if he did not, for I sense he has an inordinate amount of pride in him."

"Pride? Well, he does come from an old family, and has pots and pots of money. I suppose he has something to be proud of, even if Drusilla Thorne was afraid of him, the silly goose," Joanna offered, while staring off in the direction of the Prince of Wales, wondering how long it would be before her antagonist would come riding along with his valet and gear in tow.

Her aunt gave her a curious look, then turned back to her inspection of the little garden, exclaiming over a particularly pretty pink rose she discovered.

Joanna recalled her intention to find a dog and decided it was more necessary now than before. Putting her plan into action, she retied the ribands of her bonnet and pulled on a pair of short gloves. "I am off to locate a dog. Pray I find one with a good temper, well-mannered, as well as a dear little fellow we can like."

"You will," her aunt predicted cheerfully.

Joanna grinned, knowing that her aunt usually had the most peculiar luck of being right. That she would find the proper dog encouraged her in her quest.

She inspected each home as she walked along the street, seeming to check over the garden, but actually hunting for signs of a terrier such as she had seen earlier. He had been so playful that she had no doubt he was a pet and not a dog trained to hunt rats and foxes.

About nine houses down she chanced to espy the very same terrier—she was certain it was him—gnawing on a bone on the steps of a stone cottage that had no garden and little grass about it.

Joanna stopped, then put her hand on the gate. The terrier looked up and gave her a decidedly narrow look.

"I do not fancy your bone, dear doggy. But I would like to speak with your master if you might let me past you," Joanna coaxed.

The terrier thought otherwise and after nudging his bone into a corner came toward the gate all bristly and growling in a low, menacing manner.

"Are you in a spot of difficulty, Miss Winterton? Allow me to offer my assistance."

Joanna did not have to turn to know who was there at her side, peering with her over the gate at the terrier.

"Indeed, Sir Lucas, as you see the dear little dog does not wish me to enter."

"You are interested in the dog?"

"I wish to procure a dog to take along with me on walks," she said in a firm voice, finally giving him the cool look he fully deserved. "I would feel so much safer then, you see."

He flashed her that wry, knowing grin, his eyes alight with a gleam, then said, "There are so many vagrants about, you cannot be too careful."

"Not only vagrants, sirrah," she riposted. "There are other dangers as well."

Before things could become really interesting, an elderly man opened the front door and limped toward them, calling the dog to heel as he did so. "You want summat?"

"I wish to have a terrier such as you have there, and wondered if you might tell me where I could find one," Joanna said before Sir Lucas could collect any words he might utter.

"Have him," the man said. "He jest showed up here one day. Don't know where he come from. I already have a dog—don't need another."

Joanna scarcely knew what to say. "I, that is, if you are certain."

"Come, fellow," Sir Lucas commanded. The dog trotted over to sit at the gate, looking up at Sir Lucas with alert eyes. "And what will you call him?" he asked while letting the dog from the yard and out onto the walkway.

"Rex, for he is certainly king of all he surveys," Joanna said after a moment, wondering how she contrived to be in this position—having Sir Lucas assist her in obtaining the very dog that was supposed to protect her from him! At a look from Sir Lucas, she added, "He is such a fierce little fellow."

"And you need a protector," he said in an approving way. He also gave her a look that told her should he decide he wished to intrude on her privacy again, he could—dog or no dog.

Choosing to ignore that look, Joanna bent to examine the little terrier. He had a slightly rough coat—almost wiry—and was a caramel color, with bright, intelligent eyes that assessed her much as she assessed him.

"He is, I believe, a border terrier," Sir Lucas inserted. "They are used up in the Cheviot Border country to hunt the hill foxes. The gypsies like them, too, you know."

Joanna studied the compact little body—for the dog could not have weighed more than eleven pounds or so—with his broad, flat head, turned-down ears, and short whiskers. She smiled. Such a fierce little fellow, indeed. She hesitantly offered her hand for him to sniff, then when he approved, she scratched behind his ears, recalling she had done so with her cousin's dog and he'd liked it.

"Well done, Miss Winterton," Sir Lucas said.

In spite of her resolve to remain distant from him, Joanna felt a spurt of pleasure at his commendation. She rose to thank the old man only to find he had returned to his house, firmly shutting the door behind him, as though to close the matter of the dog once and for all.

"Come, Rex. We shall see how Aunt Caroline takes to you." Joanna snapped her fingers and wonder of wonders, the dog trotted alongside her, just as though trained to do so. She gave

Sir Lucas a guarded look. "Now if he will attack on command I shall be pleased."

"I see that I had best pick up a fine bone at the butcher shop," Sir Lucas replied with a twinkle in those dark eyes.

Joanna wondered again at the twitty Drusilla Thorne. How *could* the girl have tossed Sir Lucas aside for that simpering Captain Fortesque? It seemed to her that Sir Lucas, while he might be a trifle imposing, was by far the better catch. That is, if one were in search of a catch—which, she assured herself, she was not. At least *not* Sir Lucas.

All of this cogitation so confused her that she unthinkingly accepted that gentleman's arm and walked back to her cottage, which the cook had informed her was called *Rose* in honor of the pretty garden without. Rex the terrier trotted along beside them, accepting his new mistress with the outlook of one who has not had an easy time in life.

Aunt Caroline met them at the door, looking askance at the unlovely dog. "My, he is a, er, feisty, is he not?" she said at last.

"I told you I needed a dog who would protect me when I go for walks," Joanna said as she pulled her hand abruptly from Sir Lucas's arm, suddenly conscious of the cozy picture they must present. She studiously ignored the self-satisfied expression he wore.

"Indeed, ma'am," he said. "There are vagrants every now and again, itinerant former soldiers and the like. Even musicians and poets wander about the hills for inspiration."

"Gracious!" cried a completely alarmed Aunt Caroline.

"Never fear, Rex will guard me well. Won't you, old fellow?" Joanna inquired, crouching down beside the dog and gazing at him with fondness. He was such a champion little dog, so brave and self-reliant. One had to admire such toughness.

He studied her with a keen gaze, then, apparently deciding she was acceptable, walked over to put his chin on her knee, looking up at her with a pleading that quite undid her. Clearing her throat, she said quietly to her aunt, "See if there might be a nice bone for our new family member, would you?"

Almost as affected by the scene as Joanna, Aunt Caroline

hobbled into the house, leaving the door open behind her. Rex took one look at the open door, glanced up at Joanna, then trotted trustingly after Aunt Caroline.

"He will settle in well, I believe—and now you must do so, too, I perceive," Joanna said with a glance at the stone cottage across the street from Rose cottage. If the place had a name she could not imagine what it might be, unless it had something to do with damp and smoky.

"You are amused. I am delighted that my nearness offers you pleasure," Sir Lucas said, before bowing and striding off to his new abode.

Joanna fumed for a few moments, recalling that look of sheer entertainment in his eyes. While she was not pleased that he had moved so close to them, she thought it would be amusing when the poor man learned that the house was indeed damp and smoky. Cheered by a chilled Sir Lucas, Joanna whirled about and joined her aunt in the kitchen.

"Oh, he is a good little dog," Aunt Caroline said with approval. "He begged ever so prettily for his bone, then retreated by the fireplace to gnaw on it as though he had done it a hundred times at this very hearth. I believe he will do nicely for you, Joanna."

The front door slammed shut with the rising wind and Joanna hurried to see all was well in the other rooms. Within moments rain pelted the windows and a wind tossed the flowers in the garden to and fro. It was a good afternoon to do needlework or read a book.

"I am glad the dog is curled up at our hearth. Poor fellow would not have liked being out in the rain," Aunt Caroline said, slipping a bit of biscuit to the dog.

Joanna agreed, then settled down with one of the books she had brought along to read on just such days as this.

About an hour later, there came a pounding on the front door that made Aunt Caroline nearly bounce in her chair. Rex growled most fiercely and Joanna silently praised him.

Bodkin hurried to answer it while the two ladies of the house speculated on who could possibly be out in the storm.

Of course, Joanna suspected, even before he entered the sitting room. He came in, shaking rain from his cape and doffing his hat, ignoring the drops of water that sailed about from it.

"Sir Lucas," Aunt Caroline cried in dismay. "Whatever is the matter?"

Only then did Joanna observe that there were traces of soot on his handsome face and he looked as angry as could be. Rex trotted over to inspect this apparition, then sat back with a doggy grin on his rather homely face.

"You were right. That house is as damp as a long-standing tomb, and the fireplace smokes enough to drive me out. It is truly dreadful."

"Dreadful," Aunt Caroline echoed, bustling about with a soft murmur to do with a warm posset.

Sir Lucas was led to a comfortable chair by the gently blazing fire—in the fireplace that drew quite nicely. Aunt Caroline eased him down, then disappeared into the kitchen.

Sir Lucas gave Joanna a look that defied her to say a word about his condition, or that he had been warned about the cottage across the way.

"Perhaps you could find a clever man to open your chimney so it may draw better," Joanna ventured demurely.

"Emery is going to hunt down just such a person as soon as the rain lets up," Sir Lucas said as he leaned back against the chair and closed his eyes.

"Are you all right?" Joanna inquired, worried that Sir Lucas might have been injured and not revealed it to them.

In spite of his pride that usually forbade him from mentioning it, Lucas admitted, "Headache. It is splitting, and that blasted smoke and the aggravation did not help in the least."

"The posset may help. Perhaps," she offered hesitantly, "I might try something I used to do for my father when he suffered from one of his headaches?"

"Anything," Lucas said in a quiet voice most unlike his customary teasing tones.

Without pausing to consider what she was about to do, Joanna rose from her chair, set aside her book, then found a bottle of lotion made from a mixture of garden herbs. She poured out a bit, then began working it into his neck and forehead. Her hands at the side of his neck, she firmly made a zigzag path downward. Most daringly, she worked below the edge of his cravat, then upward again, always going back and forth. Then after a time—when she had not heard a sound from him for some moments—she moved in front of him and began a rotating motion above his eyes. His skin was firm and pleasantly textured. She wondered what his silvery hair might feel like. Was it as soft and feathery as it looked?

She studied his face and took a deep breath. He looked more at ease, like the pain had subsided. Satisfied that she might have helped him, she withdrew. She wiped her hands on a towel brought by a silent Susan, then resumed her seat, all without saying a word.

Aunt Caroline bustled in with a steaming, fragrant cup in hand, and placed it on a small table that stood beside the chair. Then, after tapping him on the arm, she, too, took her chair, exchanging a concerned look with Joanna.

Sir Lucas opened his eyes in a short while and stared wordlessly at Joanna for several moments. "Your father was a very fortunate man to have such a talented daughter. My headache is about gone." He picked up the soothing posset and polished it off, for it had cooled sufficiently to be just right to drink. He set the empty cup on the table and gave Aunt Caroline a look that conveyed much of what he felt.

"I am fortunate to have such good neighbors."

"Pish tush," Aunt Caroline said. She limped over to take the cup, then disappeared into the kitchen once again.

"Just because I eased your pain does not mean that I will permit any future liberties," Joanna felt compelled to say when she thought she caught a gleam in his eyes.

"As to that, I cannot promise a thing, my good Samaritan." He grinned at her with his usual twinkle in his eyes, and Joanna wondered if she needed to call Rex to her side.

Aunt Caroline returned and settled into her chair to softly conduct a quiet conversation, the sort that was not in the least demanding of anyone, particularly Sir Lucas.

It was about two hours later that the rain ceased and the wind abated. Joanna went to check the sky outside and stood at the window.

"My heart leaps up when I behold a rainbow in the sky,"

she quoted from the Wordsworth poem. She turned slightly and added, "I fancy he looked at just such a rainbow as this before he wrote those lines, for this is a magnificent one. Come see."

Sir Lucas assisted Aunt Caroline from her chair, having observed the slight difficulty she had, and they joined Joanna at the window to view the wonder in the sky.

"Oh, my," Aunt Caroline murmured.

"Indeed," Sir Lucas agreed, for it was a brilliant arc of color that stretched across the sky from one side of the valley to the other. It lasted but briefly before a cloud obscured the sun again.

"Lovely," Joanna said simply and with heartfelt pleasure.

"This calls for a cup of tea and some of Cook's excellent biscuits," Aunt Caroline declared, hustling off to the kitchen with Rex close behind her.

Lucas studied the quiet girl at his side, who still watched the changing sky. "Miss Winterton—Joanna, if I may—I must apologize to you. I abused your trust and yet you offered me a healing touch."

"I accept your gracious apology, Sir Lucas. But I fear it must remain Miss Winterton. Nothing has occurred to alter that position, has it?" she said with an amused little quirk of her mouth. "I am pleased you feel better. I recall how miserable those headaches made my father when I still lived at home."

"Indeed, they are such," Lucas said with understanding.

Joanna looked out of the window again, offering Lucas a view of a determined little chin. "There is Emery with a chap who looks as though he might be the sort to solve stuffed-up chimneys and damp walls."

Lucas stifled a sigh and withdrew from his pleasant spot. "I had best return there to see what goes on. Thank you again for all you have done."

He offered apologies for his departure when Aunt Caroline and Bodkin entered with the tea tray. She quite understood his desire to oversee matters and urged him to return to his house.

He left them, striding over puddles and reaching his temporary home with no incident.

Joanna observed that while he had apologized for his behavior, he had not specifically said he was sorry he had kissed her. In a peculiar way that pleased her. She would rather he not confess such a thing, and she supposed that was a shocking admission to make.

"Well, in spite of the rain we have had an exciting afternoon," Aunt Caroline declared as she settled down to her tea.

"All in all it has been quite a day," Joanna concluded.

From his cozy spot on the hearth rug, Rex, the fierce little terrier, agreed with a soft woof.

Chapter Four

Aunt Caroline bestowed a keen look on her niece, then quietly said, "That was very kind of you to rub his neck and forehead. I know your father suffered from the most dreadful headaches years ago. 'Tis nice to know you can use the knowledge gained in helping him for others."

Joanna gave her aunt a distressed look. "I fear I was dreadfully forward, for I had not considered the propriety of the matter. After all, I am a spinster and he is unmarried as well. It is not seemly for me to touch him in such a familiar manner."

"I believe there are times when propriety can be a frightful nuisance. If one is intent upon helping another with the gift of healing, I do not see how propriety can be heeded," Aunt Caroline replied in a considering way.

"He did seem much better when he left, did he not?" Joanna said with some relief and a hesitant smile.

"Indeed. Although I do believe I shall make up some of my headache posset and bring it over to his valet later. After all, he cannot come running to us every time he has a headache, can he?"

Joanna bent over to scratch Rex's head, fondling one of his dark brown ears. Rex responded by rolling over and resting his head against Joanna's shoe. It saved her having to comment on her aunt's observation.

"I believe you have a friend."

"Dear Rex—he is not a pretty dog, but I shall feel better having him along with me," Joanna admitted.

"Indeed," her aunt murmured with a highly speculative look at her niece, who was adroitly avoiding her direct gaze. "Did something happen yesterday while you were walking that I ought to know about?"

"No," Joanna said hastily. "Nothing at all. But I did see the wisdom of acquiring a protector."

"I see," Aunt Caroline said with a mystified expression on her face, indicating that she did not see in the least.

The following morning brought a fitful sun but no apparent threat of rain. Joanna announced that she and the dog would be off on a walk immediately after breakfast.

"Do you need something for a leash? He has not been with you long," Aunt Caroline said with a cautious pat bestowed on Rex's head.

"I shall take some small scraps of food with me for him. Should he wander, I can summon him with the promise of a treat."

"How clever you are," Aunt Caroline said with an admiring smile.

Joanna grimaced. Had she been truly clever, she would not have allowed Sir Lucas to kiss her yesterday, nor permitted him to assist her in selecting her dog—although, to be honest, she would have chosen Rex anyway. He was just what she needed.

Not wishing to delay her departure, Joanna stuffed a small loaf of bread, a chunk of cheese, and a bit of fruit in a small canvas bag that she toted with her to hold odds and ends. She added the promised treats for the dog and then set off again, this time on a different path.

At least she did not expect to encounter Sir Lucas today. In addition to settling in at his cottage, he might be suffering from the aftermath of his dreadful headache. While Joanna did not precisely like the man—and she did not trust him an inch—she felt genuinely sorry for anyone who was plagued by the headache.

The air was fresh and almost balmy. In the cottage garden, blossoms were drifting down from the trees and the foxgloves were coming into bloom. It was warmer than Joanna had expected. When she could she remained in the shade of the birch trees that seemed to do so well in the area, admiring the views in every direction.

Before long, she left the shelter of the trees and headed up the path into another, thinner patch of trees. It was good to have Rex for company, especially when the path grew steep and rough. She was panting when she reached a peculiar-looking gate.

Deciding it was a good place to rest, Joanna paused in some shade offered and half closed her eyes against the glare of the sun.

At her feet Rex growled and the hair at the back of his neck seemed to bristle. Joanna looked about her to find a man, one of the itinerants they had spoken of yesterday, approaching from the same steep path she had just taken.

" 'Tis called a kissing gate, lass," he said when he drew closer, gesturing to the gate. He paused at a respectful distance, most likely because of the dog.

"Indeed," murmured Joanna in a cool but polite tone, looking again at the gate. She was thankful that Sir Lucas was not about or he would have made a teasing reference to the gate's strange name that would most assuredly have put her to the blush.

"It is shaped to allow but one person to pass at a time," came a second, familiar voice from just beyond the far side of the gate. Joanna recognized it at once. After all, she thought with resignation, she had heard it often enough as of late.

She turned to note the U shape of the opening through which one must pass. Truly, only one person could go through it at a time. "So I see," she said politely. Then she looked at him. "Good morning, Sir Lucas. You rose early."

"Although the fireplace now works better, the house is still damp. Perhaps in a day or two it will be all right."

The itinerant moved closer to Sir Lucas, studying him with a narrowed gaze. He seemed about to speak, then remained silent. When offered a few coins, the man took off down the slope with a few backward glances that made Joanna uneasy.

"Rex has yet to learn to protect you adequately, I see." Sir Lucas leaned against the gate, studying the dog and Joanna in turn.

"He warned me that someone approached. The man seemed almost friendly until you came." She gave Sir Lucas a cool look, tilting her chin in defiance. Rex had *not* warned her about Sir Lucas.

"That is because he hoped to catch you unawares. I cannot rest easy with your going about like this. Even the most tranquil scene can hold dangers."

Joanna thought that her greatest danger was Sir Lucas himself but did not say so. She was too polite to argue with him, although she held her own reservations about being alone.

"You were headed up the hill?" he prodded.

"According to my map, I may reach the top of Butter Crags if I take this path. I merely follow this stone wall"—she gestured behind where he stood—"pass a small tarn, then skirt a bog, and walk along a stone wall until, there I am. There is supposed to be a spectacular view of the valley."

"That is rather abbreviated, but basically correct. I had best go along with you, for you might take a wrong turning and end up elsewhere."

Joanna was indignant. Did he think her unable to read a map? Then she recalled the itinerant and the menacing look he had given them. Perhaps Sir Lucas—as dangerous as he seemed—was better than the unknown.

She passed through the kissing gate with a wary step. Rex, right behind her, jumped over the narrow way with ease. She noticed the dratted dog did not growl at Sir Lucas. Rather, he had sniffed at the man, then trotted along between her and her unwelcome partner.

"He does guard you in a way," Sir Lucas observed with a smile. "He knows me, but trots along between us."

This served to make Joanna feel a measure safer. She gave the dog an approving look, then took a treat from her bag and bent over to give it to him.

As they climbed their way along the sometimes sketchy path, Joanna silently admitted she was grateful that she had been joined by one who knew it better than she. At long last, they skirted the bog past the small tarn and encountered a large cairn, beyond which was the expected view of the valley.

It was as breathtaking as she had hoped. Beyond them the

hill dropped away sharply to the flat, lush green of the valley floor and the village of Grasmere. Stone fences crisscrossed the fields, and patches of trees offered lovely contrast in color and texture. Above the valley the land rose again steadily into Easedale just across from where they stood. It was an awesome sight. Those who championed the picturesque instructed one to look at each landscape as though it were a picture. Even they could not find fault with this.

"How far up have we climbed?" she wondered.

"About four hundred feet I should say, more or less."

"Oh, it is splendid," Joanna said, then sank down on the ground to gaze her fill. Rex sat beside her, still keeping himself between Joanna and Sir Lucas, she noted with approval.

"That is the Scafell range over there, with other fancifully named peaks like Sergeant Man and Great Gable.

"That itinerant, I suspect he was a soldier once," Joanna said suddenly, recalling the tattered clothing the chap had worn. "I am glad you gave him some coins. More ought to be done for those who served our country."

Sir Lucas eyed her without comment, and Joanna supposed she had voiced unladylike sentiments. But she was of a practical nature and felt that if the men had decent pensions, they would not feel the need to wander about the country, begging for crumbs and coins.

She pulled the bread and cheese from her little canvas bag, thankful that she had put in extra just in case she became exceedingly hungry. She offered some of the crusty loaf to Sir Lucas, the cheese as well.

"Excellent," he murmured after sampling both.

They ate in silence for a time, merely enjoying the view, allowing the breeze to caress them. Joanna was glad for her straw hat that gave her face a bit of shade. Had she been alone, she would have been tempted to take a nap. With Sir Lucas along, she knew that to be unwise.

"Look over there," he said, pointing to a distant white building. At least she thought that was what he meant.

"There's the Swan Inn, where we can have a refreshing drink, if you will join me. After allowing me to share your bread and cheese, that is the least I can do. When Walter Scott used to visit Wordsworth, he'd sneak out of his bedroom window whilst the family was asleep, and repair to the Swan for a more substantial breakfast than the usual porridge at the cottage." He rose and offered his hand to assist her.

Joanna reluctantly accepted his help. Rex took exception and growled until she murmured something soothing that quieted the dog.

Sir Lucas didn't release her hand, but kept it firmly in his clasp. "I feel I must thank you again for your fine ministrations yesterday. I do not often have that sort of headache and when I do, it is most enervating. Cannot say I have had that sort of neck and face rub before, but it certainly did the trick. Thank you, Miss Winterton. You have my deepest gratitude."

Joanna felt her face warming, no doubt with a blush.

Lucas found himself in an odd position. He was alone in a remote spot with a pretty young woman and he felt he must exercise restraint. Strange thing for a chap like himself, who favored a bit of dalliance with a lovely creature like the one next to him. She blushed so charmingly. He would have liked to repeat their kiss; it had been most delightful. Yet his honor forbade this.

He fed the last of his cheese to the dog, then, still retaining her hand, led her along with him to where the path descended steeply. Broad zigzags dropped them down quickly to the valley floor.

She tugged her hand from his clasp and ran the last part of the way, once again reminding Lucas of that flying angel. She gave him an impish grin when she had stopped, and he hurriedly caught up to her. Rex trotted at his side, dashing up to his new mistress to check her safety when they drew near her.

"I am a frightful girl, to run like that. But it is almost like flying—like a bird, you see." Joanna brushed an errant curl from her forehead and a few wisps off her cheek. She grinned at him with the joy of doing what one wishes, regardless of the consequences.

Lucas thought her grin infectious and felt younger than he

had in years. "And here I thought you such a sensible creature," he said with a chuckle.

"Oh, I think even the most practical of us need a silly moment from time to time," she said, not denying her sensibility.

"Come, let us make our way to the Swan. I am quite parched after all that exertion."

This time she did not shy away from his hand, accepting his assistance over the little bridge that spanned the beck, then on to the inn.

It was late in the afternoon by the time they strolled back into Grasmere. Joanna felt more in charity with Sir Lucas, although it was guarded. At times it was difficult to recall he was here to recover from being jilted at the altar. She felt sure there had been no attachment to the fickle Miss Thorne. But she suspected he had suffered a blow to his pride, one that might have curious repercussions.

"You are an amazing young woman," said Sir Lucas, interrupting her reverie. "I know of no one who can walk as far on a June day and still look fresh and pretty." With a start, Joanna realized they had reached the little gate that led to Rose Cottage.

Feeling somewhat sorry for the man who had been so rudely left standing at the altar, Joanna said, "If I was able to keep you company for a time and assist you in forgetting what you came here to forget, I'm pleased."

A shadow crossed his face, and it seemed to Joanna that he froze for a few moments. "Indeed," he said in a remote way. Then, with an abrupt farewell, he turned and walked to his own house with dispatch.

Joanna opened the little gate and strolled inside, pausing to examine the flowers coming into bloom while she considered what had just happened. Quite obviously, Sir Lucas did not like her mentioning his jilt, even if indirectly. Was Aunt Caroline correct in her assessment? *Could* it be his pride that had driven him from London, more than the gossip? Or was it all of a piece?

At her side Rex gave a friendly woof, and Joanna turned to

see her aunt limping toward them, a welcoming smile on her face.

"You are just in time to go with me to pick gooseberries," she announced. "I quite enjoy a nice gooseberry pudding—and so, I recall, do you."

"That I do," Joanna agreed. With a lingering look at the little house now occupied by Sir Lucas, Joanna willingly joined her aunt in a foray to a patch of berry bushes not far away. She had been utterly weary, but the mention of gooseberry pudding was quite enough to help her keep going a bit longer.

"And how did your walk go today? I must confess I was a trifle nervous until I saw Sir Lucas had joined you at some point." Aunt Caroline paused in the midst of the berry patch to give Joanna a curious look.

"He had been up on the mountain ahead of me, then kindly showed me the correct paths to take so I would not get lost. Rex was a very good dog and trotted along between us." Joanna grinned at her aunt, then looked to where the dog stretched out in the waning sunlight. Of the itinerant ex-soldier she decided to say nothing. It would only serve to frighten her aunt. Joanna wished to continue her walks, but did it mean she must rely on her neighbor? She hoped not. She might have to consider Susan after all.

"Tomorrow I will walk along the valley toward Rydal Water. There will likely be a good many others about, so you will not have to worry about me becoming lost." Other possible dangers were not mentioned.

"I spoke to a gentleman in one of the shops regarding the next regatta, and we had best make arrangements now if we plan to attend. It does sound like a lovely outing."

Joanna felt exceedingly selfish for thinking of her walks when she heard her aunt's wistful tones. "Indeed I shall. Tomorrow I will stop in the village to take care of the matter. Perhaps a little gig would be the thing. Or we could use our traveling coach."

"We could invite Sir Lucas to travel with us," Aunt Caroline said.

"I doubt he would wish anything so staid," Joanna ventured.

But in this Joanna was proven wrong. Sir Lucas not only agreed to Aunt Caroline's hesitant invitation, but also insisted upon arranging for a small boat for them to use once they arrived at the lake and the point from which the sailing race would begin. He said they might find the viewing better.

Joanna still found his nearness upset her self-possession. She felt so very aware of him. Her nerves seemed to tingle, and every bit of her being knew of his proximity. It was very unsettling.

"I intend to take a gooseberry pie along for us to enjoy, for there is an abundance of berries this year. And I shall have Cook prepare a goodly number of sandwiches and other things to tempt a gentleman's appetite. I believe he is looking more the thing now, do you not?" Aunt Caroline asked eagerly.

Seeing that her aunt fancied herself as assisting Sir Lucas to heal his disappointment in marriage, Joanna merely nodded, willing to go along with most anything her aunt wished.

"And I do hope you will wear that new white muslin."

When Joanna cast her a startled look, not recalling any new white muslin, Aunt Caroline appeared downright sheepish. "I ordered a few new things for you. Black is all very well for those truly in mourning, but you needn't have done such penance. It merely satisfied your father and the Underhills. And I believe it asked a great deal of you, to expect you mourn him to such a degree. Had you been married. . . ."

"Thank heaven we weren't wed," Joanna fervently agreed.

That effectively ended the conversation. Both women reflected on what had transpired in London following the news of Robert Underhill's death.

"The less said about the matter, the better," Aunt Caroline concluded after a time.

Joanna agreed, picked up her full basket, then took her aunt's as well on the walk back to Rose Cottage. Utterly worn out by now, she set the berry baskets on the kitchen table and went to her room to change and rest.

"Supper?" Aunt Caroline asked, before Joanna could nod off.

Joanna groaned and wondered if Sir Lucas's valet was as

gentle a tyrant as Aunt Caroline. She joined her relative for a simple meal and felt the better for it.

It rained during the night, and come morning Joanna suspected it would be muddy walking today. She strolled about in the garden, picking off the heads of dead flowers and examining the roses for which the cottage was named.

Sir Lucas left his house and headed toward the village. Joanna did not wish to speak to the man, so why did she know a pang of regret when he ignored her?

Then, as he passed from view, she realized it would be safe to take her walk now. She quickly found Rex, packed the same sort of lunch as the day before, including a cork-stoppered bottle of water, and set off along the walk through the town to where she might pick up the path to Rydal Water.

The road led south and east toward where writer Thomas De Quincey lived in Nob Cottage. She'd avoid him. Some distance beyond Rydal Water was Rydal Hall, where the poet Wordsworth lived with his wife, their children, her sister, and his sister. She intended to avoid them as well. She was not one of those who wished to intrude upon someone merely because she happened to enjoy his poetry.

Not but what she had tucked a slim volume of verse in her sack this morning. She thought it would be lovely to read the poetry inspired by various views.

Since she wished to keep off the road and avoid any chance of encountering Sir Lucas—for she suspected he may have ridden to Ambleside to arrange for a rowboat—she followed the path that led around the far side of the water.

It was a small lake, much smaller than Grasmere. From a high point she had an excellent view of where she had been not long before. Then she plunged down the path, speculating on whether she might chance to meet anyone today. For June, there were curiously few people about.

She wondered about the ruin seen on one of the two islands in the lake. It was a curious place to attempt to build anything.

The path led her to an opening of a cave where it appeared

that slate had been quarried and might still be quarried for all she knew.

She was uneasy that the sky had clouded over so very much. It looked to coming on rain. Of a sudden the clouds opened up and what she feared occurred. Rain. Oh, how it poured.

Joanna stepped farther inside the larger of the two caves and hoped there was no one hiding back in the shadows. Water covered the floor of the cave, with stones pointing up through the murky liquid everywhere. It was not a pleasant spot. Rex shook off the water and sat beside her, shifting about uneasily, perhaps unhappy with the rain.

Leaning against the wall for additional shelter, she watched the rain fall in great sheets. Rex growled and Joanna stiffened. Who was there? In the deepening gloom caused by the heavy rain and lack of light she could see but little. Outside the caves, gulls wheeled and squawked at the inclement weather, or so it seemed to her.

She wished she was snug in Rose Cottage with a cup of tea at her side and her feet toasting near the fire.

"Who is there?" she cried in alarm when Rex growled again.

The silence of the cave, the sound of rain falling, and the gulls outside were all she heard. She watched the dog, who was staring into the depths of the cave. Joanna shivered, wondering what or who was back there, the unseen menace. Rex stood frozen, hair bristling, intent on whatever noise he heard. He sniffed, then growled again.

Joanna prayed the rain would end soon. She looked to the sky, and it seemed a trifle lighter to her anxious eyes.

And then, as suddenly as it began, the rain stopped, or near enough so that Joanna could flee the cave where she had thought to take refuge.

She ran as fast as she could back the way she came, panting with exertion as she climbed the slope to the rise, then paused to catch her breath when she felt it safe.

She stared back at where she knew the cave to be and saw nothing out of the ordinary. Not a person, nor an animal. The sun slanted through the trees, bestowing a look of tranquillity on the scene that was quite at odds with Joanna's inner fears.

"Miss Winterton! Are you all right?"

Almost welcoming the intrusion, Joanna turned about to face Sir Lucas as he climbed up from the main road to join her. She could see a dandy little gig that he must have leased. It pointed toward Ambleside rather than Grasmere and she surmised that he had yet to arrange for a rowboat.

"I repeat," he said when she failed to answer, "are you all right? Your aunt said you left some time ago, and worried about you becoming soaked in the rainstorm. But you are dry. You found a refuge, I take it."

He had the look of one who had gone to great pains for no reason at all.

Still frightened by the unknown, Joanna took a step toward Sir Lucas. "I am dry and just fine. However, I do not trust the weather. I took shelter in one of the caves along this path, the one running behind me. It was not a pleasant experience and I am quite unwilling to continue my walk today. Would you mind walking with me until we reach the road?" He offered her his arm at once.

Joanna accepted his assistance with more than ordinary thankfulness. She felt distinctly uneasy in this area and observed that Rex still glanced back toward the caves and growled from time to time. She had not imagined it. There was danger in that cave.

When they gained the roadside, Joanna found she felt considerably better. So much for leaving the well-traveled path! "Thank you, sir," she said, but could not smile yet.

"I suspect there is more to this than the weather," the very astute Sir Lucas said. He didn't pry, and for that Joanna was grateful because she suspected she would sound like a looby with her fears.

She turned in the direction of Grasmere when Sir Lucas said, "I am driving into Ambleside to take care of a small matter. Why do you not join me in the gig? It is an open vehicle and this is not London," he concluded, alluding to the proprieties that must be observed when in Town.

Since Joanna had no desire to return at this moment, before

her fears had been completely put behind her and she might still be in danger of revealing something to frighten her aunt, she promptly agreed with the offered plan.

"Thank you, Sir Lucas. That would be lovely." She cast a last look at the path that led to the caves, neither of which she could see from here, and joined Sir Lucas in the little gig with all due haste, settling Rex at her side.

They clip-clopped toward Ambleside with no hurry, which was fine with Joanna now that she was free of the caves.

"Will you tell me what frightened you back there?" he said after a time of silence during which Joanna had searched her memory to see if she could recall something of significance.

"What? Oh, it was nothing, I assure you. Merely a silly noise or something." She scratched Rex's ears and cuddled him closer to her in her lap. The dog did not resist her desire for comfort.

"And something silly made you turn pale and your eyes pools of frightened blue?"

Joanna had no desire to confide in him, never mind that he had more or less rescued her from a frightful experience. She had reached safety when he joined her, but she felt far more at ease by his side. However, no amount of coaxing could persuade her to reveal her tale.

"If you say so," she said at last. "I expect that I reacted to something quite innocent. It was the rain, and the birds, and the gloomy cave. Perhaps it was too much like a Minerva novel?"

He merely looked at her, a speculative look, then finally said, "I suspect you had better reconcile yourself to taking your maid along with you."

Joanna nodded, then sat quietly while he skillfully tooled the gig into the village and down to the pier where the rental boats were to be found. Beyond them the lake stretched out to a great distance, far longer than Grasmere.

"It is the largest lake in England, or so I've read," Sir Lucas said when he returned from arranging the rental of the rowboat.

"I look forward to the regatta on the morrow," Joanna said. "Aunt Caroline promises to bring a gooseberry pie!"

"Splendid. I'm fond of gooseberry pie," Sir Lucas said while escorting Joanna back to their vehicle.

Joanna busied herself about climbing back into the gig. Once settled with Rex, she took a last look at the lake and the pretty little boat they would use. At least there could be no danger there, she thought with satisfaction.

Chapter Five

On the way back to Grasmere they again passed Rydal Water. Any sight less likely to be threatening Joanna could not imagine. It appeared as tranquil as a Sunday afternoon in Hyde Park. Yet, she vividly recalled the sensations she experienced while standing in the opening to the cave. What had been there? She unconsciously wrapped her arms about her for comfort when they approached the place where Sir Lucas had found her.

He noticed her action and brought the horse immediately to a halt. He stared off along the path that circled the lake, a frown creasing his forehead.

"I see nothing to alarm a person," he said at last.

"Who said anything about being alarmed?" she countered.

"You were pale and wide-eyed when I found you. And now you huddle on the seat as though an ogre might jump from the bushes," he said, but not in a scolding way. It was clear he was puzzled and not a little intrigued by what Joanna had told him. Yet he did not denounce her, and this she appreciated.

"I will admit I shall feel better when we are safely back in Grasmere. It truly was peculiar. I saw nothing, but I thought I heard a noise when there ought not have been one—if you know what I mean—and Rex growled and sat most alertly on guard. And I have not a clue as to why," Joanna admitted with frustration.

"Let us hope that when we travel this road tomorrow on our way to the regatta that you are able to conceal this reaction from your aunt. I know you do not wish to upset her." Sir Lucas gave her a surprisingly understanding look.

Perhaps she had misjudged him. It could be that the rakish

facade was precisely that—an outward mien presented to the
ton and nothing more. But then, she was such an innocent,
what did she know about anything?

They resumed their drive back to Grasmere, and Joanna relaxed as they drew farther away from the inexplicably frightening spot. As to a change in his character, she would reserve
judgment on that. It remained to be seen if he would behave
himself in the days to come.

They drew to a halt before Rose Cottage, and Joanna
climbed from the gig with little difficulty. Sir Lucas remained
holding the reins, watching her.

"Thank you for being so considerate, Sir Lucas. Not every
man is so patient with a woman's little quirks," Joanna said
while helping Rex from the gig.

He compressed his mouth briefly, then said, "No one cares
to have another ring a peal over his head. However, I want no
roundaboutation in the future. If something of this nature oc-
curs again, you had best share it with me. And Miss Winterton, I really do suggest you consider taking your maid along
with you in the future. You never know what might happen."
His eyes gleamed, perhaps with the memory of the stolen kiss.

With that cogent observation, Sir Lucas wheeled the little
gig about and returned to his own stone cottage. Joanna hoped
it was drying out, but doubted it would remain so for long,
even if the roof were repaired. Rain was a frequent occurrence
around here—as Aunt Caroline had said, the green hills did
not come about without reason.

While strolling to the cottage, Joanna considered what had
happened, which actually was nothing more than her overac-
tive imagination and a peculiar feeling about the cave.

Sir Lucas would have been quite justified in heaping a scold
on her foolish head. He was a mystery. He kissed her soundly,
like the rake he was reputed to be. Then, when she was ac-
costed by the itinerant on the path, Sir Lucas reversed his own
direction and escorted her safely across the crags and down to
the valley again. Back to Rose Cottage, as a matter of fact.
And today he had been most considerate of her, not chiding
her for being foolish when she had certainly felt foolish. Yet,

she was quite certain she had not mistaken that gleam in his eyes.

He most definitely had not forgotten his stolen kiss. Although he twice suggested that she bring her maid along with her on future walks. Sir Lucas was definitely a difficult man to understand.

Joanna bent over to sniff a rose before going inside to face Aunt Caroline. Sir Lucas was not the only one who recalled the stolen kiss. Joanna did as well, and it no doubt put her cheeks to a blush as pink as the rose whose rich fragrance she sampled.

"Hello, dear girl. Home so soon?" Aunt Caroline queried with a glance at the mantel clock.

Since Joanna felt she must make some explanation regarding her early return, she avoided the matter of the cave and her fears, saying instead, "I did walk some distance to Rydal Water, but the rain made walking unpleasant. Fortunately for me, Sir Lucas chanced by on his way to Ambleside to reserve a rowboat for us on the morrow."

Joanna strolled across the room to lean against the highback chair. "And 'tis a good thing he did, for the inns are full to capacity and there is scarcely an available bed to be found in a private home. I understand the butcher is renting out his rooms over his shop—he, poor fellow, is bedding down in Farmer Hadgley's barn. I feel sure that all the boats will be spoken for by tomorrow."

"You drove to Ambleside with Sir Lucas?" Aunt Caroline said, pouncing on the one interesting fact in Joanna's recital.

"He was all that was kind and proper, dear aunt," Joanna said. "Amazingly so, for one deemed a rake." She busied herself with brushing Rex and checking his paws for dirt. Aunt Caroline did not appreciate dirt tracked into the cottage.

"Hmm. Somehow I had not associated kindness with Sir Lucas. Nor propriety. One thinks of a rake as a sneering, starched-up sort of man, not one given to kind deeds and certainly not propriety. I doubt Robert Underhill would have behaved so well under the same circumstances. Yes, I find Sir Lucas charming—but still suspect."

At this comment Joanna looked sharply at her aunt, strong

denial on her lips. Then she remained silent. How could she reveal his behavior following the encounter with the itinerant without alarming Aunt Caroline? And how could she explain how understanding he had been when Joanna had been frightened of a nameless, unseen thing without truly horrifying the dear lady?

"One never knows, does one?" she said, forcing herself to a mild reply.

Aunt Caroline was silent for a few moments, then said, "I had a letter from your father."

Startled, Joanna forgot about cleaning up the dog and rose to face her aunt. "And?"

"He plans to marry again, a widow, Gwendolyn, Lady Parry. Her late husband was Baron Parry of Langdale. She is about your late mother's age, perhaps younger, and apparently a pleasant companion, sharing your father's taste for country life. He writes he is buying a new bed, one of those elaborate things with a fancy dome complete with draperies and a crown atop it. He has also ordered one of those Grecian couches that Sheraton makes. I wonder if the blue salon will turn into a Grecian chamber?" she said with a note of irony in her voice. She offered the two folded sheets of crisp white paper to her niece.

Joanna accepted the letter, which she quickly perused before reading it more carefully a second time. Letters from her father were rather rare and deserved careful study.

"It seems your father does not have headaches anymore, does he?" Aunt Caroline inserted. "Perhaps a second wife will ease his mind and give him peace." Aunt Caroline sank onto a Windsor chair close to hand and watched Joanna.

"I expect he has been lonely. Mama has been gone many years, and then I denied him any grandchildren. It would seem he has given up hope of having any. What a shame he did not have a son. The entailed estate must go to one of my cousins." Joanna exchanged an expressive look with her aunt.

"Unless Lady Parry is able to provide an heir. It would not be beyond her at her age. She has two daughters and a son by her first marriage. Stranger things have happened." Aunt Caroline shot Joanna a commiserating look.

"Do you know, I hope she does. I believe Father would quite dote on the lad." Joanna smiled at the thought.

"As he did not dote on you? Never mind, my dear. I think I doted enough for the two of us," Aunt Caroline said with a chuckle.

Joanna smiled and chatted for a bit, while thinking it might have been nice to have known just a bit of attention from her father. She knew he had hoped for an heir, but to so totally ignore her, only entering her life long enough to insist she marry that utterly dreadful Robert Underhill! Well, it was all behind her now, if Society would permit her to return without constantly making reference to her supposed loss.

She had done so many things to try to capture Papa's good graces. Massaging his neck had been her best attempt, for he took to sending for her whenever he was so afflicted. As he grew older, he had ceased having the headaches. That they stopped after her mother died was a coincidence that had caused Joanna no little curiosity.

"Well, you had best come to inspect Cook's gooseberry pie and offer a few words of praise. The crust looks particularly light. I believe we were very lucky to find her." Aunt Caroline rose from the chair and led the way to the kitchen where Joanna duly admired the pie.

The following morning dawned bright and reasonably clear. The few clouds in the sky did not seem the sort to disappoint the crowd and bring rain.

Joanna dressed in an ankle-length nautical-blue gown decorated with white trimming down the front and on the sleeves. Aunt Caroline had declared the white frill at the neck most flattering. She was tying the dark blue satin bows of her bonnet under her chin when her aunt called out that dear Sir Lucas was patiently awaiting them.

Precisely when Sir Lucas had earned the "dear" was a mystery to Joanna, but she was pleased that her aunt would not be uncomfortable in his presence.

Joanna well knew that even if her aunt was willing to overlook a mishap now and again, she would *not* have ignored the matter of a stolen kiss had Joanna reported it to her. But as

Joanna had no wish to be forced into another arranged marriage, she thought the matter best swept under the rug as it were.

Aunt was garbed in a cheerful lavender India muslin print topped with a pretty silk shawl—the sort that is yards square and printed with flowers. Joanna complimented her on her choice for the day.

"Well, dear girl, I am not half so well done as you. How appropriate," Caroline said with her usual approval.

"I have no doubt that no matter what I wore you would applaud." Joanna grinned.

"Well," her aunt said with a frown, "I cannot like that divided skirt you have. Perhaps I am old-fashioned, but it seems scandalous to me."

"Enough," Joanna murmured. She closed the door behind them, carrying the basket of provisions for their picnic out to the coach that Tom Coachman had readied for the excursion. Rex trotted along at her side.

Sir Lucas joined them by the coach, quickly relieving Joanna of her burden.

"The horses are restless," he said with a look at the coachman who waited patiently for them and restrained the horses with difficulty.

"Plaguy things—eat their heads off, then resent being put to the traces again," Joanna said with a moue of disgust.

She tried to keep her gaze from settling on Sir Lucas in his understated elegance. His breeches might be a sensible brown, but fit him to perfection. His fawn waistcoat and corbeau coat fit him beautifully as well, she admitted, while trying to equate this polished gentleman with the more casual man who had joked with her on the way down the mountain to the Swan Inn.

Joanna managed to ignore the path that led around Rydal Water because just as they approached that area Sir Lucas began telling outrageous gossip about several people her aunt knew. Even Joanna had to laugh, and the disturbing spot was passed before she was aware of it.

The rowboat was a neat little craft. Joanna found to her amazement that Sir Lucas was quite capable when it came to rowing, and decided he must have learned the skill while at

Oxford. Rex jumped in and quickly settled in the front of the boat beneath the seat Joanna claimed.

Aunt Caroline sank back against her pillows with a contented sigh, tilting her parasol to shade her face, and chatted to Sir Lucas in an amusing manner.

Joanna—sitting to the front of the boat—watched his back. She ought not, she supposed, for he had removed his coat and she had a view of muscular arms and shoulders through the fine cambric of his shirt. But she would quite understand his not wishing to possibly ruin his coat, since those objects were not made to actually *do* anything in while being worn. Although, she realized, his coat did not fit as snugly as some. She had no doubt that some gentlemen required two men to assist them into their coats as she had heard.

Once well out on the lake, they dropped anchor—Joanna agreeing to this task—and waited for the regatta to begin.

"It is quite splendid," Aunt Caroline cried, forgetting to relax against her cushions in the excitement of seeing a dozen sailboats vying for first place. They skimmed across the water, sending sprays of droplets arching into the air, capturing the sun so that it seemed each boat trailed a necklet of diamonds.

A fresh breeze whipped up little waves and Joanna relished the smell of the water, clean and sharp, the scent of country. Even at this distance, she could hear the flap of sails, the shouts of the various crews. While watching the race she trailed her fingers in the cool, clear water, thinking how different it was from the vile stuff in the Thames.

Lucas watched the two women in his rented boat, sitting astride his seat in order to do so. Aunt Caroline was delightfully girlish, not untypical, he supposed, of spinsters. Pity she had the limp, for it most likely stopped a gentleman from finding that quiet wit she so ably revealed when given the chance.

As for Joanna Winterton, he could not explain why he was so drawn to her. He had been so certain that there was not a trustworthy woman to be found anywhere. Yet she had not told her aunt about that admittedly unwise kiss. Had she done so, it would have meant an immediate betrothal, since Joanna was a gently bred young woman. And he was aware that he was no small catch. Even if he had no pride in his family name, he would acknowledge that his wealth was a magnet for an unmarried girl.

And she was considerate of her aunt in other ways. He had observed her go off to pick gooseberries when she must have been extremely tired after her long walk. She had endurance, for certain. It seemed that she would not disappoint her aunt.

There was the matter of her betrothal to Robert Underhill. There was a mystery there, for he could not understand why it had been necessary for her to mourn a chap so totally unworthy of such an emotion. Had her father insisted on the marriage? There were a number of things that did not add up here. She seemed to have forgotten her husband-to-be, going for walks unchaperoned and coming close to being in trouble. Had she any notion of what might have happened to her that day? It had been a dashed smoky situation.

Rex stared at him from beneath Joanna's seat, a reminder of that day when he had helped her find a protector. The dog gave a soft woof, then settled his head on his paws, totally uninterested in sailing races. Even so, he seemed to snooze only lightly, ever ready to defend his new mistress.

Which brought Lucas back to his first mental wanderings. Why did Joanna Winterton interest him? She was passably pretty, certainly a practical chit. She seemed to be perceptive as well, knowing when to keep silent and when one desired conversation. She watched the boats race across the lake without constantly chattering, only making an occasional remark.

It must be, he decided after several long looks at Joanna, that it was propinquity. She just happened to be near when he desired female company. That he might have elected to pass the time with the bosomy barmaid at the Swan Inn was ignored.

Several of the itinerant musicians joined together to play music for the occasion. They sat in the shade of the trees and put forth jolly, happy tunes that prompted one to tap toes. The music floated across the water, a lovely counterpoint to the slapping of the waves on the shore.

When the race concluded, Joanna pulled up the anchor and he rowed along the shore rather than return to the pier as might have been expected.

Aunt Caroline exclaimed what a treat it was to be on the water. "What a kind man you are, to be sure," she concluded, with a shy smile at her benefactor.

Lucas hadn't thought of himself as being *kind*. He had been called many things, and *kind* wasn't one of them. He raised the oars to allow the boat to drift so Aunt Caroline could watch some ducks at play. This enabled him to half turn and watch Miss Winterton. Joanna. The name fit her, somehow.

They drifted closer to shore and Rex sat up to stare at the passing land. Then his hair bristled and he emitted a low growl.

"Is that familiar?" Lucas asked Joanna softly.

"Indeed. I heard the same yesterday."

"Oh, look at those dear little ducks. Something must have frightened them, for they scurry along, some taking to flight. Some nasty animal, no doubt," Aunt Caroline said, with an indignant sniff.

"Do you believe that?" Lucas asked Joanna.

"No," she said, shaking her head while studying the shore. "Do you suppose there could be someone following us, walking along the shore? There are enough bushes and trees for him to hide in quite easily."

"You think it a man?"

"Unlikely to be an animal. I doubt it is a woman. Unless you are given to having women trail after you?" Joanna said with a teasing smile. Rex subsided and she relaxed.

She did not want him, Lucas realized. There was no desire in her eyes, no repressed longing in her voice. She was, he acknowledged, treating him like a brother. It was most lowering, he decided upon reflection.

"Do you have a brother?" he abruptly inquired.

"No, I am an only child," she said.

"Joanna's father is to marry again," Aunt Caroline announced from the rear of the boat, an indication that she was not as unaware of what was going on as Lucas had thought.

"Mother died some years ago and I expect he has been lonely," Joanna said quietly.

"I had not realized your father was still living," Sir Lucas replied, startled at this news. He was surprised that the young woman lived with an aunt rather than her parent. It seemed to him that the aunt normally came to live with the girl and her father, not the other way around.

"Joanna very much resembles her mother. I suspect it was more comfortable for George to live without constantly being reminded of the past," Aunt Caroline said with a narrow-eyed stare at a passing duck. "And now he will be married. No need for Joanna to go home now."

Lucas had no idea how that remark might be construed. That Joanna looked faintly embarrassed stopped him from making further and possibly intrusive inquiries.

Still, none of this explained why she treated him with such a lack of flirtation. She boasted no fluttery lashes, no coy glances, no suggestive smiles. And, he realized, she was a discreet creature. Another girl might have babbled on with perfect resentment about a neglectful father. Joanna imparted the facts, nothing of her inner feelings. Judging from the aunt's words, there might be just cause for bitterness on Joanna's part.

This was contrary to what he had observed of other women of the *ton* in the past, and he looked at Joanna Winterton with curiosity. Was she one of a kind? Or could there be women in the world who were discreet, sensible, and pretty as well? Somehow he doubted it. He had been serious when he declared a pox on all women.

Yet, *this* woman did not want him. The knowledge piqued his pride. Never had such a thing happened to him before. She had enjoyed their kiss—he would swear to that. Did she bury that shared joy somewhere in the back of her mind? That must be the case, he decided. It was not to be considered that she actually scorned an interest in him.

It certainly appeared that she was not the little baggage he had first suspected. He had thought her a pretender, grieving for a man who did not deserve it in the least. Now he was not so certain. Perhaps all women were not dishonest, scheming jades.

After having had another hasty nap beneath Joanna's seat, Rex sat up, alert and staring off at the shore again.

Lucas quickly grabbed at the oars and began to row away

from the land, thinking it better to be on the water if there was a danger present.

"Why is that dog making a fuss?" Aunt Caroline demanded to know when Rex growled.

"I suspect he saw a cat," Joanna improvised.

"We had best return to the pier. I would like to sample that gooseberry pie you promised," Sir Lucas said. He began to row faster, as though he could not wait for his treat.

Joanna was more than a little concerned. Rex was behaving the same way that he had at the cave.

There was a loud report. Rex barked madly. From the side of the boat a fountain of water began spilling into the craft.

Aunt Caroline sat up and said, "I do believe we shall sink, unless you row very fast." She clasped her hands before her and wore a very worried look on her plump face.

Thankful her aunt was so sensible and calm, Joanna searched about to see if there was something she might use to stop up the leak, and could find nothing at hand. Rex sat back and growled but did nothing to help matters.

Joanna scrambled past Sir Lucas and sat down on the damp floor on the opposite side of the boat in the hope that it would be enough to tilt the boat above the waterline and so stop the influx of water. Her plan worked. The spouting ceased.

Sir Lucas rowed as though entered in a competition and determined to win.

They reached the pier and Lucas put the boat in at the rocky shore, hoping Aunt Caroline could be helped from the boat before she might raise an alarm. He rose, letting the oars drop where they were, and nearly tugged the poor woman from her seat, assisting her across the boat and to shore rather forcefully, he feared. The sooner he got both Joanna and her aunt on dry land, the better. Rex jumped out, then sat to one side to watch, eyes alert.

Lucas went off to explain the situation to the chap who had rented him the boat. It was not going to be a simple matter. He put forth the suggestion that someone had been shooting at a duck and the fellow seemed to accept that idea—somewhat reluctantly.

Joanna gently guided her aunt across the rocks and up the

bank to a sheltered place. Tom Coachman stood not far away, ready to bring the basket of lunch when needed.

"I should like to know what is going on," Aunt Caroline said simply after she had settled on a cushion in the shade.

"I suspect Sir Lucas would as well. I heard him tell the man that it might have been someone shooting at a duck."

"Fiddlesticks. No one with any sense would shoot off a gun in an area such as this. Too many people about."

"Well," Joanna said with a look around her, "there are a great number of people without the sense God gave a flea."

Sir Lucas returned to join them, accepting a proffered cushion from Joanna with thanks and settling down beside Aunt Caroline with flattering attention.

"Do not try to gammon me, young man," Aunt said with a solemn stare at him. "What is afoot here?"

"To be honest, I truly do not know." He glanced at Joanna, then off to where the fellow who had rented the boat was repairing the hole with a mixture of pitch. "Dashed peculiar thing to happen, and I cannot tell you how sorry I am if this has upset your day."

"Not in the least," Aunt Caroline denied with a bracing air. "One needs a bit of shaking up from time to time. Keeps one from becoming staid and dull."

Lucas nodded and smiled, thinking this pair of women were two of the more unusual people he had come across in his years. Rather than have hysterics, Joanna Winterton had the presence of mind to tilt the boat so the water would not enter. And the aunt had sat quietly rather than adding to the confusion. His own mother would have fainted, possibly falling into the lake, given her size and the size of the boat. The notion made him smile.

"Well, if you can still smile, the matter cannot be too serious," Aunt Caroline declared, relief apparent in her voice. "Come let us have our lunch. I declare, this is a lovely spot and the breeze most welcoming. I trust you are hungry after all your exertion? I fancy that Joanna will do justice to her portion."

The trio put aside the problem of the stray shot at the rowboat, and set to with a will to demolish the appealing lunch Aunt Caroline and Cook had prepared.

"The gooseberry pie is outstanding," Sir Lucas concluded after a bite. "You went to pick the berries after we returned from the Crags?"

With a flash of her eyes that told him she had not mentioned this to her aunt, Joanna quietly said, "Indeed."

Caroline Staunton uttered a horrified gasp and scolded her niece, "I had no idea you had walked that far. You ought to have said something. You must have been extremely tired."

"I would not have missed this pie for anything, nor the pudding we shared the other evening. It was well worth the effort." Joanna said, casting another blue-eyed look at Lucas.

Lucas lounged against the tree, watching the play of shadows of the overhead branches on Miss Winterton's expressive face.

Then his gaze went beyond the two women to the strolling crowd. Who was out there who wished one of the trio ill? Why would anyone wish Joanna Winterton dead? He discounted his own danger, he had no serious enemies. But could she?

Chapter Six

They strove for a mood of gaiety, but each of them was wondering precisely what had prompted that shot at the boat. That not one of them believed it was an accident was rather curious, Joanna thought. She was certain that someone from Sir Lucas Montfort's past had come to haunt him. Either it was an irate husband out to dispose of a man who had courted his wife, or a father disappointed when Sir Lucas had wooed his daughter, then failed to come to the sticking point.

Lucas, on the other hand, looked at the two women and dismissed the possibility that Caroline Staunton was the target. No, it had to be Joanna Winterton. Could it be something to do with her deceased betrothed? Perhaps one of his family who sought to put a period to her existence, thinking it unfair that she lived while Underhill was dead? While unlikely, it was not impossible. Stranger things happened every day and even stranger people existed. Why, one of those itinerants might be the chap they sought. And there was no way they might know until he struck again. That he would strike, Lucas was sure. He just could not figure out when. Or how. Not to mention why.

Caroline cast a worried look at both Joanna and Sir Lucas. Who would wish either of them dead? Since she could not imagine who might have a grudge against her niece, she fastened upon Sir Lucas as the likely target. She suspected he was a man of many parts and most apt to have a shadow in his past. What that might be, she neither knew nor wanted to know. But there was little doubt that he was the target, and she hoped she might find a way to help the poor man. He had been most besieged of late and did not appear to deserve it.

The musicians struck up a jolly tune and the trio in the

shade of the spreading oak watched a group of merrymakers join in an impromptu dance.

"How pleasant this is," Aunt Caroline declared. "What a pity it must come to an end. They have given out the awards and the participants are leaving." She sighed rather wistfully, then began collecting the remnants of their al fresco meal. Not a crumb of the gooseberry pie remained.

"I fear it will rain again," Sir Lucas said with a jaundiced glance at the clouded sky. He motioned the groom over to assist with gathering up cushions and the like.

"As Aunt Caroline said, all this lovely green grass must have water to grow." Joanna set the last of the plates in the hamper, placed the clothes on top, and stuffed the cutlery into one basket corner.

"Not to mention gooseberries, brambles, and all the other treats that grow around here," Aunt Caroline said in a determinedly happy voice. "I believe I shall encourage Mrs. Hawkins to cook us some jam."

Joanna allowed Sir Lucas to carry the basket and then assist the ladies into the carriage for the ride home.

"Just one moment, good ladies. I see an old friend with that sailing group. Permit me to greet him?"

Without waiting for a reply, Sir Lucas strode off to where a portly gentleman in a nutmeg bagwig, elegant tricorne hat, and a smashing plum coat decorated with a row of large brass buttons down the front watched the dancers. Well dressed in his slightly outdated style, the older man beamed a smile of welcome for Sir Lucas.

Joanna was surprised. She had not thought Sir Lucas would tend to friends among the older set. Why, the man must be as old as her aunt! She was doubly surprised when the two returned to the carriage together.

"Miss Staunton, Miss Winterton, may I present a good friend of mine, Lord Osborn. He came up from Oxford for the regatta. I have persuaded him to visit with me for a time."

Lord Osborn bowed quite nicely, smiling politely in greeting, and said all that was proper.

Aunt Caroline turned pale, then a delicate rose as she viewed the distinguished gentleman. "We met some years ago, although I daresay you have long forgotten the occasion. I am pleased to meet you again, Lord Osborn."

"My pleasure, I assure you, madam," he said, clearly trying to recall the event.

Joanna pleasantly greeted the new addition to their little group while wondering if this man had something to do with the shot at the rowboat. That her aunt had met him, and quite obviously admired him, made it unlikely. But then, as Sir Lucas had said, there were strange people in this world.

"Have your man come along with your baggage. The chap at the Prince Regent Hotel can tell him where to find us."

They waited while Lord Osborn did as suggested. He rejoined them, climbing in and shutting the carriage door behind him. He settled down to face Caroline with a smile.

"I have it now. You were a trifle insubstantial back then, which is why it took me a bit of time." To Joanna he added, "I have never been one to notice those thin, poor creatures. Make no mistake, I know there are fellows who favor them, but not me." He shook his head sadly, then beamed again at Caroline. "You look as fine as fivepence, ma'am. And I recollect we met at your sister's wedding. She married Winterton—your father and mother, I suppose," he said to Joanna before turning to Aunt Caroline again. "I cannot credit that you have remained single. I married where my father commanded, of course. My wife went aloft some years ago, you know. Alone now."

He lapsed into silence after this garrulous beginning.

"Lord Osborn is something of a sleuth," Sir Lucas said with a pointed glance at Joanna. "He has solved a number of mysterious occurrences around Oxford these past years."

"Oh, it merely takes a bit of reasoning and mousing about, you know," his lordship said with modesty.

"You are precisely the man we need," Aunt Caroline cried, then blushed. "You see, we have had a most curious happening today. Someone shot at our rowboat while we were drifting along the shore. And there was not a soul to be seen," she concluded with astonishment.

"Other things are not as they ought to be, either," Sir Lucas murmured quietly.

Joanna glanced at him, wondering just how much he intended to reveal to this stranger.

They passed Rydal Water with only the briefest of comments from Sir Lucas, who merely pointed out the locale to his guest.

Joanna picked up Rex and cuddled him on her lap. He had not growled at Lord Osborn, rather accepted him with doggy good grace. She listened to the amiable chatter of the others while studying the view from the window. The rocky show of Rydal Water receded, and they climbed up and over the rise that led to the village of Grasmere.

There was no doubt about it, she would have to have Susan go along with her on her walks, not that the maid would be much help against a gun. Joanna wondered if she ought to begin carrying a weapon. It would be bulky, she supposed. Heavy, as well. But *if* someone was out to do her in, she ought to be prepared to defend herself. Why would anyone wish to dispose of her? It was beyond her. No, she decided, it could not be herself. It must be Sir Lucas. Yes, she could think of a number of reasons there.

Caroline chatted pleasantly with the baron, pointing out places of interest.

"You are pensive," Sir Lucas quietly said as they rolled through the main part of Grasmere.

"I keep wondering if there truly is someone out to do away with me. Or is it you he seeks?" she said in an undertone. She gave him a concerned look, then turned her gaze out of the window again.

"Since I doubt it is your aunt, and you are young and pretty, it is possible you might have an enemy. And," he acknowledged, "I suppose I've not led a blameless life. Although if there were a chap annoyed with me, I would hope he would seek out a face-to-face confrontation, not sneak around behind my back, endangering innocent people as well." Sir Lucas looked indignant at the danger Joanna and Aunt Caroline had been subjected to while in the boat. "No, I wonder if it is someone associated with the Underhill family. Were they angry with you when you left London?"

"Well," she said, recalling a few irate words she had exchanged with Mr. Underhill after the ring had been returned. "Had anyone said that I might be a target for a murderer a few days ago I would have laughed in his face," she mused. "Should I acquire a—" and she glanced to note that her aunt was still in earnest discussion with Lord Osborn, "gun?" The final word came out in a near-whisper.

At first, Sir Lucas was obviously taken aback at this suggestion. Then he appeared to reconsider. "I see what you mean. Let me see what I can do."

Joanna observed several things. First of all, he believed that *she* was the intended victim, so he likely did not have a worry in his head regarding himself. Secondly, he did not pronounce her silly, or helpless, or unable to shoot the largest target in Grasmere much less a person. Thirdly, he was willing to help her. She gave him high marks for all three. But, and she frowned slightly at the very thought, why was he so sure he had nothing to fear?

The coach rolled to a halt before Rose Cottage. Lord Osborn was quick to assist Aunt Caroline from the vehicle. He paid not the least attention to her limp, but accommodated his gait to hers as they strolled slowly to the house, deep in discussion of mutual acquaintances.

"He is a very nice man," Joanna observed. "I am pleased you invited him to visit with you. Did he truly solve a number of mysteries in Oxford?"

"Indeed, I thought perhaps another head, and a good one at that, would not come amiss." Sir Lucas smiled down at Joanna, making her feel a warmth that had nothing to do with the fitful sun. That gleam crept into his eyes again and she just knew she must be blushing. The dratted man was positively gifted with the ability to make a girl blush.

She captured the basket from his hand, then gave him a hesitant smile. "Join us for tea? I believe your friend is already seated in the front room. Mrs. Hawkins will have something delectable for us. We are in the habit of having a cup of afternoon tea, you see, which makes the day more pleasant."

"I believe I will."

Nothing exciting happened the rest of the day, Joanna decided upon climbing into her bed that night. Of course, it would have taken quite a bit to top being shot at.

The next day Joanna peered from her bedroom window to see Sir Lucas and Lord Osborn dressed in sensible clothes, off on a walk first thing in the morning. They looked to be headed down to the center of the village.

When she joined her aunt at the table, Aunt Caroline had donned her best muslin and lace cornette, the one with the tiny roses embroidered on it, and a pretty rose muslin gown. She looked flustered and dithery and most engaging with a silver-touched curl peeping from beneath the edge of her lace-trimmed cap.

Joanna had worn the first gown she found in her wardrobe, refusing to allow herself the pleasure of catering to that man across the street. Or to anyone else, for that matter.

"I told you a white dress would look charming on you," Aunt Caroline said, beaming an approving smile at her niece. "What a nice change from that horrid black. Yes, white is most becoming to you," her aunt declared while smoothing down her rose muslin gown and taking small peeks at the front windows. Little could go on in this part of the village that could not be seen from those front windows.

"Enjoy your breakfast," Joanna said, suddenly feeling foolish, as though she had especially dressed to please someone when she hadn't.

Aunt Caroline was clearly disappointed when the two gentlemen from the cottage across the street failed to return.

"I would wager that our neighbors are off mousing about the area. Perhaps Lord Osborn is hunting for clues?" Joanna said in order to be helpful. "Why do we not take a walk into the village and perhaps stroll about the area ourselves? That is, if you feel able?"

Aunt Caroline gave Joanna a self-conscious look. "Well, I do not mind walking even if I do limp. It seems that not every gentleman thinks ill of me for my disability."

"And it is high time, too," Joanna declared stoutly. "There are a good many to-be-pitied men in England who have missed the charm of your company because they do not bother to look beyond the surface."

"Oh, Joanna," her aunt said, quite flustered.

Joanna hoped that her dearest aunt would enjoy Lord Osborn's company. She was so vulnerable. Joanna determined that she would see to it that he did not lead her aunt a foolish dance. Joanna smiled and nodded, hoping that Lord Osborn was on the lookout for a second wife, or at the very least for a friendship with her gentle and good aunt.

The two women set off into the village, pausing to look at various gardens, taking note of the inhabitants and the pretty cottages.

"Do you see anything of interest?" Aunt Caroline asked while studying a child playing in one yard.

"Nothing that applies to what I think you want. Come, let us visit the artist in the next cottage. I learned that he sells his paintings of Grasmere, and I've a mind to buy something as a remembrance of our stay."

The ladies knocked, then entered when welcomed. The painter, Michael Wilson, greeted them with a paintbrush in one hand and a sheaf of sketches in the other. He was utterly charming in an absentminded way. Dark brown hair flopped over a surprisingly pale brow, considering he must spend a fair amount of time out of doors while painting and sketching. His hazel eyes held a somewhat pensive expression in them. He had what Joanna considered the tall, slender aspect of a poet. But then, perhaps artists and poets were all of a muchness?

Aunt Caroline fell in love with a view of the lakeshore and village. She exclaimed over the church with the mountains rising majestically behind. You could see the various cottages here and there on the slope that comprised Grasmere. Caroline was certain she could pick out Rose Cottage in the midst of a cluster of trees in the upper part of the village.

While Joanna strolled about the room, her aunt purchased the watercolor. Joanna found what she wished shortly after. It was a view from Butter Crags, much the same view that she had seen when she had been with Sir Lucas that day. The lake shimmered in the valley, with the island surrounded by several sailboats. St. Oswald's church could be clearly seen to the right of the picture, with other of the cottages scattered along the road through the village. Behind the lake the mountains rose in craggy splendor.

"Never say you went up that far on your walk," her aunt said in dismay when she came over to see what Joanna had selected.

"I quite enjoy the climbing. Sir Lucas was all that was proper, Aunt," Joanna replied softly. "And this is a lovely view." She promptly paid for her choice, suspecting the artist would welcome the two sales. She devoutly hoped that he had other income on which to live. Perhaps his family assisted him?

"You enjoy walking?" Mr. Wilson said after tucking her money in his small leather purse, clearly interested in so unusual a young woman. "I walk many miles in my pursuit of an appealing scene. Grasmere is a good location for me, for there are so many such scenes to be found." He gazed at the watercolor Joanna held and added, "I am pleased that you found this to your liking. I particularly enjoy that view."

Joanna exchanged pleasantries with him regarding the various walks that might be taken, her delight in the Swan Inn, and mentioned the regatta at Windermere the day before. "The water was so lovely, and the ducks so cunning," she concluded. Of her aversion to the caves at Rydal Water or the shot at the rowboat she said nothing.

The women were about to take their leave—not before Mr. Wilson begged permission to call on Rose cottage—when Lord Osborn and Sir Lucas knocked and entered the house. The door had been left wide open, so Joanna supposed they might have seen her and her aunt inside. She wondered what their motive for joining them could be.

"I quite liked the painting of yours I bought when last here, Wilson. Had a good many compliments on it. In fact, I intend to buy another," Lord Osborn said with a pleasant smile. Then he turned to greet Aunt Caroline and Joanna with a proper bow.

Joanna was surprised that he had come with the intention of adding to his collection. Although, she chided herself, there was no reason for them to seek out the two women just because they had spent time with them the day before.

"You found something to your liking?" Sir Lucas said in a quiet aside.

Joanna was of mixed emotions as to showing him the scene she had bought. What would he think of her selecting the view from Butter Crags? She hoped he would not read more into her choice than he ought. It would be horrid were he to assume she fancied her memories of their walk and bought the painting merely for that reason.

Reluctantly, she brought forth the painting and with a gentle hand lifted the protective sheet that covered it.

"The view from Butter Crags? Very good," Sir Lucas said with obvious approval.

Joanna watched to see if his dark eyes caught that special gleam again, but she noticed nothing out of the ordinary. Which was to say, his eyes looked their usual attractive rich brown hue.

"I liked his colors and the way he drew the valley. He has captured a lovely mood, I think. I also like the way he has done the island. He seems very talented." When she looked up, she caught an arrested expression on Mr. Wilson's face. He smiled at her, but not in a manner to make her blush.

"Indeed," Sir Lucas said with a nod. He handed the painting back to Joanna and strolled about the room, pausing at a particularly well-done picture of Rydal Water.

"Do you like to hunt, Mr. Wilson?" he suddenly asked.

"I do a bit of it when I go to my parents come fall. Otherwise, I have no time for it," Mr. Wilson replied politely. "Saw a chap up there shooting birds when I did that painting of Grasmere from Butter Crags not many days ago. Had a couple of dogs with him, and he seemed determined to bag a few birds for his table."

"Indeed," Lord Osborn said. "Can you recall what he looked like? Anything about him?" Lord Osborn held a picture of Grasmere from another aspect that was quite as captivating as the one Joanna had bought, and she envied him for it. She had not expected to be so captivated by the place she'd elected to visit.

Mr. Wilson explained that he had been too far to note any-thing in particular about the man. "For he wore a hat with a broad brim that covered him well. And there is nothing un-usual about a brown coat and breeches."

Lord Osborn agreed, then purchased the painting. The four left the little house in amiable conversation. Each carried a painting tucked under an arm. Joanna glanced back to see that the artist watched them walk up the path in the direction of Rose Cottage, the pensive look returned to his face.

The child they had seen earlier ran toward them from where she had played, the shy look on her thin face catching Joanna's interest. She looked to be a sweet child, with a win-some manner about her.

Joanna stopped to smile down at her. "You are enjoying a nice day?"

"Yes'um," the child said with a dip of a curtsy.

On closer inspection Joanna noted that the girl's gown was much patched and faded with washing, and the curls about her thin face had not been brushed for some time. "What is your name, child?"

"Mary, ma'am," she replied with a look at the curious lady dressed so fine in her white gown.

Joanna felt there was something amiss that this sweet child should be so neglected when the house was as neat as a pin and the garden well tended.

"Is your mother to home, Mary?" Just what Joanna intended to do she had not the slightest idea.

"Not my mam," the girl protested. "She keep busy with her bakin'." Mary gestured to the house, then turned and ran away.

"What a strange child," Joanna observed, "I sense a mys-tery."

"I believe you are seeing a mystery wherever you go," Sir Lucas said, clearly amused.

"Not so," Joanna denied. "But I found that girl oddly ap-pealing, so shy and sweet and terribly neglected. Did you not think it strange that the house is well-ordered and the girl treated so?"

Sir Lucas looked back at the neat cottage, then turned to

Joanna. "Your interest and compassion does you well. I do not see what you can do about her, however."

"I see you are not the sort to interfere," Joanna said quietly. Privately, she decided to inquire of the child. She wondered where the girls's mother might be and was afraid the woman was most likely dead. There were a great many mothers who died young, leaving children to be reared by others. Often that created a hardship for the one who took the child or children in to raise as their own. Joanna suspected Mary was just such a case.

They arrived at Rose Cottage and Aunt Caroline invited the gentlemen to join her and her niece in nuncheon.

"As Sir Lucas has a somewhat unusual cook, we shall accept with pleasure," Lord Osborn said with a jovial smile at his younger friend.

Sir Lucas said, "My valet has been doubling as cook and does well only on simple things. Tell me, what magic did you perform to acquire such a gem?"

"Not magic, sir," Aunt Caroline said, "merely good luck. We chanced to hire her when her previous employer left the area." She glanced shyly at Lord Osborn, then added, "We would be pleased were you to join us for dinner. Mrs. Hawkins does excel at whatever she prepares."

They had a pleasant nuncheon, mostly because Lord Osborn regaled them with amusing tales of his life in Oxford and his sleuthing. Joanna perceived that Sir Lucas had done well to persuade his friend to join him, and wondered if her aunt would contrive to invite the gentlemen to have a good many meals at Rose Cottage. Or perhaps she might offer to share Mrs. Hawkins—at least once in a while.

"You capture a memory of your walk, perhaps?" Sir Lucas said, gesturing to her painting when she placed it on the mantel so as to view it from a distance.

"The view, certainly," she said with a nod. "This is truly a lovely area. I had not thought when I selected it that it would prove so charming. All I had hoped for was a pleasant enough place in which to rusticate while waiting for Society to forget about me and turn its attention to someone else."

"How well you put it," he murmured, "I left London for not too dissimilar a reason."

"You were not smothered in sympathy, however." Then thinking that she had said quite enough, Joanna suggested they take another stroll, this time to the church. "I should like to study the interior when not attending divine service."

Replete with an excellent, although light, meal, the others agreed and within minutes bonnets had been donned, parasols found, and Aunt Caroline was having her silk shawl draped about her shoulders by a solicitous Lord Osborn. He supported her while they slowly ambled along the lane.

Joanna looked for the child, Mary, and glimpsed her in the garden to the rear of the cottage. She was weeding among the cabbages and carrots.

"You ought not encourage the child. You do not do her a favor," Sir Lucas said with a frown.

"I would never harm the girl," Joanna said when she turned away. "But I am concerned about her," she concluded with a twirl of her rose silk parasol.

Sir Lucas merely glanced back at the child, then gave Joanna a narrow look that indicated to her that while he might enjoy her company, he had no faith that she might do the girl a kindness. It appeared that he had no trust in women. Not in the least.

The door shut behind them with a thump and Joanna advanced down the earthen aisle of St. Oswald's with curious eyes. Dried rushes rustled beneath her feet as she walked toward the nave. Above her the unusual raftered ceiling gave evidence of the building's age. To the front were five plain windows, although a pretty little stained glass one was off to one side. The altar was a simple affair, with an elaborately carved pulpit more than compensating for the somewhat stark interior.

They left not long after, Aunt Caroline recounting the history of the church as she had heard it. "It is named after Oswald, who once ruled Northumbria. The oldest part of the church dates back to the thirteenth century. Goodness, how very ancient it is. 'Tis said that the Saxons worshiped in this place as well. Those rushes are left from the rush-bearing ceremony held each August. I believe it is necessary, for they bury the dead beneath the church floor so the rushes help disguise less pleasant odors."

Joanna glanced back at the church, then minded her steps lest she stumble and fall. The paving stones were treacherous, even with her good jean half-boots on her feet.

They passed the cottage where little Mary lived and again Joanna paused to look for the child. The others strolled on ahead, Aunt Caroline doing very well with Lord Osborn's gentle assistance.

Mary saw Joanna and came running to say hello, with only one backward glance to the house.

"Do you get enough to eat, child? How old are you?" Joanna asked softly, wishing she might brush those curls.

"I be seven, ma'am. And yes, I'm fed."

The answer was not complete, for it did not tell Joanna if the girl was as hungry as she looked to be. Joanna had thought her five years of age. It was a shock to learn she was seven.

"Come, Miss Winterton, the others await us."

She apologized, then after saying goodbye, she hurried along.

Lucas was hard pressed to believe that Miss Winterton was not merely trying to impress him with how caring she was. He had seen young women do the like before, always with the view of affecting the sensibilities of the viewer—usually a gentleman who was likely to be looking for a wife.

Mr. Wilson, the admittedly talented artist, joined them on the path, and Lucas scarcely repressed a snide remark. Really, the chap was too much. Bowing to the ladies and nodding to Lord Osborn as though an equal. Yet, Lucas said nothing, for Miss Staunton accepted the fellow with a warm generosity of spirit he could not fail to admire.

"You disapprove of our befriending the artist," Joanna said while watching Wilson speak to her aunt. "Aunt Caroline is always wanting to feed up the thin and care for the needy. 'Tis a pity that she never had a family of her own."

"I cannot approve of your friendship with the man. What do you know about him? He painted a remarkable picture of Rydal Water, showing an intimate knowledge of the place.

And that business of his seeing a man with a gun on Butter Crags—most likely it was himself."

Joanna stopped by the gate to stare at her neighbor. "On that we must disagree. I find him charming company. Which is more than I can say for you at the moment, sir," she concluded in gentle reproof.

She opened the gate and marched into the house, pausing to collect Mr. Wilson and bring him along with her, flattering him with generous praise.

Lucas was as angry as he could recall being in some time— and the worst of it all was that he wasn't sure just why.

Chapter Seven

It was a very hot morning. Even the birds seemed disinclined to sing. A light breeze saved the day from becoming totally impossible.

Aunt Caroline reclined on a wicker chaise longue in the shade behind the cottage wearing her softest, thinnest lawn gown with a muslin pillow beneath her head. She even had left her muslin cap untied, the ribands dangling indifferently to either side of her face. She plied a fan languidly back and forth, as though the mere effort of cooling herself was too much.

Joanna joined her, strolling listlessly about the little yard, plucking a spent rose or tweaking an expired flower head from a stalk.

"I had no notion it would be so hot here. Mercy!" Aunt Caroline said quietly.

"I have little desire to be ambitious. Perhaps I may take my parasol and stroll along the shore of the lake. Do you mind? It would seem that the mere sight of all that water might be cooling," Joanna said, brushing off some dried petals that had fallen onto her white muslin gown during her small efforts.

"If you wish. Even walking seems too great an effort in this heat." Aunt Caroline bestowed a fond smile on her girl, as she preferred to think of her.

"Here comes Lord Osborn to entertain you. He is wearing a linen coat. What a clever idea for a hot summer day." Joanna took a step toward the cottage, then added, "I shall have Mrs. Hawkins send Bodkin out with lemonade for you both."

"Take Susan and that dog with you, dear. I am not comfortable with the idea that someone may lurk in the shadows, intent upon doing you harm."

Joanna nodded, greeted Lord Osborn with pleasure, then gave the request for lemonade to Mrs. Hawkins. The cottage was slightly cooler than the outside—a result of the thick walls, no doubt—but it lacked the bit of breeze, and the scents of the flowers and water. The lake water had a distinct fresh, sharp smell that Joanna relished.

She called Rex to her side and was about to summon Susan when she saw Sir Lucas at the front doorway, the door having been left open to encourage a flow of air.

"Good day, Sir Lucas," she said politely, vividly recalling how they had parted the day before. Then, her manners and breeding nudging her, she added, "I must apologize to you for my somewhat uncharitable words yesterday afternoon. I was rude to you, and while I felt I had cause, that is no excuse for my language."

"You are too gracious," Sir Lucas said, clearly surprised at her admission. "I am also at fault, for it is none of my affair if you chose to invite Wilson into your home for tea."

"I am sorry you did not join us. Between Lord Osborn and Mr. Wilson we had a jolly time. Do you know they are both gifted with the ability to tell amusing stories?"

Lucas did not comment on that, for he had regretted his words and missing out on the ample and delicious tea Miss Staunton usually presented. Rather, he glanced at Miss Winterton's parasol in hand and the dog waiting patiently at her feet, then said, "Are you off on a walk even in this hot weather?"

"I was just about to call Susan to go with me. I thought perhaps if we strolled along the shore it might seem cooler." She turned to find her maid when he lightly touched her arm. "Sir?" she said in surprise.

"You said you enjoyed fishing. Would it not be better to go out on the lake, reaping full benefit of the water and that admittedly gentle breeze?"

"Indeed," she agreed promptly. If this was an atonement for his behavior of the day before she would accept it, for the thought of a morning on the lake was vastly appealing.

Word was given to her aunt, who—quite taken with Lord Osborn—scarcely paid them heed.

Joanna and Sir Lucas, trailed by an eager Rex, walked down the short distance to the lake and crossed the rocky beach to a dandy rowboat Sir Lucas had obtained for his use while staying in Grasmere.

"With it being so warm, I doubt if any fish will nibble our bait," Joanna said, ever practical. "However, just being on the water will compensate for the lack."

Lucas grinned at his guest for the morning expedition. She was so calm and sensible about all this. He rather liked the change from the usual dithering females he had encountered over the years. He was forced to admit that Joanna Winterton was requiring him to revise his opinion of women. Perhaps not all of them were heartless, rapacious creatures who wanted him for his vaunted expertise as much as his fortune.

The dog jumped into the boat first, followed by all the poles and gear deemed necessary for fishing, plus a basket Emery had packed and brought down in anticipation of their being two on the little voyage.

"Were you so certain I would join you?" Miss Winterton said after a look at the overflowing basket.

"Had you not wished to go along, I would have had Emery go with me," Lucas replied, having been ready with that sort of answer. She sounded a trifle piqued, which suited him fine.

He pushed off from shore using one of the oars, then when they had drifted far enough, he set it into the lock and began to row after first removing his coat. It felt good to get the exercise, even if the day was hot. And with the thin cambric as the only covering on his upper body, he was far cooler. Sitting here he could observe Miss Winterton's expressive face—apparently she did not often see a gentleman in his shirtsleeves.

Joanna watched Sir Lucas from her cushioned seat in the rear of the little boat. He was very strong, she realized. His arms drew the oars through the water with seemingly little effort. She could glimpse his muscled arms through that sheer cotton, the fabric straining as he moved. And he had a capable look about him she had not observed before. It made her feel enormously safe and secure. Fortunately, they were far enough from shore so she need not worry about a gunshot.

Although she knew a wind could come up quickly, making

the waves dangerous, she felt Sir Lucas could cope with anything. What a pity he had such a wretchedly nasty tongue at odd moments. She suspected that his temper stemmed from being jilted. No one likes rejection, even if the heart is not engaged.

She relished the feel of the breeze through her curls, but was careful to keep her parasol positioned so as to guard her skin from the sun. She had no wish for a freckled or burned face.

"I believe this ought to be as good a spot as any. I saw a chap pull in some large trout here the other day." Sir Lucas set the oars, then went forward to drop anchor.

Joanna watched as he went about the business of baiting her hook, then his own. She accepted the pole, then swung it out over the water, allowing the line to sink to the proper depth, the same as Sir Lucas.

Then they settled down to silence. The water slapped gently against the side of the boat. Rex settled in the shade of the basket, sniffing now and again at the intriguing contents. Peace.

It was an oddly comfortable time, at first. They murmured inconsequential nonsense about one thing or another. And then Sir Lucas turned to what was evidently a matter that still annoyed him.

"Tell me, what do you really think of Wilson?" he asked in a manner that was slightly too studied to be casual.

"He seems a pleasant young man," she said tranquilly.

"Nothing more than that?" Sir Lucas asked skeptically. "He is a handsome chap, if you like the poetical look . . . was Robert Underhill also pleasant?"

There was a long, somewhat painful, silence while Joanna searched for words to express how she felt about her late betrothed.

"Mr. Underhill was my intended husband. I must say nothing ill of him," Joanna began, only to be interrupted.

"Yet you cannot say anything good! He was a gamester, a womanizer, and a fool. Forgive my blunt words, but I cannot see how your father could align you with such a man, nor you accept his suit. You cannot grieve for him—I forbid it."

Joanna was astounded at the spate of angry words from Sir

Lucas. She hastened to reply, "You have not the right to do so, nor to say such things to me."

She paused, testing her line that most assuredly was getting little nibbles. Her action gave her a few moments to collect her thoughts.

"My father made an agreement with his father when I was yet in the cradle—you must be familiar with that sort of arrangement. Sometimes they are actually acted upon. With my mother gone, there was no one to intervene on my behalf, although I doubt if my father would have paid her any heed. Father blinded himself to the less desirable aspects of Mr. Underhill's character. He seemed to believe that they would mend once he married. I give leave to doubt that. It is my observation that men seldom change once married. Once a rake, always a rake, if you ask me." She tossed him a defiant look that dared him to deny her words.

They faced each other, the tension growing as the minutes passed. Crazily enough, Lucas wanted to kiss those impertinent lips, mold her to his will. And he couldn't so much as move, for he might upset the boat. He could swim, but he doubted if she could.

Joanna gazed into those dark eyes with sherry glints in them, so taunting and cynical. If he held such contempt for women, why did he chastise her about Robert Underhill? Or care if she mourned someone who was so unworthy of grieving?

He puzzled her . . . but he also drew her like a lodestar, the pull a tangible thing. How fortunate she dare not shift about while in the boat. She had been taught to swim—Aunt Caroline declaring every woman ought to know how—but perhaps Sir Lucas had not. She also admitted to herself that, could she move, she might be so foolish as to creep into his arms and attempt to persuade him that not all women were false.

How many other women had sought to convince him of that very thing and been rejected? The mounting tension was broken by a pull on Joanna's line that nearly unseated her.

"A fish!" she cried, momentarily forgetting what had just passed between them.

Diverted from his own brooding thoughts, Lucas quickly grabbed the net to help her land the fish.

"That is a very nice pike—must be all of four and a half pounds if an ounce," he declared as the netted fish safely flopped about in the bottom of the boat. Rex sat back with a funny expression on his face, as if he didn't quite know what to make of this odd, smelly creature.

"Yes," Joanna said, feeling quite superior that she had caught the first fish on a day that Sir Lucas had said might net none.

Sir Lucas strung the fish on a length of line, then looped the line around the oarlock so the fish might remain in the water, and the dog would not be tempted to play with it.

Then the silence descended once again.

Joanna repositioned her parasol, which had been cast aside when she had attended the fish. She darted little looks at Sir Lucas, thankful he had not the least notion of his effect on her senses. Heavens, but he tempted a girl. She could well understand why all those London belles chased after him, why mamas with girls making their come-outs either cast appraising looks or dire glances his way. And she wondered at her own daring at being alone with him.

She could not think of anything to say and wondered if the heat had affected her brain or if Sir Lucas simply had rattled her senses completely.

About a half hour later, Sir Lucas felt a tug on his pole. "I have one," he whispered. And so he did. In very short order he brought in a beautiful trout.

"If mine was over four pounds, yours must be at least six. It's enormous!" Joanna cried, generously willing to acknowledge his supremacy in this matter.

Once the fish had been dealt with in the same manner as Joanna's, Sir Lucas placed his pole aside and leaned toward the basket, uncovering it to reveal the contents.

Rex sat up, alert to possible treats.

They feasted on lemonade—a trifle warm, but refreshing— and sandwiches made with thin slices of beef. Little cakes from the Prince Regent Hotel completed the repast. Joanna leaned back against the boat, quite satisfied.

"Did your gown become wet when you entered the boat?" Sir Lucas suddenly asked.

She glanced down to see that the lower part of the skirt of her gown was decidedly wet. It had not been when they left the shore. "Oh, dear!"

"I believe water must be seeping in somewhere. Look, Rex is dampish as well." As though to prove this statement, the dog—having consumed his portion—rose to shake himself off, sending droplets of water in every direction.

Too concerned to chastise Rex for doing what came naturally to dogs who became wet, Joanna joined Sir Lucas in checking the boat. Without a word, he searched the front of the boat while Joanna combed the rear.

"Here!" she cried after moving the basket. "There appears to have been a patch or something that has come free. I daresay the basket rubbing over it loosened it."

While Sir Lucas examined the hole, Joanna searched about to see if she could find whatever it was that had been stopping the water from entering the boat.

"I do not recall seeing this before," Sir Lucas muttered.

"Well, I daresay it is something you might not notice, if it was all the same color. I cannot find it. Not anywhere."

"What?" he said, looking puzzled.

"That stopper, or whatever it was. Maybe it was cork, and it swelled because of the heat and popped right out into the lake." she said, inventing a far-fetched tale for lack of anything better.

He attempted to stuff a napkin into the hole, but in short order it was sopping wet and could do little but slow the water coming into the boat.

"Here," he said, handing her a glass. "Begin bailing out while I pull anchor. We had best return to shore before we sink. Can you swim, by the by?" He began to row, using long pulls on the oars that ate up the distance.

"Indeed," she said, then added, "I was thinking earlier that Wordsworth wrote a poem that began with the words, *Surprised by joy—impatient as the Wind*. I might have been surprised and joyful when I caught that pike, but now I truly am as impatient as the wind."

"I row as fast as I'm able. I suggest you concentrate on bailing out the water."

She looked at his grim face and impishly said, "Perhaps I should have Rex try to lap up a portion? Would that help, do you think?"

He did not appreciate her attempt at humor.

"Well, we can both swim, the dog can most likely paddle enough to make shore, so ease your mind on that score. But do row hard." She had tried to conceal her worry behind humor but it had not helped matters. No doubt he thought her a trite, frivolous female. She had felt that it would do no good to become hysterical, no matter if she felt panicky. That shows you what being stoical does for a girl, she decided.

The water now entered the boat faster than she could bail it out. Her hem was sodden, the skirt absorbing more and more water. Rather than have it worsen, she set down the glass, raised her skirts high about her knees, and after first wringing them out as best she could, wrapped them so they would not be soaking up more liquid. If Sir Lucas received a view of her legs, so be it. This was not the moment for modesty.

"Do you think we shall make shore before the water overcomes my poor efforts?" she said lightly.

"I'll try," he said in that same grim tone. The distance between the boat and shore lessened rapidly.

Just as Joanna felt her arm would give out and that the water would overwhelm them, she heard the scrape of the boat bottom on the rocks. She raised her head to look at the rock-lined shore with aching relief.

"We made it," she said quietly, tired and spent with the effort and the heat. She slumped against the back of the boat for a moment, then gathered herself to leave.

Sir Lucas pulled off his shoes and stockings and went over the side of the boat. He picked up Rex, depositing him on the rocks with surprising regard for the dog. He waded back to the boat, wet up to his chest, to bring the basket ashore along with the line that still held the two fish. Then he came for her.

Joanna braced herself for his touch, not sure she could trust herself not to collapse against him.

"I had best carry you, for it is too rocky for you to wade

from the boat to land, even with your skirt so fetchingly gathered above your knees."

Joanna had no doubt but what his relief at reaching shore was adding to his high humor, but she had thought he might ignore her state of exposure.

"A true gentleman would not comment on that," she said primly.

"True gentlemen either miss a great deal or keep it all to themselves," he riposted. "I do neither."

"At least we have the fish," she said, scrambling over the central seat to reach the front of the boat and his arms. Keep on neutral topics, she reminded herself. His touch, being held in his strong arms, will not affect you.

Oh, my, she was wrong.

It was a bit like electricity, she decided, recalling her participation in a demonstration of that phenomenon. She felt those same zinging tingles dancing through her, rushing from where his hands and arms cradled her outward to her very toes and fingers. She could not help but gasp.

Drat the man, he looked amused.

He snuggled her against that strong chest and slowly made his way across the rocks that were submerged beneath the water—a treacherous path, indeed.

It was Rex who caused the accident. He saw his new mistress being held by his friend and thought to join in the fun. Rex dashed into the water to jump up at Sir Lucas.

Sir Lucas lost his precarious foothold.

They landed in the cold water with a resounding splash.

Both went beneath the water, rising to gasp and spew out lake water, flailing their arms to gain a balance, perhaps find a rock upon which to perch.

"It's a good thing my shoes are safely on the shore," he said, grinning down at a very wet and most assuredly bedraggled Joanna.

It might be well she'd restored his good humor, but she was furious that it had been done at her expense. Joanna gamely fought for a footing on the slippery rocks. She prayed that no one would come close enough to view her. White muslin conceals precious little when wet. She could see every detail through the shirt Sir Lucas wore. There was little doubt in her mind that he had the same opportunity. And he took it.

That wicked man. His grin broadened a moment before he sobered and offered her his hand. Not only had he looked at her, he also had observed every detail possible. And she had no doubt but that there was much visible she preferred not to have seen by him—or anyone else, for that matter.

"You might have the grace to look elsewhere, you know," she said with ill temper. "I quite realize that I am a dreadful sight." Her hair dripped about her face, her dress was plastered to her body in a most indecent way, and she was so chilled by the lake water that she began to shiver.

Then he scooped her into his arms and she faced a different set of troubles.

The heat from his body did little to help her, for it stirred up all manner of alien sensations that disturbed Joanna no end. Her breasts tingled from the pressure of his chest where he clasped her against him. Her insides ached, and not from the fall. She was conscious of his scent, accentuated by the wetness. She had the bizarre notion that he would taste quite as lovely as he smelled.

He solved the matter by placing a kiss on her trembling lips, cold and wet, enticing and frightening. Indeed, she realized when he withdrew, he certainly did taste as lovely as he smelled. She gave him a bemused look, collected herself and ordered, "Put me down, sirrah. There will be no more taking liberties."

"Pity, that," he said with a grin that showed he was not the least penitent.

Ashore, Rex danced back and forth, not seeming the least contrite for his behavior. Joanna felt surrounded with misbehaving males.

When Sir Lucas placed her on her feet he retained his hold of her, explaining when she raised her brows, "Even on shore the rocks are precarious. I'd not wish you to fall."

"I'll chance that, if you please, sirrah," she said with the slightest snap in her voice. "And have the kindness to look elsewhere than at my poor self," she concluded, bending over to release her tangled skirts and wring out as much water as possible from her gown.

He laughed, a deep, rich, wonderful sort of laugh that Joanna failed to appreciate at the moment. "My dear, it would take a stronger man than myself to do that. The view from here is most charming."

"Odious creature," she said vehemently, glancing up to catch him watching her. She picked up her parasol from where it had fallen and unfurled it, in so doing affecting a cover of sorts, at least from him. Fortunately, the sun began to dry her. Although it would most likely take hours to do the job completely, it did stop her shivers.

Lucas could not help his laugh. What a delightfully absurd girl, to think any red-blooded man could refrain from looking at her garbed in that clinging length of white muslin. It was most fetching, the revelation of Miss Winterton's many charms. She was delectable and enchanting in her déshabillé. However, if he lay claims to any pretensions to being a gentleman, he had best ignore her for a few moments until she had herself in hand once again.

He cast a look at the boat he had leased for his stay. He pulled it to shore and up over the rocks until the area where the hole was located could be seen.

"Give me a hand, will you?" he said absently to Miss Winterton, ignoring her indignant gasp. "I want to know what caused that leak. I do not think it was an accident."

With that remark, Joanna put aside her parasol—which had done little but ease her feeling of exposure—and helped him turn the boat upside down. She joined him in examining the hole, putting her head against his. There was little doubt in her mind that someone had carefully drilled that hole. The edges were perfectly round.

"It could not have been done with intent toward me," she said thoughtfully, sitting back on her stockinged feet. "No one could possibly have known you would invite me to go fishing with you today."

He glanced back at her, raking her with his gaze. "I rather think he might have thought that."

Joanna knew she blushed but refused to give ground. There

was nothing remaining of her that he had not already seen. The idea that he might have viewed other women in such a state crept into her mind, causing a strange, aching pain.

He turned away from her and renewed his study of the hole in the boat, picking at it with his finger. Joanna backed away, lamenting the loss of her slippers, for the rocks were hot and hurtful to tender feet.

There was a large cloth in the basket, intended, she supposed, as a tablecloth. Joanna extracted it and wrapped it about herself, feeling much more the thing. Even the heat of the sun could not dispel the chill within her. She could not escape the knowledge that someone wished one of them ill. And she truly did not feel it was herself. No, rather, she believed more then ever that someone from out of his past had caught up with Sir Lucas.

It remained to be seen where and how he would strike next. The why of it all was beyond her.

"Oh, sir, what has happened?" called Emery, dashing up to them as best he could, given the rocky shore.

"Someone put a hole in the bottom of this boat. I have the unpleasant feeling that he also would like to put a hole through one or both of us. Why, I cannot begin to guess."

Joanna wondered if he truly felt that way or was merely pretending not to know. She began to walk in the direction of Rose Cottage, feeling dreadfully conspicuous, and hurting, for her almost bare feet were no match for the rocks and other debris found on the shore.

"If I might suggest, sir, the young lady? She needs to be taken home at once. And you might do with a change of clothing as well." The valet discreetly gazed out to the center of the lake while Sir Lucas glanced up to where Joanna was gazing at the gig with a wistful gaze.

"Right," Lucas said, moving away from the boat toward the road where his little gig sat waiting. "I'm glad you brought the gig," he said to Emery in a low voice. "The sooner I bring Miss Winterton home, the better. Stay here and guard the boat. I shall return as soon as possible."

With that instruction, he donned hose and shoes, then clambered across the rocks to join his wet and bedraggled companion. He lifted her into the vehicle, ignoring her little noise of protest.

"You cannot deny that you had best return to Rose Cottage as swiftly as possible. You are most fortunate that no one has seen you yet."

The words hung in the air between them all the way home. Joanna sat straight, the tablecloth draped about her, eyes focused ahead. She decided that if she pretended she was supposed to look like this, with no air of apology about her, that anyone who chanced to see her would scarce make note of it. Rex sat like a king, looking pleased with his efforts at a bit of fun.

The gig came to a halt before the cottage, and with hurried thanks Joanna climbed down and fled to the interior without a backward look. Had she chanced that look, she would have captured a most peculiar expression on her escort's face. He looked quite bemused.

Peering from the front window, Aunt Caroline saw it and wondered greatly. Then she turned to view her niece.

"I know you were hot, but isn't that an extreme method to become cool? Do change your gown, then tell me all about what happened. I'll wager you have a story that will put me all agog. And I have a feeling that there is more to this than a mere boating accident. I have not forgotten that dreadful shot in the side of the rowboat on Windermere."

Joanna went to her room to disrobe. She scrubbed herself with a towel, then donned blessedly dry clothing. She had a tale to tell, to be sure. The only thing was, the most fascinating part was one that she would have to keep to herself. It would not do to reveal that naughty and outrageous kiss.

Chapter Eight

When Joanna returned to face her aunt some time later, having tarried as long as she dare, she discovered that her erstwhile escort on the fishing trip was ensconced in the sitting room having a cozy chat with her aunt. Apparently, *he* had changed garments in record time while Joanna dawdled.

He rose, bowed most politely to her, then turned to her aunt. "It is regrettable that our little excursion on the lake was so precipitously cut short. I feel sure that your niece would have caught enough fish to feed a sizable crowd. She is an excellent fisher. She neither chats overly much nor acts like a silly widgeon. I hope that by bringing my trout over with her pike I redeem myself somewhat."

Joanna was bereft of speech.

"I shall of course have Mrs. Hawkins prepare them both and we shall feast on them, all of us," Aunt Caroline replied. "I trust," she asked with a hint of coyness in her manner, "that Lord Osborn enjoys a tasty morsel of fish?"

"Indeed, ma'am," Sir Lucas smoothly replied.

Joanna longed to burst into speech, to denounce this . . . this cad for what he was. But then, she was compelled to admit in all fairness, she had done little to resist that dratted kiss, nor had she given him the proper dressing down that he so rightly deserved. And now he had wormed his way into her aunt's good graces with two fish, for pity's sake, one of which was her own.

She nodded with forced politeness to the odious creature who joined her aunt by the unlit fireplace. "How kind you are, Sir Lucas. I trust you will like the way Mrs. Hawkins prepares fish. She is an excellent cook, as you may have noticed."

"Now would someone please explain to me how Joanna came home all sopping wet and looking like a thundercloud?" Aunt Caroline demanded in her sweet way.

Both attempted to explain at once.

"It was Rex, you see," Joanna began.

"The boat was sinking," Sir Lucas said, then, seeing that Aunt Caroline looked confused, he paused for her next question.

"Rex caused the boat to sink?" she said in a bewildered haze.

With a dark look at Sir Lucas, Joanna began anew. "There was a slight problem with the rowboat and Sir Lucas rowed us back to shore. He placed Rex on the beach, then returned to assist me. I suppose that dear Rex took exception to Sir Lucas carrying me ashore, for he plowed out into the water and jumped up, causing Sir Lucas to lose his footing—those rocks are dreadfully precarious," she explained. "We both fell into the lake with a dreadful splash, hence my wet, bedraggled appearance." Of the remainder, Joanna said nothing.

Lucas eyed Miss Winterton with new respect. She could have made his life quite miserable by telling the whole of it. He had taken advantage of the situation, and she had every right to call him a cad and worse. Could it be that the young woman, who was not only pretty but had a delightful body as well, did not *wish* to be compelled to marry him? The thought did not sit well at all. He studied his nails rather than look at her. He did not like to see what would be reflected in her expressive eyes.

To Miss Staunton he said, "What she says is correct. I do not believe the dog meant any harm—he was merely joining in what he perceived to be a game."

"I should like to know," Aunt Caroline said in her soft, but determined manner, "precisely what was wrong with the boat."

"It had a little leak," Joanna said hastily.

"And you had not noticed this before, obviously," Aunt Caroline said, looking most confused.

"Because it had not been there before. Good lady, you deserve to know the whole of it," Sir Lucas began when Joanna popped up and declared, "Tea! I am famished for a cup of tea. Would you not wish a cup of tea, Sir Lucas? And dear Aunt Caroline? I shall request it this instant. And those lemon biscuits as well. Or ratafia, perhaps?"

With a whirl of her soft lavender skirts Joanna fled to the kitchen to order a dainty tea for the trio in the sitting room. If Sir Lucas was going to confess all, she did not think she wished to be there.

And yet . . . perhaps she had better, merely to correct or deny whatever he chanced to say. She rushed back to the sitting room to find her aunt frowning at Sir Lucas.

Joanna's heart sank to her toes.

"Well," she said with forced brightness, "it cannot be as bad as all that, can it?"

"Sir Lucas believes that the hole in the boat was put there deliberately. Some man expected Sir Lucas to take that boat out and did not wish him to return."

Joanna sat down abruptly, thankful there was a chair directly behind her. "Oh," she said with an explosive rush of air from her lungs. She was saved. The frightful kiss had not been mentioned.

"Dreadful matter. And you have no clue at all?" Aunt Caroline gently demanded. "What does Lord Osborn say?"

"When I informed him of the happening, he immediately went down to examine the boat. I came here to reassure myself that no harm had befallen Joanna in spite of her plunge in the lake."

"That was most kind of you, I'm sure," Aunt Caroline murmured while keeping an eye on her niece, who studied the toes of her lavender slippers with downcast eyes and pink cheeks.

"I feel it must be investigated, however," Sir Lucas said firmly.

"But how?" Joanna said, concern for the danger involved clearly revealed in the gaze she raised to his.

"I suspect," Lucas replied, "that a clue may be found in the caves at Rydal Water."

"Oh, no," Joanna cried. "I doubt that there could be anything there. Why, those caves are littered with rocks and there is a great deal of water on the ground. Who could take refuge inside such a place?"

"I intend to explore them. Tomorrow, as a matter of fact," Lucas asserted with the assurance of a man who dares to do anything.

"I suppose nothing would dissuade you," Joanna said, lowering her gaze to her clasped hands to conceal her fears.

"Why, I shall go armed, and perhaps I may persuade Lord Osborn to join me. I fancy he will relish putting his skills to the test."

Joanna visibly relaxed against her chair. "How providential that his lordship has such knowledge of sleuthing."

Mrs. Hawkins bustled along the hallway to open the front door, having anticipated the arrival of their guest by the simple means of keeping a sharp eye on the main walk up from the village.

She ushered him into the sitting room with the dignity of a London butler. "Lord Osborn, ma'am."

Sir Lucas rose to greet his friend, giving him what Joanna considered a very searching look.

"You have just come from the boat?"

"Indeed," his lordship replied after bowing over Miss Staunton's lace-mitted hand. "It is precisely as you suspected. Someone bored a hole through the boat bottom with a good tool, for the edges are clean and sharp, not dull and chewed up. He knew his tools, too, for the job was expertly done. 'Twould be an easy matter to botch it up," he explained to Aunt Caroline. "The pitch put over the hole was badly applied—on purpose, no doubt."

Joanna watched the byplay between her aunt and his lordship with concern. If this high-and-mighty lord thought he was going to have a bit of amusement with her precious aunt, Joanna would personally correct his impression. She would keep a careful watch. Just how she would know when it had gone too far, she was not sure. But she would protect the woman who had been her mother all these years past.

Then she had another thought. "You ought to take Rex, you know. He is an excellent dog for sniffing out trouble," Joanna said.

"How did you learn that, dear?" her aunt inquired.

For once Joanna was stumped. If she revealed all that had transpired while she was in the caves, her aunt would forbid Joanna to ever go walking again.

"Did you not tell me that the dog had warned you against some rather scruffy sheep? Guarded you from them, as it were?" Sir Lucas said quietly and calmly.

"Indeed," she said gratefully. "He is a very good little watchdog."

"But evidently not to be trusted when it comes to water, it seems," was her aunt's dry rejoinder.

"To be sure," Sir Lucas murmured with a cautious look at Joanna Winterton.

Joanna wasn't sure why Sir Lucas chose to come to her aid, but she was much obliged to the man. That he should step in to help her was unexpected. Perhaps he just was thankful that Joanna had not peached on him to her aunt.

"Well," Lord Osborn intoned, "I suspect you may have a good reason for searching around Rydal Waters. When I was mousing around the village, as I am wont to do when investigating a matter, I came up with a few tidbits. It seems there is a feeling that several of the itinerants make camp in that area. Nothing wrong with that as long as they do not create trouble. After all, a goodly number doss down in a hayloft with no complaint from anyone—as long as they leave the place tidy."

"I think it a pity that our great and wonderful government can send these men off to fight for our country and then treat them so shabbily when they return unable to work at their old jobs because of an injury," Joanna declared with some spirit. "Something ought to be done about it," she said, giving a polite but somewhat defiant look at his lordship.

"I agree," Lord Osborn said with a nod. "Some of the men in Parliament truly wish to help, but there is a limit to what we can do for these men without changing a great number of laws. There are many peers who are only concerned with their own matters. Indeed, they rarely, if ever, come to sessions."

Joanna nodded, feeling far more kindly toward the gentleman who looked at her aunt with such amiability.

"Joanna, would you please inform Mrs. Hawkins that there

ill be five for dinner this evening, and to prepare the trout
long with the hares that Mr. Wilson brought us earlier."

Thinking that her dear aunt had surely put the cat among the
igeons, Joanna popped up to leave the room. She was not sur-
rised when Sir Lucas also rose and followed her.

"I am able to locate the kitchen, thank you," she said with
n amused glance at the man who so plagued her life, one way
r another.

"You invite Wilson here? for dinner?" he demanded softly,
o not to be heard by the others.

"I believe I mentioned that my aunt takes pity on thin and
oetical gentlemen. She loves to feed them, and Mr. Wilson
ooks in need of feeding."

"And you have no objection, of course," Sir Lucas said,
oming closer to lean against the wall with one hand, effec-
ively blocking her way.

"Why should I? My aunt has a perfect right to invite guests
o the house. You do not understand how it is here. My father
ives her a generous allowance to provide for me. Whatever I
pend comes channeled through my aunt, not directly to me
rom my father. She is in charge."

"As is proper. A young woman cannot be expected to know
ow to handle finances," Sir Lucas said with a nod of approval
or the sensible Lord Winterton. He had never given the baron
igh marks before. He must now.

"But," Joanna replied with what she felt to be perfect logic,
"if she does not try, nor attempt to do so, how will she ever
earn?"

"Her husband will take care of all matters," he said with the
assurance of the polished gentleman of the world.

"My aunt never wed," Joanna countered gently. "It is well
that she had an unconventional governess who insisted the
girls of the family be taught their numbers and how to reckon.
They were also taught to detect when they were being
cheated." She gave him a triumphant look that almost bor-
dered on the flirtatious had she not been proving a point. Still,
she looked terribly appealing with those blue eyes flashing,
her smile dazzling even as it taunted him.

Lucas stared down at the slim girl who so sweetly put him

in his place. For she had the right of it, blast it all. She knew whereof she spoke. Yet her aunt had done as ordered by her brother-in-law. Curiosity piqued Lucas to ask, "Did she never teach you some of it?"

"Of course, sir. She obeys my father in all things he has requested, but she has added a few that were not mentioned." The girl gave him a sweeping look, then dipped under his arm and disappeared to the kitchen regions.

Lucas wandered back to the sitting room where he sought a chair again, only to sit in silent reflection while he waited for the shining and increasingly delightful Miss Winterton to return.

The group that gathered around the table at Rose Cottage for dinner late that afternoon chattered about the events of the day, in particular, the boating accident.

"What is the world coming to," Mr. Wilson demanded to know, "if a fellow cannot go fishing without risking his life and limb?"

"Fortunately, I know how to swim, but he would have no way of knowing that. I believe you taught your niece how to swim as well, Miss Staunton," Sir Lucas said approvingly. "Well done of you, for it would be better if all were so equipped when boating."

"I believe that knowledge of all sorts can only be beneficial," Aunt Caroline said with her customary modesty.

Lucas finished the portion of excellently prepared trout on his plate and smiled to himself. What would the redoubtable Miss Staunton say to the knowledge that her niece had acquired since coming to the Lake District? He looked at Joanna Winterton, who was pleasantly conversing with the artist. Thoughtfully rotating his wineglass between his fingers, Lucas wondered if the young woman entertained any predatory thoughts on the fellow. He had never met a woman who did not set out to snare a chap with her charms. To his way of thinking, it was an automatic thing with them.

"La, sir, I quite like your representation of Rydal Waters," he heard Joanna say. What was she up to now?

"It was an excellent painting," Lucas agreed.

"I go down there from time to time. It is best to go late in the morning after the itinerants have left for the day, and leave before they are likely to return."

"So," Lord Osborn inserted, looking narrowly at Mr. Wilson, "the itinerants do spend time there."

"Indeed, my lord. I believe they camp out there for the night, for the roof of the cave offers a haven in the rain. And you must admit the area receives a great deal of that."

They all chuckled over the obvious remark.

Joanna could see that Sir Lucas had firmed his plan to investigate Rydal Water on the morrow. Well, she had her own intentions in that regard, but she'd say nothing about them now.

"It promises to be a lovely evening," Aunt Caroline said when the final course, a brambleberry pudding topped with delicate chantilly cream, had been served. They gazed upon the delectable confection with proper reverence before anyone answered.

"Shall we take a stroll?" Lord Osborn proposed. "I ate well and could do with a constitutional following my dinner." He bestowed a look of flattering regard on her aunt.

"How delightful an idea," Aunt Caroline murmured with a fluttering of her lashes.

Joanna nearly choked on a mouthful of pudding. Her dear, sensible aunt was behaving like a schoolgirl. It was a good thing that Joanna was not similarly fascinated by some man, as they would soon be in dire straits. She leaned over so that her words might be heard only by Sir Lucas. "I wish to speak with you later."

"I am flattered, dear lady," he replied with a knowing smile and his London polish. Normally, he used such behavior with a woman who sought an assignation for purposes he was quite certain that Joanna did not entertain, much less know anything about. But how he enjoyed baiting and teasing her, for she rose to his lure so beautifully. And, he thought with an inward sigh, she was a delightful little baggage.

Only that was the trouble. She was hardly a baggage—she was the daughter of a respectable baron and quite wealthy in her own right. Miss Staunton had casually revealed in conversation that Joanna had inherited her mother's portion and would receive Miss Staunton's as well. All this, plus the generous dowry already settled upon the girl, would amount to an income of several thousand pounds a year. Small wonder the artist fawned over her like a lovesick fool.

By the time they left Rose Cottage, the moon had risen and beamed gently across the valley. It surprised Joanna how well they could see. There was little difference between the lovely candlelight within the cottage and the moonlight. Sir Lucas joined her, placing her hand on his arm in proper assistance.

"I gather you wish to speak with me?"

"I do," she declared with a tranquil air.

"About what, pray tell?" he not so gently prodded.

"Tomorrow. I shall go with you." Joanna said, having decided during dinner that it would be best if she were to accompany the men. Her feelings were greatly mixed, but somehow evolved around safety. She thought that were she along Sir Lucas might not do terribly rash things.

"You are daft, woman," he said, swiftly refusing her.

"I think not," she replied calmly. "You must take Rex with you and I am his mistress," she explained, quite as though that took care of everything.

"We'll leave the blasted dog at home," Sir Lucas said, obviously determined that Joanna not join them.

"I go, or I tell everything," she stated. It was a simple yet dire threat.

Lucas stared down at her. Her features were lit with the soft moonlight, giving her face an illusionary delicacy. What a farce. This young woman could chance anything.

"Everything? Surely you would not wish to reveal . . . everything," he said, infusing his voice with a sensual tone he had been told sent shivers down a shapely back.

Joanna merely halted and gave him a straight look. "I do mean everything. I have considered the matter. My aunt would never be so silly as to force me to wed where I would not— you are safe from that, at least. But from her censure, no. And you do not fear that, you have never been at the angry end of ay aunt's tongue-lashing."

"It is unseemly for you to join us. It might be risky," he aid, giving her a look that was most reproving.

Joanna considered that look. It certainly was not the look of man enamored of a woman. It was unlikely he would kiss er again, so she was quite safe from unwanted attentions— hich is certainly what they were. Why, she would far prefer he company of the gentle Mr. Wilson to that of the dashing nd dangerous Sir Lucas Montfort.

As if aware of her thoughts, Mr. Wilson pulled a flute from is capacious pocket and began to entertain them with prightly tunes.

"Ah," Joanna said quietly, "To pipe a simple song for think-ng hearts," she quoted from one of the Wordsworth poems he had been reading. "Hart-leap. Wall. Wherein the lands of a night who kills a hart is forever cursed."

"I recall that one. Do you agree with the rest of it?"

"I do not believe that mere nature can punish the guilty; punishment comes from above. God uses nature to achieve His means. There is a difference. Besides, the stag was placed n earth to serve man. To believe that killing the stag would ring a curse upon a family and lands is ridiculous," she con-cluded.

Lucas was struck by her simple statement. He had heard others debate the topic endlessly. Her brief remark con-ained much wisdom, remarkable in one so young. But that did not mean he trusted her. She was in effect coercing him o allow her to go with them tomorrow. She was like the rest of the women he knew—she wished to get her way by any means.

Joanna sensed a withdrawal in Sir Lucas, although he still walked politely at her side along the path to the lake. She slipped her hand from his arm and walked ahead of him to be by herself.

Mr. Wilson noticed this at once and joined her, chatting with an amiability that set Lucas's teeth on edge. She would get her way. Lucas had no desire to endure the threatened censure from Miss Staunton. But, by Jove, that chit would behave herself, or he would know the reason why. He stalked after the others in silent fury, only to stumble over a rock near the water's edge.

"Lovely night, is it not?" Joanna caroled.

That said it all.

The following morning Joanna rose early, snatched a bit of bread and jam from the kitchen, and with Rex at her side slipped out of the side door to stand watch. Her vigilance was rewarded when, moments later, she espied Sir Lucas and Lord Osborn leaving the cottage across the street. Joanna hurriedly walked over to join them.

"Good morning," she said with forced cheerfulness. She was uncertain how she might be received today. Sir Lucas could deny he had agreed to let her come. Lord Osborn might be so shocked that she would be compelled to stay behind.

Rex insinuated himself into the group, wagging his tail and bestowing a doggy smile on all.

"We are here and ready."

Lucas almost groaned. He had hoped that by rising early they would leave Joanna behind. Yet here she stood, wearing a strange garb consisting of a brief jacket over a long black skirt. Divided, he guessed. She might carry a proper parasol, but that was the only proper thing about her.

Lord Osborn, rightly figuring that this was something between the two younger people, said nothing. He gestured to the gig.

"I forgot," Lucas said with a smile, "the gig will hold only two of us."

"Not to worry, old chap," Lord Osborn said, "My man will bring my mount around in a trice." He motioned to the man who had stood by the horse hitched to the gig and he disappeared around to the rear of the cottage. In less time than Joanna would have believed, he returned with the saddled horse for Lord Osborn.

Joanna had anticipated this and had climbed up into the gig, pleased that her divided skirt permitted her to do so with ease

nd, better yet, without Sir Lucas's help. He just stood and
lared at her.

Sir Lucas picked up Rex, thrusting him at Joanna. She gath-
red the dog close to her and sat quietly while they set off toward Rydal Water.

"I would have thought this was the last place on earth you
vould wish to visit," Sir Lucas grumbled as they started up the
ise from Grasmere.

"I must," she insisted. "And I would not have you go
lone."

"Lord Osborn is along," he pointed out in as reasonable a
one as he could muster.

"You shall need Rex. Where he goes, I go as well."

They had driven in silence for perhaps half a mile when
Lord Osborn signaled them to halt.

"I suggest we stop here and approach on foot. Are you
game, Miss Winterton?"

Joanna nodded. "I am, sir. And I shall keep Rex close to my
ide and not allow him to run off or frighten anyone away."

"How do you propose to do that? Hold the dog all the
ime?" Sir Lucas said with a smug look.

Joanna withdrew a leash from the pocket of her skirt and
clipped it onto the pretty collar she'd had fashioned for Rex.
"Like this, sir," she said.

Now that she was here, with two strong men along, her
fears had subsided, although they had not left her completely.
There was still something menacing about the place that bothered her greatly.

So with much care they began to walk toward the caves.
They had to cross a kissing gate, which brought back disturbing memories to Joanna. She avoided looking at Sir Lucas and
primly made her way through it.

Off to one side she could see the glimmer of Rydal Water,
with its silly little island in the morning sun. The water
slapped against the rocky shore in an enticing rhythm. Ahead
of them yawned the first of the caves. The entrance was
flanked by a growth of bracken.

There was quite a scramble to enter it. Once they managed
to reach inside, it was a gloomy place, just as Joanna remem-

bered it. Water trickled down a far wall, dripping monoto-
nously into the shallow pond below.

"Look here," Lord Osborn whispered. "Signs of a fire
against this wall. My guess is that they catch fish or hare, then
bring them up here to cook."

"It would keep one out of the rain as well," Joanna added
with a look outside. The sky was changing, and a misty cloud
had drifted overhead.

"There is nothing wrong with any of this," Sir Lucas
pointed out. "These caves have been quarried for years. I believe the larger one still has slate removed from it for roofs,
and the like," he concluded.

"It would be an excellent spot for someone to hide. Most
people would not think to look here," Joanna whispered. The
place had that effect on them all, reducing them to whispers
and careful steps.

Rex growled low in his throat. Joanna froze. She could
sense someone watching her. Forcing herself to be calm, she
methodically searched the walls from left to right. She could
see nothing. But then, if a man dressed in slate gray and dirt-
ied his face, he could become invisible.

"What is it?" Sir Lucas said softly in her ear.

"There is someone here," she mouthed back to him.

"You cannot find him?"

"Look," was all she whispered.

And look they did. Not one of them could locate the menace
that made Rex growl. Joanna sensed that Lord Osborn was
more than a little frustrated. His sense of honor compelled him
to find the threat and dispose of it.

They prowled the area, poking into corners, stepping across
the puddles of water with care, yet finding no one hiding in the
shadows. Joanna suspected that they had come too late, that
the man had gone from here.

Rex followed Joanna closely, growling from time to time,
then, finally, he subsided and she felt a change. Whoever had
been watching them had left. She was sure of it, although it
would be difficult to explain.

At last, utterly mystified, they scrambled from the cave.
Joanna breathed easier once they reached the mist. It drifted

down with quiet charm, cloaking the bracken with shimmering droplets of water.

"It's almost raining. We had best return," Sir Lucas said. It was then he espied the note on the seat of the gig.

Exchanging a look with Joanna, he picked it up and began reading.

"It says that I will meet the fate I deserve whenever and wherever he decides."

"I knew it was you he wanted," Joanna said, but with no sense of pleasure.

Chapter Nine

The drive back to Rose Cottage was silent for the most part. Joanna shivered, and not from the cooling mist that drifted and swirled about them in ever-increasing amounts.

"He certainly is a shrewd fellow. How clever of him to lurk about, watching us, then leave the note while we searched for him," Sir Lucas said sarcastically. It was plain that he was more disgusted in not finding the chap than he was frightened of the threat.

"I doubt he was there when we left," Joanna said. "Rex did not growl. Of course he might have been downwind, and Rex did not catch his scent."

"Somehow that is not much comfort," Sir Lucas said. He fell into a reflective silence.

Any hope of keeping the morning's results to themselves was dashed when Lord Osborn left his horse with his man, then marched across to meet Miss Staunton, who left the security of the covered entry to greet him, parasol in hand. His lordship was a rotund man, but they both managed to find shelter beneath the broad oiled-silk covering.

"I perceive you have not had a very good morning," Aunt Caroline declared as she led the way back to the cottage. Her parasol dripped with moisture, but it seemed not to bother her in the least.

"As to that, Miss Staunton," Lord Osborn said, "I must confess that we did find evidence that one or more persons use that area as a camp of sorts. Remains of a fire, bits and scraps of food—bones and the like. I have no doubt that some farmer is missing a chicken."

"They might have earned some money to buy one, or perhaps some kind soul gave them a bird," Aunt Caroline said with hope, while pausing beneath the covered entry to the cottage. She shook out the umbrella, then proceeded to furl it.

"I doubt it."

"And you," Aunt Caroline said to Joanna, who had left the gig and reluctantly crossed the stone walk, "I cannot believe you would go with the gentlemen on such a potentially dangerous errand. What have you to say for yourself?"

"I thought perhaps Rex might be of some help. So far he will not obey anyone else but me, so I could not merely send him along. He did growl at one point and we suspect the man was watching us. He left a note in the gig. I fear Sir Lucas is his target." Joanna turned to survey Sir Lucas with more than a little sympathy. He had handed the gig to his man and hurried through the mist to their sides.

"How difficult to fight an enemy when you cannot see him," Aunt Caroline observed, turning again to lead the way inside.

"I propose we have a spot of coffee and whatever Mrs. Hawkins can produce," Joanna said.

"You must, all of you, be chilled to the bone. What a difference from yesterday. 'Tis like going from summer to fall," Aunt Caroline observed. She left the trio with a motion for them to enter the sitting room while she pattered off to the kitchen.

Joanna led the way, walking over to stand by the fire. Although it was not cold out, exactly, the damp had seeped through her and the warmth felt good. Sir Lucas joined her, holding out his hands to the fire.

She turned to look at him, speculating on what he might do now. Having an enemy you could not see, while not knowing what might happen next, must be daunting. Sir Lucas did not seem the sort of person to avoid confrontation.

"You cannot hide indoors," Lord Osborn said, giving voice to Joanna's thoughts.

"Perhaps I shall go out at night when the fellow is asleep." Sir Lucas favored them with a jaunty smile.

"You shall catch cold at that, for it will not take him long to figure out your plan," Joanna pointed out.

"Pity no one has seen a suspicious-looking man lurking about the houses—for we are over here as much as we are across the street," his lordship said pensively from the chair close to the fireplace.

Sir Lucas suddenly turned to Joanna and said, "I hope I do not place you in any jeopardy. I would not have you or your aunt injured."

"I feel sure we are quite safe," Joanna assured him, inwardly wondering if there was any real danger from associating with Sir Lucas. Surely the assassin could have done harm this morning had he so chosen. No, she began to suspect that he wished to make Sir Lucas worry and fret some, to frighten him.

"It might be a sort of game," she said. "Perhaps he is merely trying to give you a bad fright?"

"Could be, I suppose," Sir Lucas agreed. "Someone with a macabre sense of humor."

Aunt Caroline bustled into the room with Mrs. Hawkins right behind her carrying a tray overflowing with tasty sandwiches, little pastries, and pots of tea and coffee.

They settled down to a light meal—for each discovered an appetite—and continued to speculate on the would-be killer.

"How very analytical we are," Joanna said at last. "Poor Sir Lucas is the object of terror from some idiotic man, and we sit around and discuss it like it was a sort of game."

Lucas gave her a startled look. Never in his life had anyone voiced pity for him. It was rather unsettling. Was he past his prime? Had he descended into the realm of has-been rakes? Those pathetic creatures who believe themselves fascinating, when in reality they are nothing more than objects of pity and derision? Heaven forbid. But, he reminded himself, he *was* slipping. First Miss Thorpe ran away from him, and now Miss Winterton revealed no sign of being enamored of him—rather, she pitied him! Horrid, indeed.

"We are scarcely a part of one of Mrs. Radcliff's novels," he reminded the others. "We had best *be* analytical in our approach. I doubt emotion will achieve a thing."

Joanna looked across at him over the rim of her teacup. A wayward thought fluttered into her mind that she could most likely become very emotional with Sir Lucas, given the right setting and situation. She banished the notion and took a sandwich instead of further and most likely fruitless contemplations.

So they sat and visited, speculated, even tried to plot out the rest of the day and the next.

Outside the mist ceased and the air began to clear. By midafternoon a fitful sun had appeared.

"A walk," Joanna declared as though she had discovered a clue. "I think a walk might do us all good. And I believe we should all surround Sir Lucas. Surely the man will not attempt anything when Sir Lucas is among friends."

It was agreed upon. After they had repaired the ravages of the morning—which meant that Joanna changed out of her somewhat shocking divided skirt and into a demure white muslin gown—they began their stroll through the village and on to the lake.

"Why is it that wherever we intend to go, we always seem to end up by the water?" Joanna said to Sir Lucas, with a gesture to the expanse of azure blue ahead of them.

Sunlight shimmered on the water. Birds darted about, delighting in the warming weather. The breeze was just sufficient to prevent the rising heat from being uncomfortable.

He favored her with one of those arched-brows, wickedly knowing looks and said, "Perhaps you have a fondness for the lake? Pleasant memories? I know I do."

"If you refer to what I suspect you do, you are not a gentleman," Joanna said in a quiet miff. She tilted her chin up and marched ahead before she recalled that she was supposed to be acting as a part of the guard for her nemesis. She turned to face him, suddenly aware that she wore the same white gown she'd worn on their fishing trip.

"I suppose others have told you that you blush delightfully," Sir Lucas said in that teasing way he had.

"I rarely have cause to blush, sirrah. 'Tis only you that seem to take pleasure in tweaking my nose." Joanna darted a scornful glance in his direction.

"And such a pretty nose it is, too," he countered.

"Naughty boy—behave," she whispered as the others waited for them to catch up.

Again Lucas felt put in his place. Not only did Joanna Winterton refuse to flirt with him, she also seemed impervious to his flattery. It was a lowering reality. Could she actually view him in that light?

Aunt Caroline paused to greet a couple she had chanced to meet several days before. Within a brief time, the four strollers were invited to a little gathering at the Plumptons' that very evening. A simple, casual affair with visiting, perhaps cards, and a bit of dancing if the local fiddler remained sober.

"It will be good for you," Joanna observed to Sir Lucas. "If you are at a party surrounded by people, you will be able to forget your dilemma for a while."

"You will contrive to remind me, I have no doubt," he said.

"Well, I cannot see how," she countered. "And why should I?" Annoyed with the impossible man, Joanna drifted forward to walk next to her aunt, exclaiming over a bird she'd not seen before. Lord Osborn reluctantly gave way to her, joining Sir Lucas.

"At least we don't have that blasted painter along," Lucas observed to his old friend.

"You don't like the chap? I think he is very good."

"Perhaps at painting," Lucas admitted. "However, I cannot like his attentions to Miss Winterton. She inherited a sizable amount of money, with more to follow. Stands to reason that he would be interested in an heiress. Ever know an artist who did not need money?"

"Cannot say I have," Lord Osborn confessed. "Now look here, we are off the topic that needs to be discussed."

"It was rather nice for a bit," Lucas said with a grin.

"Be serious. This evening ought to be safe."

"That is just what Miss Winterton said. I suppose if I had any brains, I would leave for London in the first available post chaise." Lucas exchanged a caustic glance with his friend.

"While you have Bow Street at your disposal there, you have the problem of a great many more people as well."

"You are assuming the chap has the means to travel. I give leave to doubt that." Lucas laughed at the notion he would be so fainthearted as to flee the scene. "No, I shall try to bait the fellow and see what happens then."

"What will you use for bait?" his lordship wondered.

"Why, myself, of course," Lucas replied with a grin.

"How fortunate that I had Susan pack your pretty pink sarcenet. I hoped we might find congenial company while here, and the Plumptons are delightful people. I believe I went to school with Mrs. Plumpton's older sister." Aunt Caroline hovered about Joanna, patting the dress here and tugging there to achieve the properly elegant line.

Joanna could not help but be pleased. The gown had a high waist and low neck edged with satin binding of a deeper rose. The tiny sleeves were slashed, showing the same deeper rose inside. The sarcenet fell to her toes in a graceful cascade of colorful silk that floated about her when she moved.

"We can only hope the fiddler remained sober today. I fear I could not concentrate on cards this evening."

"I asked Mrs. Hawkins about that, and it seems he is her cousin. She slipped down to order him to stay away from the drink, or he'd not be receiving any more of her pies. He promised. That is a very good threat, you know. She is famous for her pies." Aunt Caroline stood back to admire her girl.

"I am aware of her talents. As are our neighbors. I vow they eat more meals with us than at home." Joanna formed a moue with her lips before grimacing. How could she deny her dearest aunt the pleasure of a gentleman's company? Was this not precisely what she had prayed for so many times?

Both gentlemen were dressed to the nines when they came to escort the ladies. Lord Osborn offered his arm to Aunt Caroline, saying, "Miss Staunton, it gives me great pleasure to squire you to the party. In that blue gown, you look every inch the London belle."

Aunt Caroline blushed and tapped his hand with her fan. "Dear man, what an agreeable person you are, to be sure."

Joanna watched them stroll down the lane, the group having decided that it would be folly to have the horses put to just to go a brief distance.

"I trust that friendship meets with your approval?" Sir

Lucas said quietly to her. "Osborn is a good chap and as sound as they come. Tidy income, nice home in Oxford. All in all, a good catch for an older woman."

"I don't know that my aunt is on the catch for a husband," Joanna shot back quickly.

"Nonsense, every woman must be on the catch for a husband, good or otherwise. Although I suppose the better he is, the happier she and her family will be."

"Do I detect a note of bitterness in your voice?" Joanna replied. "Poor fellow, are you so put upon, then? I cannot imagine why you should be so chased after. Perhaps the field is a trifle narrow," she concluded with a trace of glee in her voice.

"Young woman, were I your father you would receive a good spanking," he said in return.

"Were you my father we should not be having this conversation. Besides, I rarely talk to my father and certainly never like this. Fathers are awesome creatures who look down from on high to make lofty pronouncements like, 'You are to attend Miss Featherstone's Academy for Young Ladies of Quality,' or 'You are to marry where I tell you and there will be no discussion on the matter,'" she said in gruff accents.

"And I suppose you heard both those statements. What a trial that must have been for you," he said, tightening his hold on her elbow as they crossed the street before reaching the Plumpton house.

"There was nothing to be done. He is my father and I must obey him. Not only the church but also the law says so. And I have been a dutiful daughter." Joanna made a face at this remark, thinking she would rather have had a father in whom she might confide and whom she could love.

"I know, for I endured much the same thing."

"Only, he did not order you to marry, or select your bride for you," she said thoughtfully, quite aware that she trespassed on a tender subject.

"No, he could not choose her. He would have deemed her acceptable, for she has fortune and breeding. Or did have," he added after a moment.

"I hope Captain Fortesque is kind to her. It must be a diffi-cult position to be in—little money and no help from any-one."

"He might have gambled less, saved more, and perhaps con-tented himself with a girl who was not bespoken." Sir Lucas paused before the Plumpton house and looked down at Joanna. In the waning light he did not look angry, but rather like one who had been crossed and was annoyed.

Privately, Joanna thought that Captain Fortesque had actu-ally done Sir Lucas a great favor. Surely somewhere there must be a girl with the same qualifications who was also lov-able.

She knew she had overstepped the bounds of what was polite. But so had he. "Shall we join the others?" she said, hoping to break the spell he was beginning to weave around her.

"Indeed. I would not have our host and hostess think us ill-mannered," he murmured, escorting her to the door in time to greet Mrs. Plumpton with his customary social smile.

The lady was clearly impressed by the elegant guests from London. Everyone in the village had speculated on the four persons living in the cottages at the end of the lane. There was little doubt but that Mrs. Plumpton felt she had contrived a coup of sorts to have them all at her little gather-ing.

"I believe we cut quite a nice figure this evening," Joanna murmured to Sir Lucas. Indeed, those attending might be from a little village, but they seemed most agreeable and were dressed in excellent style.

And so it proved. They were requested to lead out the first dance, and Joanna vividly recalled the last time she had danced with Sir Lucas in London. It was just before the disas-trous wedding that did not take place.

"It has been some time, has it not?" she said lightly as he lifted her hand in the first pattern of the country dance.

He twirled her about, then faced her with a wry expression on his face. "I also remember."

"You were quite odious that evening, as I recall," she said while they waited for the next pattern to begin.

"Why? Because I told you Underhill was not worthy of your grief? It was the truth, and I more than suspect you know it."

Joanna was saved from a reply by having to step through the next measure of the dance. When she again faced him, her hand held firmly in his, she said, "I have no desire to be disrespectful—to him or his family."

"His family and yours would most likely have the greatest effect on you. You were wise to leave off your mourning attire. I must say you looked the veriest fright in black."

"You do amaze me, you really do," Joanna said with a falsely sweet smile. "However did you manage to survive a Season without being killed?"

"Perhaps it is not a man who seeks me but one of those frightful Bath misses after me for merely giving her a setdown," he replied with a grin, twirling her again.

"You *are* wicked, you know," Joanna confided, stepping on the toe of his patent-leather slipper by design and feigning a look of innocence. What a pity her soft leather slippers would make no mark. She was too insubstantial to put a dent in his slippers—or in his ego, for that matter.

"I believe you are rather naughty yourself, my dear girl. Delightful, though," he murmured as he bowed over her properly gloved hand at the end of the dance.

Joanna felt strange as she looked down into his eyes. The candlelight cast a delicate golden glow over his face and silvery hair, giving him a truly angelic look. The pale blue satin of his coat enhanced the image and Joanna was almost awed by this apparition. Then she sought those dark eyes and knew the angel had a very roguish soul.

Mr. Wilson arrived late and begged a dance with Joanna. Sir Lucas frowned but Joanna happily granted the dance and counted Mr. Wilson most accomplished.

Then Lord Osborn begged a dance with her and Joanna gratefully accepted. He was skilled, and Joanna chided herself for being so absorbed that she had not paid attention to her aunt performing what had to be her very first dance.

"I believe my aunt must have enjoyed dancing with you, sir," Joanna said when they went down the line.

"Indeed, I believe she did. Didn't want to dance. Said something about a trifling limp, as though that mattered. She did well, though. Very well indeed." His lordship looked over to a delighted Miss Staunton and exchanged a smile with her.

After that Joanna danced with every gentleman present and a second time with Sir Lucas.

"How fortunate this is a small gathering. I'd not be likely to see you otherwise. I am surprised to see Wilson here. You certainly have been occupied," he complained.

"That is only proper. It would be bad form to refuse one gentleman, then dance with you, and you know it." Joanna gave him a look she devoutly hoped was cool and collected.

He merely whirled her about in the waltz he had requested and said nothing. Because there were many who disapproved of the dance, and others who were merely tired, and still others who wished to see the waltz performed by those from London, Joanna and Sir Lucas had the floor to themselves. She also became silent, allowing her feet to skim over the polished boards, ever turning in circles as was done in the city ballrooms.

At the conclusion, there was a scattering of applause and murmurs of "well-done" from those assembled.

"Sir, you would have us become a byword?" she whispered as he drew her along to where her aunt and Lord Osborn awaited them.

"From time to time it is acceptable to instruct others on how the waltz is properly performed. I must say, you are an excellent dancer."

Joanna was forced to swallow her ire at this handsome compliment from such a polished gentleman as Sir Lucas. That he was most likely emptying the butter boat over her head with false flattery, she ignored for a moment. The dance had been most enjoyable—too enjoyable. She wished she might dance with him always, and that could not be.

"What a lovely couple you made in that waltz," Aunt Caroline declared, beaming a smile on her dearest niece.

"I propose . . ." Sir Lucas began and Joanna glanced at him with wide eyes, wondering what he planned now.

There was a flurry of activity on the far side of the room.

Mrs. Plumpton invited them all to join in a light repast, a mere cold collation. Joanna suspected the table would be groaning and it was.

Sir Lucas did not continue his sentence. She would most likely never learn what he intended to propose. No doubt it was something innocuous. But the thought entered her mind that she would entertain a proposal from him and that surprised her. She did not like him. Or did she? He was a wicked man, make no mistake. He teased, kissed, mocked Society's dictums, and did as he pleased wherever he went.

He ought to have learned something from his jilt. It seemed he had not. Joanna wondered if she could teach him a lesson— And then she wondered what manner of lesson she could teach.

After the delectable collation that Mrs. Plumpton had set forth, Joanna wandered out to look at the lake.

Mr. Wilson joined her to gaze at the moonlit view.

"How lovely it is," she murmured, reluctant to speak loudly less she break the spell.

"I brought my pad and pencil with me, my paints as well. I had thought I might try to paint a scene by moonlight. Most moonlit scenes are imagination. I would like to attempt one." He laughed. "Most likely it is impossible."

"You will never know unless you try," she reasoned.

"True. Would you join me? I could use an extra pair of hands and I may need a candleholder."

Joanna laughed, not the least bothered that she had been asked to serve as a candleholder. Mr. Wilson was not the threatening sort.

"I must seek out my aunt for permission. I fancy they may wish to spend some time in this glorious moonlight as well." As she hunted for her aunt, Joanna considered that it would do the budding romance no harm for her aunt and Lord Osborn to enjoy the lovely and almost magical evening together.

"You were on the terrace," Sir Lucas said when he joined her.

"I was. 'Tis a beautiful moonlit evening," Joanna said, deciding to ignore that his voice was a trifle accusing. "Have you seen my aunt?"

"I believe she was in the middle of a card game and was winning the last I observed."

"Goodness, that is unusual. It must be the company," Joanna said, a mischievous glint in her eyes. "Aunt is an indifferent card player. She must be inspired."

"You wish to go home?"

"On the contrary. Mr. Wilson desires to sketch the lake by moonlight. I thought to go along and watch him. He does not mind in the least, and suggested I might be of assistance— holding a candle if needs be," she said, aiming for the table where it appeared her aunt had just completed her game of cards. She had won, if the dazed expression on her face was anything to go by.

"Would you like to go on a little walk, perhaps do something a trifle unusual?" Joanna said quietly once she had extricated her aunt from the players.

"By all means yes," Aunt Caroline said. "This has been a lovely evening, but all good things must come to an end."

Joanna hastily explained what Mr. Wilson proposed to do and her dear aunt, bless her heart, agreed with alacrity.

In short order the five had bid their hosts a pleasant farewell, declaring it a fine evening, and left for the lake.

"There is not the slightest need for you to join us if you would rather go to your cottage," Joanna said politely to Sir Lucas.

"And leave you to the painter with desires and suggestions? Not likely." Sir Lucas stepped on a stone that threw him off balance. He murmured words better not heard.

Joanna smiled. She was feeling the stones through the soles of her slippers as well, and wondered if this was a wise idea. But she was not about to give it up and admit defeat.

Mr. Wilson found what he declared a perfect spot. The gentle moon shed light over the lake, creating a silver path that led to the shore. Trees could be seen with amazing clarity and not far distant a lone fisherman sat in his boat, fishing by moonlight.

Joanna could not understand how the artist could see to

sketch the scene, much less paint it. While the moon was bright, was it bright enough?

Evidently she was proven right, for shortly after, she was asked to hold the candle that he pulled from his pocket. He lit it for her, and she sat down on a convenient rock to shed light for him.

"This is the outside of enough," Sir Lucas murmured. "I can think of a hundred better things to do in the moonlight with a pretty girl. This is not one of them."

"I suppose you must be right. For instance, I have heard of picnics, and balls, and even games in the moonlight," Joanna said with what she hoped was a demure look.

"Baggage," he replied. He leaned over to see what Mr. Wilson was sketching, and in so doing placed his hand on Joanna's bare shoulder.

"Sir?" she said with a tremble that had nothing to do with the mild breeze that wafted across the lake.

"Merely wished to see what our artist creates." Sir Lucas took a second look and added thoughtfully, "If this turns out, I should like to purchase it. It really is a fine scene."

Aunt Caroline and Lord Osborn strolled down to the lake, then along the shore. They would return from time to time to chat and see how the moonlit scene progressed.

Eventually, Joanna tired of holding the candle. She poured a bit of wax on a large stone, then placed the taper on top, thus affixing it reasonably well. Then she also left, promising to view the completed painting tomorrow.

"At last. I thought you would turn into a statue."

"Shall you really buy the painting? I ask because if you don't, I will."

"I will," he declared. Then they strolled along behind the older couple, holding hands and enjoying the night and the moon.

Of course it had to end. It was around three o'clock when Joanna bade Sir Lucas a good evening before the gate to Rose Cottage. "It was lovely," she said in conclusion.

"Memorable," he agreed.

"And do you know, nothing dire happened to you all

evening." She yawned, swiftly covering her mouth with her gloved hand.

"True. Perhaps he has given up?" But Lucas knew that something had happened. Only he couldn't put a name to it and thought perhaps he had better not try.

Chapter Ten

Joanna hurriedly stepped into the parlor and was most surprised to see her aunt sipping tea. "What a slugabed I am. Why, we were often up late while in London. I have grown too accustomed to country ways, I believe. Did you sleep well, dear Aunt?"

"Tolerably, Joanna. It was a lovely evening. I cannot recall when I have so enjoyed myself."

"And about time, too. I vow your limp is better. You even danced last night!" Joanna exclaimed.

"Indeed," Aunt Caroline replied, her face beaming. "It was excessively pleasing, to be sure. I believe I might risk a dance when we return to London—that is, should someone ask me." She gave her niece a coy glance, then turned a pretty pink hue.

"How long will Lord Osborn remain here?" Joanna asked, her mind leaping from the matter of her aunt's possible partner to the gentleman who had been showing her particular attention.

"He says he will not leave until the mystery is solved and the villain uncovered. It may take time, he says."

Joanna noted that her aunt seemed pleased with the prospect of entertaining the gentleman in the interim.

She went to the kitchen, found a bit of bread and cheese for a late breakfast, then accepted a pot of tea from Mrs. Hawkins. She returned to join her aunt and enjoy her light meal.

Across the street Lucas left the cottage—which had been much improved by having the chimney cleaned and a proper fire to dry the interior—and headed down the lane to the village, his stride purposeful.

When he reached Wilson's little house, he swung open the gate and marched up to the front door, now closed.

He rapped with his cane, then waited.

"Good day, Sir Lucas," Mr. Wilson said, seeming most surprised to see anyone at his front door. The fellow was in disarray, hair going every which way and daubs of paint on the front and sleeves of his white shirt.

"I wish to see you about the watercolor you did last night. Did you finish it?" Lucas.

"Indeed I did, sir. I think it one of my better paintings, if I may say so."

His modesty did him credit for he was very talented, Lucas thought.

Wilson led Lucas over to where the completed watercolor could be seen on the largest table in the room. Little tables were scattered here and there, each overflowing with paints, papers, sketches, and the like. Mr. Wilson was an exceedingly untidy man.

"Ah, and so it was," Lucas exclaimed in an undertone. The scene was precisely as they had viewed it last evening, right down to the silvery ripples on the lake. "How much?"

The sum named seemed more than reasonable to Lucas and he quickly agreed on the price, only requesting a mat be placed to protect it until he could find a frame.

Within a short time he left the house and marched up the lane again to the gate that led to Rose Cottage.

"Am I in time for tea and a biscuit?" he inquired after Mrs. Hawkins had ushered him into the sitting room.

"What an interesting person you are, Sir Lucas. You show up at noon requesting tea and biscuits with a parcel under your arm," Aunt Caroline observed.

He supposed he looked smug, but he was pleased he had beaten everyone else to the painting. "I have a surprise that must be celebrated properly. I doubt you have champagne, so I ask for tea."

"Goodness, what can it be?"

"I suspect a painting. Am I right?" Joanna asked.

"Not just any painting, but the one from last evening.

Ladies, for your approval." Lucas unwrapped his little treasure and was gratified to see their delighted response.

"How like the scene it is, quite as though we were looking at it all over again," Aunt Caroline exclaimed.

"That is what I felt as well. Miss Winterton, may I present this to you as a memory of your visit to the lakes. When you return to London, perhaps this will make you think of fresh air and the lakes and a lovely summer evening."

"It is too much," Joanna protested, accepting the painting with a mixture of delight and proper hesitance. It would not do to be overly eager. "I do thank you, sir. It is a very nice thing of you to do. I had thought to buy it myself, for this has been a memorable holiday."

"I am pleased that I may redeem myself in this manner. May I trust I am in your good graces again?" he murmured, while holding the painting for her to examine more closely.

Joanna shot him a questioning look, then recalled the number of liberties he had taken without her leave.

"Perhaps," she allowed. "I shall consider the past breaches of propriety forgotten," she said very softly.

Lucas suspected that she might declare them forgotten, but he wondered if she forgave him as well. It was odd how she drew him when she was only passingly pretty with no pretense to stunning beauty or fascinating charms. But he could not deny there was something rather special about her. Her earnestness and common sense quite appealed, not to mention her delectable figure. Yet what compelled him to return to her side again and again eluded him. She captivated him, and he could not quite explain why.

Mrs. Hawkins bustled into the room bearing the requested tea and biscuits, with sandwiches and buns as well. The painting was placed where all might admire it.

Joanna poured Sir Lucas's tea, offering the cup and saucer with a demure smile. "Biscuits?" she asked after assuring herself that he had the proper amount of milk in his teacup.

Lucas found that the appetite he'd thought satisfied earlier had returned, and he filled a plate with the sandwiches, a bun, and several ginger biscuits.

"So," Aunt Caroline said, "the villain did not strike last

evening. Do you think he has given up and gone away? Or is the chap likely to renew his attempts on your life?" She was not one to beat about the bush when it came to important matters.

"I wish I might say the latter. I honestly do not know what to think. He's not quite rational, is he? I can only be on my guard." Sir Lucas favored them both with a serious look, one that revealed some of his worry.

"I thought I might go visiting today and perhaps make a few inquiries," Joanna said. "We met so many of the local people last evening that I feel I might knock on a few doors without being intrusive. This is not London, so I daresay I need not be quite so formal." She gave him an inquiring look, unsure she was correct.

"I feel sure that wherever you chance to go you will be welcome." A persistent imp that had bedeviled him in the past reminded Lucas that the girl might have a few pounds to her name, but every young woman looked to gain more and that through marriage. Did she plan such a thing? Goodness knew that lately she sought his opinion, chanced to be with him, was tangled into his life from one end to the other.

The thought came to him that he was overdoing his attentions. He did not wish them to be misconstrued. Lucas finished his tea, then bid her a distant good day.

Once the door had snapped shut with a click, Joanna rose to look at the painting where it sat propped up on a table. "He was in an odd mood. At first he seemed so friendly, then he turned so cool." She turned to give her aunt a frowning look. "I do not understand him in the least."

"I understand that is not at all uncommon," her aunt replied before rising to peer out of the window. "He has met Lord Osborn and they head off to the village. I doubt we shall see them again today."

"Perhaps I annoyed him with something I said," Joanna suggested. In her mind she went over what she had spoken and could not think of anything that might be deemed unacceptable. "Unless . . . do you think I ought not have asked his opinion of visiting?"

"That is not the problem, I feel sure of it. But I wonder," she mumbled to herself, "does Sir Lucas know his own mind."

Sometime later Joanna and her aunt, properly equipped with parasols, reticules, and neatly engraved calling cards, left the house for the village.

Their first stop was to see Mrs. Plumpton. After expressing their delight in the lovely evening, Joanna ventured a question about little Mary.

"The child Mary, the girl three houses down from you, what do you know about her?" Joanna fiddled with her reticule, waiting with surprising anxiety for the answer.

"It is such a sad story. Her parents were killed in a boating accident, and she was left all alone. A neighbor took her in out of pity, but it is not easy to care for a child not one's own when others come along."

"She is an orphan. That explains a good deal. Poor child, to be so unloved."

"She is that," Mrs. Plumpton agreed.

"Then that couple did not adopt her?" Joanna asked, not sure why, but she had to know.

"Never bothered. Why? 'Tis an expense they could ill afford." Mrs. Plumpton shrugged her shoulders as though that concluded the matter.

Aunt Caroline turned to another topic, begging to know the recipe for the delectable punch for which Mrs. Plumpton must be famous. The two older women put their heads together, chatting comfortably about various beverages until it was the correct time to leave.

"What sort of bee do you have in your bonnet now, my love?" Aunt Caroline wished to know as they strolled along the lane to the next house where they planned to call.

"I do not know, precisely. 'Tis only that I feel so for that child. She reminds me of myself at that age, you see."

"But she is not at all like you," Aunt Caroline felt obliged to point out.

"Perhaps, but there is something I see in her that draws me." Joanna said no more on the matter, and they walked on to chat briefly with another woman they had met the evening before.

Two hours later, and after a goodly number of calls paid on

the people they had met, the two women trudged back to Rose Cottage.

"I fear we did not learn much of use," Joanna said sadly.

"Not so far as the villain is concerned. Everyone sees the itinerants, all ignore them except to hand out an occasional coin with the hope of ridding the area of their presence. Either these itinerants have led a horrible life, or they are gifted storytellers. Each person could tell one tale that made you wish to weep." Aunt Caroline shook her head, then brightened when they drew near the cottage. "I believe little Mary has come to call on you."

"Best tell Mrs. Hawkins to fix us a large tea, one with great quantities of biscuits and sandwiches and treacle tarts." Joanna hurried forward to greet the child, then escorted her into the house. Here she showed her the lovely painting of the moonlit lake, then promised a nice tea.

"Pretty," Mary said, then gave Joanna such a smile of devotion that it made her feel most humble. To think a bit of kindness should affect the child so.

The child stuffed herself on a little of everything on the table, asking politely and nibbling at an impressive speed. When finished, she shyly chatted for a time, then properly begged her leave.

Joanna stood by the gate and watched the child skip her way down the lane to the village.

"Good afternoon, Miss Winterton," Lord Osborn said, coming from the other direction.

Joanna spun around and immediately noted that the gentleman was alone. Clearly, Sir Lucas was maintaining his distance from Rose Cottage.

"Good afternoon. I trust you have had a pleasant day." Then she glanced about her and asked, "Have you learned anything new about the villain? Aunt Caroline and I went mousing about the village earlier and did not learn a useful item. There are so many itinerants passing through this area that they scarcely take note of any one in particular."

"Alas, we have found the same to be true. They are tolerated and pitied, but little more. Most of the local people are

only a little better off, I believe. They have precious little to
spare."

"Sir Lucas is safe? We saw him this morning. He brought
the lovely painting of the moonlit lake to me as a gift."

"I left him chatting with the fellow who lets the boats. No
more attempts on his life so far. It does tend to make him a
mite edgy at times. Might I see the finished painting? Lucas
said it was quite good."

"More than good," Joanna promised. "I think it excellent."

Aunt Caroline pretended surprise when they entered the
house, although Joanna would have sworn she noticed her
aunt's face at the window. It might explain why she had
changed to her best day cap and draped a pretty fichu around
her neck.

"What a splendid picture," Lord Osborn exclaimed when he
entered the room.

It seemed to Joanna that he looked at her aunt rather than
the painting. Small wonder that Aunt blushed like a schoolgirl.

Joanna decided to leave the two to chat and begged off, saying she had forgotten something she needed.

Grabbing her reticule, she hurried from the cottage and
walked down the lane at a fast clip. Rex trotted at her heels,
sniffing the air but never leaving her side.

Just in front of the house where little Mary lived, she encountered the gentleman who occupied far too many of her
thoughts. "Good afternoon, Sir Lucas. Lord Osborn came to
call and my aunt showed him the painting. He thought it
prodigiously fine."

"Lovely," Sir Lucas replied, obviously somewhat preoccu-
pied.

"You went to speak with the boating man. Did you learn
anything of help?" Joanna cast a glance at the lake, then back
to Sir Lucas.

"Very little. I have never encountered so many blind alleys
in my life. The fellow is able to disappear at will and is garbed
such that no one pays the least attention to him. It is like chasing a phantom."

"I can see how frustrating that must be for you. At least
there have been no more attempts on your life."

"Or yours. I have not forgotten that when you first entered the cave by Rydal Water, you were terrified by an unseen presence." Sir Lucas gave her a considering look.

"He did not harm me," she reminded. "I think perhaps I merely intruded at a moment he did not expect anyone. And I doubt he liked my dog. I wish you would permit Rex to go along with you." She turned to the dog and snapped her fingers. He obediently trotted to her side, looking up as though to ask what she wished of him.

Joanna looked to Sir Lucas. "See what a good fellow he is? Now tell me, would you not wish for company on your rambles?"

"I have no wish to deprive you of a guardian."

"I shall take Susan when I go for a walk. Please, I would feel a great deal better were you to have Rex."

"Very well. Come," he said to the dog. Rex looked to Joanna, quite as though requesting permission, which she readily gave.

She watched her little companion trot off up the lane for a bit. Then Sir Lucas veered off in the direction of Rydal Water. Joanna shivered when she thought of the possible danger he might be in.

She saw little Mary playing close by and called her a hello before going on to complete the fictitious errand she had created so as to leave the house and her aunt with her guest. Goodness, what skullduggery. At this rate she would become a most devious person.

Joanna bought a packet of pins, a tin of Bohea tea, and several ribands she could use for trimming her gowns. She spent time sauntering about the little store, then at last, with her purchases tucked into her reticule, she headed for Rose Cottage.

All was very quiet around the house, she thought. Mrs. Hawkins was busy preparing supper. The maids were at their tasks. Her aunt had disappeared, for a stroll, most likely.

Joanna left the cottage to rest in the wicker chair when she smelled smoke. Whirling about, she saw a man running from the yard.

Calling out to him to halt, she did not pause to wonder what she would do with him if he should obey. Then she dashed around the corner only to find little Mary beating at the flames with her hands. A fire licked at the wood trim on the side of the cottage. A bit more and it would be inside.

"Get away, child. You might be hurt. Please," Joanna cried, tugging at the child. Mary fell back, obedient as ever.

Joanna recalled that her aunt had left a bucket under the spout to catch rainwater. She ran to the rear of the cottage and caught up the bucket, then poured the water over the fire, nearly dousing it. Thankfully, she was able to stamp out the remaining flames.

She slumped to the ground, shocked and frightened. She had little doubt the man she had seen running away was the man they sought, the villain, as they had dubbed him. He had disappeared into the brush and trees so swiftly that she could not recall one thing about him.

She had been so certain that the man was after Sir Lucas—indeed, the note had indicated such. Then why attempt to burn down Rose Cottage?

By this time Bodkin and Susan, along with Mrs. Hawkins had come running from the house. They cried in alarm when they saw the smoke.

"Calm yourselves," Joanna said wearily. "It is out now, thanks to little Mary. She tried to put it out all by herself, poor child." Joanna slipped an arm about the girl, resting her chin on the delicate little head.

Mary whimpered and Joanna stared at her before realizing what had happened. The thin little hands were badly burned!

"Mercy, child, how terrible! Come with me at once. We must do what we can," Joanna cried. "Mrs. Hawkins, have we any cold water? and oil? and linen for bandages? The child has burned herself trying to put out the fire."

Seeing that Mary was in such shock, Joanna picked her up, thankful for once that the girl was under proper weight.

The four women hurried into the cottage, each intent on finding what she could. Mrs. Hawkins brought a pitcher of cold water, just drawn from the well.

Joanna poured the water into a basin, then plunged the little hands into the cold water. The tears ceased at once.

"I have never seen that done before," Mrs. Hawkins observed with a frown.

"All I could think when I saw the burns was that she must wish to be cool." Joanna held the girl in her lap, adding a little more cold water to the basin.

Mary nodded, her relief plain in her eyes.

"I shall fetch more at once," Mrs. Hawkins said. She took the pitcher and headed out the back door for the pump.

"I found some oil, ma'am. Miss Staunton uses it for her skin. It has no scent. Will it do?" Bodkin asked.

"I think so," Joanna replied, wondering anew what it was that compelled that man to such hatred.

"And here is a piece of linen we can cut into strips for a bandage," Susan added, looking at Joanna as though she had suddenly acquired a halo.

"I will not have this child scarred for life all because she tried to save mine. The fire was set just below my window. She must have thought I was still in the house." Joanna tried not to think what might have happened had the fire taken hold and she truly had been in her room.

She sat in the kitchen chair with brave little Mary on her lap for what seemed like hours. In time, when the child could stand to have her hand out of the cold water, Joanna poured the oil over the nasty burns, then wrapped each little hand with infinite care.

"She will stay here with me," Joanna informed Mrs. Hawkins. "The woman she lives with has enough to do without the added problem of a burned child. I shall care for her myself. Oh, and see if you might locate a doctor." She gathered Mary in her arms and gently carried her along the hallway and into her own bedroom, where she tenderly placed the child on the bed, then covered her up with a soft shawl. She sat at her side until the girl slept. Joanna gazed at her a moment, then tiptoed from the room down the hall and into the sitting room.

"What has happened?"

Joanna whirled about to find Sir Lucas staring at her with alarm.

"That horrid man tried to set fire to Rose Cottage. Little

Mary saw him, thought I was in my room—for the fire was set right below my window—and tried to extinguish it all by herself. Poor little girl, her hands are badly burned."

"You are keeping her here?"

"She must not be moved. Indeed, I shall watch over her with greatest care, you may be sure." Tears trembled on Joanna's lashes, then ran down her cheeks. She put her face in her hands and cried briefly before determinedly rubbing her eyes and swallowing with care. "This will accomplish nothing. Only, you see, she is so very small, and so very brave. And she is in such pain."

Sir Lucas stood at the door to the sitting room, Rex quietly at his side, looking thunderstruck. "This will not do. We cannot have such things happening." He strode into the room and began to pace about.

Joanna watched him until she felt dizzy. "He must be found before he kills someone."

A sound in the hall alerted Joanna that her aunt had come home.

"What has happened? Joanna, you look a fright. Why is your gown wet and rumpled and your face all sooty? What has been going on here?" Aunt Caroline demanded to know as she bustled into the room, with Lord Osborn directly behind her.

"A fire, dear Aunt. And my brave little Mary was burned," Joanna replied, sinking down on a fortunately convenient chair. She did not think she could have walked very far.

"Fire!" Aunt Caroline turned to look at Lord Osborn, then Sir Lucas. "What is she talking about?" Then she sniffed the air and nodded. "I do smell smoke. Well, I am waiting."

Sir Lucas, after looking to Joanna for permission and getting no more than a tired nod, said, "That fellow set a fire right beneath Joanna's window. Why, I cannot imagine. I was under the impression that *I* was his target. Why he has included Joanna, I do not know. At any rate, little Mary must have come up to see Joanna and seen the smoke. She tried to put out the fire herself and in so doing was badly burned." He turned to look at Joanna again. "Is that correct?"

"Indeed," she whispered. She had dispassionately observed

that Sir Lucas had called her Joanna—a clear breach of propriety. Perhaps manners went by the wayside at a time like this?"

"How did you treat the child?"

"Cold water—lots of it. Oil and bandages after. She is sleeping now," Joanna said, rising from her chair to go to the hall. "Let me just see she is not pulling at her bandages. I am sure those hands must pain her dreadfully."

"Joanna means to nurse the child here," Sir Lucas informed Miss Staunton.

"Of course, the poor girl would scarcely do otherwise. It is dangerous to move someone who has suffered so badly."

"Will the child be scarred, do you think?" Joanna asked from behind them. "I do not wish her to have visible reminders of this day."

"Only time will tell, that and how bad the burns are. There must be something we can do that has not been done yet. This is an intolerable situation," Lord Osborn observed. "Has a doctor been summoned?"

"Mrs. Hawkins will," Joanna said wearily.

"We have not seen this villain, nor can we explain precisely what he has done, other than set the fire. All else was meant to frighten us," Sir Lucas said.

"What about the boat?" Joanna reminded. "He drilled a hole in the bottom, with the hope you would sink, possibly drown. Not everyone can swim."

"How could we prove to a magistrate that it was a life-threatening measure? Anyone might have done it. We are stumped at the moment, I tell you. And I believe that we will have to solve this on our own. There is nothing else to be done about it." Sir Lucas looked at the others, then motioned to Lord Osborn.

"Let's look around outside. Perhaps he left some sort of clue there."

The two men left the sitting room and all was quiet for a moment.

"This is terribly serious, my love. What if this man had come late at night to set that fire? You might have been killed." Aunt Caroline crossed the room to stand by her niece, running a fond hand over her tousled hair.

"Then why didn't he? Come late at night, I mean. There is a full moon out, he could see clearly. Upon further reflection, I believe he meant for the fire to be detected and put out. He merely wanted to frighten us half to death. He did not count on harming an innocent child."

"Poor girl. I hope she will be all right."

"Aunt, I mean to take her home with me," Joanna declared in a tone that meant she would not be dissuaded. "I have thought it over. The woman with whom she lives does not want to keep her. The child does not have enough to eat. I have more than enough. It is the least I can do for someone who cared enough for me to risk her very life to save me."

"Indeed," Aunt Caroline whispered thoughtfully. "Of course, you must. I will help you."

The men returned to the sitting room.

"Did you learn anything?" Aunt Caroline demanded politely.

"Nothing of help," Lord Osborn said, frowning at their failure.

"Well, we cannot sit here and do nothing," Joanna concluded with a snap. They could escape from here to London, but she knew Sir Lucas desired to find out the truth of the matter.

"Agreed. But what?" Sir Lucas wondered.

"We need a plan," Joanna declared.

Chapter Eleven

"I believe we all agree that whoever is responsible for all that has transpired is one of the transients," Sir Lucas said. He paced back and forth across the sitting room, hands clasped behind his back and face set in determined lines.

"I cannot fathom who else might be responsible," Lord Osborn said, rubbing his chin reflectively. "I doubt there is anyone locally who knows you well enough to wish you ill." He leaned against the fireplace mantel, staring off into space as though searching his mind for a clue that might have been missed somehow. "I mean, that Wilson chap hardly looks the type to set a fire, does he?"

"Not unless he wished to paint a burning house," Sir Lucas murmured with a glance at Joanna.

"What a nasty thing to say. I believe he is utterly harmless," Joanna swiftly countered, coming to the defense of the young artist.

"No man is utterly harmless, my dear," Sir Lucas replied with a look at Joanna that sent her pulse racing for no particular reason she knew, other than he seemed to do that sort of thing quite often.

Joanna stood close to the doorway so she might hear if little Mary stirred. Susan was capable at nursing, but Joanna sensed that Mary would wish her, not a stranger, to be close by.

"Well, I declare something must be done," Aunt Caroline said in a highly affronted manner. "We simply cannot have these frightful things happening to us. Who knows who might be next? Joanna said we need a plan, but I'll be amazed if any of us can think of one." She turned to Lord Osborn with a questioning look, clearly expecting him to calm her fears.

"Never fear, dear lady, we shall come about right and tight just you see," his lordship replied with a kindly smile.

Joanna was not so sure about that. She felt that whoever had set the fire and caused all the other evils was not in his right mind. How did one second-guess a madman?

"Miss," Susan cried from down the hall, just in front of Joanna's bedroom door, "the child be calling you."

"Excuse me," Joanna murmured, hurrying away from what she thought a fruitless discussion.

Rex trotted after her, then assumed a position at the foot of the bed, head on his paws, looking as though he had lost his best friend.

"She will be just fine, Rex," Joanna said with more optimism than she felt. An inspection of the bandages revealed nothing had changed.

"My hands hurt," Mary said with surprising stoicism.

"You are a wonderfully brave girl. Did you see the bad man who started the fire?" Joanna asked with little hope the child would recall anything of value.

"He was one of those beggars, as mam calls 'em. She alus shoos them away, said they could find work iffen they tried hard enuf." Mary raised one of her hands to inspect the bandage and shook her head. "My, that would 'ave made a fine petticoat."

"You shall have a fine petticoat, my dear, if you will sleep and try to get better fast." Joanna turned to accept a cup of broth from Mrs. Hawkins, who was of the strong opinion that no one improved without chicken broth.

Mary obediently sipped the broth. When she finished, she sank back on the soft pillow covered with the finest linen and smiled, albeit a trifle wanly. "Nice," she said, then slipped back to sleep.

"Mrs. Hawkins, will you watch her while I inform her 'mam' that Mary has suffered an injury and that she will be remaining with us."

"Permanent-like?" The cook and housekeeper knew Mary's story, and also knew of Joanna's interest in the child. In a village, very little goes unnoticed when it concerns one of their own.

"Yes, I believe so. She is such a little girl to have endured so much. I think it is time that something good happens to her."

Joanna rose from the bedside and quickly left Rose Cottage by the back door, mostly to avoid being drawn into the debate on a plan how best to snabble the villain. She tied the ribands of her bonnet as she hurried along the lane. Soon she came to the gate leading to the house where Mary had lived since her parents died. What to say?

She pushed open the gate and walked slowly to the front door. When it opened to reveal a tired-looking woman, Joanna said, "Ma'am, I must tell you that little Mary has been hurt—burned in a brave effort to save our cottage from fire. I propose to keep her there . . . permanently, if it is possible. Would you agree to let me take Mary? She seems to like me and my aunt."

It proved to be far easier than Joanna had expected. The woman, Mrs. Hanks by name, was relieved to have Mary off her hands. Joanna could see why, what with four little tots clinging to her skirts and another on the way.

Joanna was about to leave when Mrs. Hanks suddenly said, "Why do you want her? You ain't goin' to sell her, are you? I don't hold with sellin' children."

Shocked to her core that anyone could think such a thing of her, Joanna swiftly said, "Indeed, not! Mary shall live with my aunt and me in London and receive an education such as any girl should have. She will be well cared for, I assure you."

And that was that. It took but several minutes to gather Mary's few belongings. Joanna left as much behind as she could, feeling that the growing Hanks girls could use the items, and knowing she could provide Mary with better. When she left, Joanna felt a weight lifted from her shoulders and knew she had done the right thing.

Back at Rose Cottage, she handed the small pile of clothing to Susan and said, "Please take measurements from these so I may order new things, then wash them."

"I suspect they will be too small soon," Susan said with a glance at the sleeping girl.

"I will buy her some dresses to wear while here, then more when we arrive in London."

"London?" Sir Lucas said softly from the open doorway. "You intend to take the child to London?"

"She has no parents, as you recall, and the people who have cared for her were only too happy to be free of their burden. She is such a dear little soul. I will be happy to care for her." Joanna smiled down at the sleeping child and missed the look of skepticism that crossed his face.

Lucas gave Miss Winterton high marks for trying to gain his sympathy. True, it appeared she seemed to care for the girl, but he suspected that once in London, Mary would be shunted off to a maid. He had seen this sort of thing before—a woman would do a generous deed when it cost her little or nothing in order to impress him. He had hoped better of Miss Winterton.

"Good luck, my dear." he said wryly.

The child moaned and held up her hands, obviously in pain. Miss Winterton soothed her, persuading Mary to drink a distillation of willow bark, and checking the bandages.

"Bring me some water—as cold as possible. I believe I will try to soak her hands again," she instructed a hovering Susan.

"Cold water?" Lucas said. "Never heard of such a thing."

"When I first saw her, all I could think of was trying to cool the burn. If I were burned, I believe I would want to be cold. It calmed her and seemed to ease the pain a great deal," Miss Winterton replied, not casting him a flirtatious look, not even glancing his way.

Lucas stood there a few moments longer, watching as Joanna tenderly removed the oiled linen, then soothed the child with gentle words. Joanna—as he was coming to think of her—ignored *him* completely. Of course it was right and proper, but it was not what he was accustomed to in the least.

It shook him to realize that here was a woman who looked on him as merely another person. All his life he had been spoiled—and he freely admitted that—by adoring women. He discovered that he had come to expect it, want it. Dash it all, other chaps envied him his luck with women. And now that he had found a woman who actually interested him, she disdained to pay him the least attention.

It was a staggering revelation for the premier rake of London to find a miss who ignored him. He discounted Miss Thorpe. He had been bacon-brained to ask her to wed him in the first place. He suspected life with her would have been boring beyond belief. Now with Joanna, he doubted one could become bored. You never knew what she might do next.

Well, he thought, as he quietly left the room where he clearly was not wanted or needed, he could survive without Joanna Winterton. There were dozens of prettier women in London who would eagerly welcome his attentions.

The trouble with that idea was that he had met them all and passed them over. This one was too eager and he deplored her fawning on him, that one had a wretched voice that grated on his nerves. Another who had pleased him at first turned out to have an appetite that promised to make her as round as a pumpkin before many years had passed. Now, Joanna was willowy slim, with a pleasing voice, and she certainly did not fawn on him. Drat and blast.

Perhaps a new girl would arrive in Town to suit his tastes. Joanna Winterton could dwindle into an ape leader for all he cared. Of course there might be a chap who liked the managing sort, the intrepid type like Joanna.

Blast it all, what was he to do?

"Fishing?" Lord Osborn said as he joined Lucas in leaving the house after paying a lingering farewell to Miss Staunton.

"What? Oh. Fishing." Lucas considered the matter and decided he might as well do something.

He ambled along the lane at his friend's side discussing the problem he faced with the itinerant villain whom no one had noticed, no one knew, and he suspected no one cared one speck about.

Joanna propped Mary up against the pillows and proceeded to soak her hands in cold, clear water. The child shivered, but was game about it. She looked at Joanna with wide eyes and said, "The hurt be better, ma'am."

"Is better," Joanna automatically corrected. She smiled encouragingly at the little girl, so brave and dear. What a pity the doctor was over in Ambleside. She would have to do the best she could without him. "I have decided that you are to be educated, just as I was. Would you like to go to London to live with my aunt and me?"

"With you?" Mary said, her eyes even wider and most disbelieving.

"If you please," Joanna said, inspecting the little hands that were so red.

"Yes, ma'am, I should like that," Mary said carefully, revealing to Joanna that the child had once spoken a better sort of English.

"Good. Do you know how to read?" Joanna had little hope the child had learned, but her answer might reveal a desire for such.

"No, ma'am. I helped in the house. Miz Hanks said there was no time for schooling." Mary gave Joanna what appeared to be an embarrassed look, then added, "I think it would be nice." "Nice" seemed well on the way to becoming her favorite word.

"How does she do, Joanna?" Aunt Caroline said from the doorway.

"She does very well. I am going to wrap these little hands up in the oiled linen again and, after a nap, Mary is going to begin learning how to read." She did as she had said, and soon Mary was reclining on the pillow, lids drooping. Within moments she was asleep again, her pain eased, and her future looking rosy indeed.

Joanna left the bedside and joined her aunt. "I have accepted the care of her. Mrs. Hanks was thankful to have me take her. Too many mouths to feed on too little money, I suspect."

"You really do intend to bring that child back to London with us?" Aunt Caroline stopped in her tracks, staring at Joanna as though she had suddenly acquired two heads.

"Indeed, so. I expect Sir Lucas thinks me daft—perhaps I am. I only know that I owe her a debt that I must repay in the best way I know how. Poor dear," Joanna said, suspecting that the road ahead would not be an easy one.

"You realize," Aunt Caroline said with caution as they walked to the rear of the house and out to the garden, "that your taking the child along might make it difficult when you go back to London."

"Why? They can scarcely accuse her of being mine." Joanna plumped up a pillow for her aunt's back, then helped her settle on a chair.

"Joanna!" a shocked Caroline cried, dropping back in alarm.

"I tease," apologized Joanna.

"I should hope so. What I meant was that there are not many men who will accept the charge of a child who is neither yours nor his, and has no expectations of any inheritance." Aunt Caroline gave Joanna an earnest look, taking one of her hands to assure she kept her attention. "This is not something you should undertake lightly, my dear."

"I realize that. Why not see how Sir Lucas reacts. I believe he is a fair example of London gentlemen. If he shuns me, we shall know the worst."

"Oh, dear me," Aunt Caroline murmured into her handkerchief. She leaned back against the chair and closed her eyes for a time. Life had abruptly taken a turn, as it often did, living with Joanna.

When the child awoke, it was to pain and discomfort. Nothing Joanna did seemed to help. Her hair was untidy and her dress less than pristine when Sir Lucas poked his head around the doorway to see how matters went.

"Trouble? We brought two trout and a pike back with us for dinner. I trust that earns us an invitation."

Joanna gave him a tired smile. "You really ought to find a cook, you know."

"Why?" he said with a grin. Then Mary moaned and he became serious at once. "She really is in pain, and I suppose you have not left her side for hours. Where is your maid?" he demanded.

"I sent her to rest for a bit. I am fine, just a little worried." She smoothed the tangled hair back from Mary's brow, then wrung out a cloth to place on her forehead.

"Not that it does much good for those hands, but it calms her," she whispered to Sir Lucas.

"Let me sit with her for a time, and you rest somewhere else," he ordered, quite surprising himself in the process.

"But . . ." Joanna said.

"Go," he repeated. He settled down on the chair at the bedside, wondering if he had taken leave of his senses. What did he know about an injured child? He frowned, trying to recall what had been done for him when he had suffered an injury. He'd never been burned, true, but surely there must be something he remembered. A story!

"Let me tell you about a young fellow I knew," he began, totally capturing Mary's attention with his rich voice and confiding air. He kept her utterly enthralled with his tale of his boyhood escapades, which were not only numerous and dangerous, but highly diverting.

Susan tiptoed in once with a glass of barley water, which Lucas persuaded Mary to consume with not so much as a grimace. She was caught up in the story of the time when Lucas had tried to catch frogs in his mother's lily pond. He had nearly drowned, but he'd had glorious fun before he'd been caught and punished. One did not go into the water wearing one's best clothes. Lucas had completely forgotten that his grandmother was expected. She had frowned on the dripping boy with water-lily stems draped about him.

"That sounds remarkably like something you might have done," Joanna said from the doorway.

"I think he must have been very naughty," Mary observed.

"She looks better, don't you think?" Lucas said to Joanna.

"She does indeed. And I feel much more the thing. Thank you for your thoughtfulness," she replied with a heartfelt smile.

Sir Lucas gave her an odd look, then rose from the chair. "I believe a stroll in the fresh air will prepare me for dinner. Will you join me?"

Joanna studied the child, then nodded. "I believe she is so much better that I can." She sat down and proceeded to check the burns, gently pouring oil over an area that had dried a trifle. She forgot all about Sir Lucas and the walk.

Lucas watched for a time, then quietly left the house, feeling rather useless. Odd, he had not minded telling that scrap of a girl about his childhood, making the stories vivid and outrageous. He supposed that soon, quite soon, he must select another bride and begin his own nursery. The prospect did not appeal very much.

Lord Osborn joined him. Then Mr. Wilson came up the lane with three hares he had shot and was bringing to Rose Cottage in the hope he might be asked for dinner.

Lucas was irritated until he realized he and Lord Osborn had done just the same thing and then he laughed.

Dinner proved to be charming. Mrs. Hawkins had outdone herself, offering a sauce with the fish that was worthy of a London chef. Mrs. Staunton provided polite conversation that did not center on the ailing child down the hall.

Joanna appreciated the efforts to cheer her and take her mind off her new responsibility, but Mary lingered in the back of her mind.

Following dinner, Lucas sought her out and demanded to know what bothered her now.

"Mary had a very good look at that man. Suppose he takes it into his twisted mind to eliminate her as a possible witness to his attempt to burn down the house? He might kill her!"

Lucas drew Joanna away from the others and urged her to sit down. He studied the floor for several moments before attempting to set her mind at ease. The trouble with doing that was that her fears were well-founded. "You might try to get her away from here."

"And leave you alone at his mercy? What manner of friends would we be then?" she said, sounding indignant.

Friends? Lucas wondered if that was an apt description for what he felt, but didn't belabor the point. "You will have to keep watch over her until we catch him. I feel certain that one of these days he will either become bolder and make an attempt at me when I can catch him, or he will give himself away in some other manner."

"I hope so. This is not quite what I had in mind when I left London to seek peace and quiet for a time. This has been anything but peaceful, and the quiet, when it comes, is frightening. One of us must always keep an eye on the child once she leaves her bed. I shan't trust the man not to harm her.''

Lucas felt the very same, and so could not give Joanna the sort of assurance he suspected she wished.

Joanna frowned, then turned to Lucas, saying, "I mean to teach her how to read, but I have never done that sort of thing before. How did you learn?''

Lucas thought back. "We had a slate and wrote our letters on it until we knew them. I do not recall it being very enjoyable. My tutor was a dull, stuffy fellow. I was not sorry to leave him when I was nine and go off to Eton, I was an Oppidan, being an only son." He gave Joanna a wry look. "Father felt it too hazardous to expose me to the rigors of a Colleger's life." Lodging in town was softer for a boy considered by his doting mother to be of delicate health. Lucas had endured a great deal while at school, but so had all his friends. It was a part of Eton, the bullying and the flogging that was too common to excite comment.

"I was sent away to Aunt Caroline after mother died,'' Joanna said reflectively. "Although I'd had a proper nanny, it was my aunt who taught me my letters; thankfully, unlike most girls, I was not only taught to read, but also to think. Behind Aunt Caroline's sweet face lies a woman with quite determined ideas about female education,'' Joanna said, smiling. "However, I did spend a year at a boarding school before my first Season." She paused, looking at Mary once more. "I daresay I might find a slate in the village,'' she said with no enthusiasm whatsoever. "But there ought to be a more appealing way.''

"It worked for us, it will still work, I trust. The child seems bright enough.''

"Yes, she does,'' Joanna murmured, then turned to face her aunt, who had called her. "What is it, Aunt Caroline?''

"I propose we play some cards. Now,'' she added when she saw Joanna about to protest, "you will be right down the hall from Mary, and Susan has shown herself most capable. The little one is improving, thanks to your excellent care. I believe you need a change, and so a game of cards it is.''

Mr. Wilson proposed to sketch those who played and then

perhaps amuse Mary with some little drawings. Joanna gave him a grateful look and agreed, taking her seat at the card table with a graceful swish of her skirt.

Lucas glared at the artist, wondering how he might earn such a look from Joanna; he found he quite desired it.

The play went rather well, with Miss Staunton and Lord Osborn soundly trouncing the other two, who admittedly allowed their minds to wander, although both denied anything of the sort.

Joanna went to check on Mary and found her sleeping fitfully, but at least sleeping. When she returned to the others she pronounced, "I believe she is out of the woods now. At least she seems much better, poor dear."

"In spite of her burns, I believe her one very blessed child, to have you take her up," Lord Osborn said with an approving nod.

"One thing I must say for Joanna, she is a generous girl," Aunt Caroline said with a fond glance at her niece.

"Mary must learn to write, or make her mark, as she says," Joanna inserted, uncomfortable with all this praise when she felt she had done only what *ought* to be done. "The thing is, I cannot use the slate for teaching, although it will be useful later on. I must think of another way."

Lucas studied the pasteboard cards in his hand. Then he had an idea, although he said nothing of it to the others. Too often an idea proved impossible or impractical. He wished to present a completed project.

"I feel sure you will think of something. It will be a few days before she can hold a piece of chalk in her fingers," Aunt Caroline reminded.

"That is just it," Joanna replied, looking adorably frustrated. "I wish to begin immediately, before she changes her mind or loses interest. What better time to begin than when she is captive in bed?"

Aunt Caroline exchanged a look with Lord Osborn, then slowly nodded. "I suppose so, as long as you do not overtire her."

"Have you nothing to add, Sir Lucas?" Joanna demanded.

"Not I," he protested, his mind busily figuring out where he might find the supplies he required.

They played another round of cards and again Lord Osborn and Miss Staunton won handily. "I declare, I wish I had this sort of luck while at the London card tables," Miss Staunton said to her new friend, Lord Osborn.

"I should think you would be so busy flitting from one party to the next that you'd not have time for such dull stuff as cards," he riposted gallantly.

"Oh, la," Miss Staunton said with a rosy blush.

The gentlemen left shortly thereafter.

Before he departed, Mr. Wilson presented Joanna with a charming drawing of the four at cards. Joanna thought she looked quite earnest, Sir Lucas dashingly handsome, Lord Osborn wondrously distinguished, and of her aunt, she could only note the back of her elegant cap and the fall of her lovely gown.

"Do promise you will do her face for me. I have no portrait and you do a splendid likeness," she said.

Mr. Wilson bowed and said, "It was the least I could do for such an excellent dinner. Another might sing for his supper, I sketch."

Joanna laughed and closed the door behind him. She took the sketch over to where the candlelight revealed the lines more clearly and studied it again. In the drawing she was looking at Sir Lucas, who languidly studied his cards. Did her face reveal what she was growing to feel for this man? Or was it just her imagination?

"What is that, dear?" her aunt said when she came in to light her bed candle.

"The drawing Mr. Wilson did for us. Since your back was to him, he promised to come again and have you pose. I should like to have your picture." Joanna offered the pencil sketch to her aunt.

"How lovely," her aunt murmured while she studied the drawing. "He captures a person well. I should be pleased to have him paint me. And he need not bring any more hares, as good as they are. I shall pay *him* for a change." Aunt Caroline chuckled, lit her candle, and went off to bed with a smile and a cheerful good night.

The following day, Joanna was occupied with Mary most of the time. The treatment for the burned hands seemed to be proving most effective. True, the flesh did not look pretty, but Joanna suspected that beneath that outer skin was lovely new skin. As long as infection could be prevented, all would be well. And since the skin had not broken yet, Joanna hoped that was a good sign.

When Sir Lucas appeared at the house wearing not only his usual perfect garb but also a proud smile, Joanna wondered what had happened now.

"Look," he urged. "I have something I think cannot but please you."

Joanna stared at the pile of pasteboard rectangles he held in his hand, utterly mystified. "What is that?" she asked cautiously.

With the air of a conjurer, he produced the first of the pasteboards. On it was beautifully printed the name MARY. Then he held up the second, which featured the word DOG, with a sketch of Rex. After that he held up several other cards, on each of which was inscribed a letter of the alphabet.

Joanna squealed with delight, immediately comprehending what he had done. "Oh, you wonderful man!" she cried and gave him an impulsive kiss on the cheek before she had time to dwell on the propriety of her action.

Lucas grinned and allowed that a kiss on the cheek was a good deal better than a mere thank you. It did not hurt to be called wonderful in that splendid manner, either.

"We can take turns teaching her, if you like. By the time she is able to hold a chalk in her hands, she will most likely know her alphabet, her name, and perhaps a few other simple words. We can make more as needed," Lucas said.

"How can I ever thank you enough?" Joanna said with a glowing smile.

"Go for a drive with me tomorrow. I would see roses bloom in those cheeks once again."

Joanna blushed and nodded. "Very well, a drive tomorrow it is."

Then she went over all of the cards, marveling at the neat hand and clever drawings that decorated the corner of each card, and which she had failed to catch on her first perusal.

"An apple for A is not original, but very apt," she said, chuckling at the fat bumblebee drawn on the following card. "I suppose there is a frog for F?" And there was. "What an excellent teacher you would be, and a wonderful father, too, most likely." Then before she thought about what she had said, she turned to call out to her aunt.

"See what Sir Lucas has done. He is quite, quite splendid." Joanna offered the cleverly done cards to her aunt, who accepted them with a puzzled look.

She examined several of them, then glanced up at the pair before her. She saw her niece, aglow with delight, then Sir Lucas, who looked as proud as punch, and allowed a smile. "Indeed, he is that."

Chapter Twelve

The following days were totally occupied with nursing little Mary. The child was obedient but restless. Joanna found herself trying everything she could think of to entertain her.

The main problem was to keep the bandages on so that there would be no possibility of infection. Treatment had gone from a poultice containing plantain, comfrey, marigold, and lady's mantle, to a decoction of coltsfoot and sweet flag in which Joanna washed Mary's hands, taking care not to injure the skin.

"How does it go?" Sir Lucas asked the fifth morning after the fire. He poked his head around the corner, then entered the room when he saw Mary was awake.

"Well enough, I suppose," Joanna said with a tired smile. She brushed her dark curls away from her forehead and leaned back against the chair that had been pulled up beside Mary's bed.

"You look pale," he said with a frown. "If the rain lets up, I believe you ought to take a drive in the fresh air. Perhaps by this afternoon?"

"I do not know," Joanna said uncertainly, with a cautious look at her little patient.

"Mary will take a nap and promise not to touch those bandages." He gave the girl one of those bone-melting smiles, and the little girl responded as hundreds of others must have over the years. Smiling a bit wistfully, she said, "I will, sir."

Sir Lucas disappeared, and was shortly heard conversing with Aunt Caroline down the hall.

Joanna resumed teaching Mary her letters. "R is for robin, so perky and fat; S is for snake, who consumes the bad rat."

"I do not like snakes," Mary confided. "But I like robins."

"Do you see the letter R almost looks like a fat robin?" Joanna took a pencil, added a few tail feathers, a wing, and a splendid head with an open beak, quite as though the bird sought food. Mary giggled at that.

The child looked at the other letter and said, "The snake looks like an S, does it not?"

Joanna agreed and they went on to the next letter with no further discussion on snakes, good or bad.

An hour later, Mary ate a nice little nuncheon and was tucked under the covers for a pleasant nap, to be watched over by Susan.

"I am pleased she is doing so very well," Joanna said, sinking onto a chair by the front window of the sitting room.

"It has been hard on you," Aunt Caroline observed. "You could do with a bit of a change."

"Sir Lucas wishes me to go for a drive with him this afternoon. The rain appears to be on the wane."

"There ought to be a splendid rainbow if the clouds cooperate," Aunt Caroline mused, resting her tatting in her lap for a moment.

"Must you sit at home this afternoon? It seems to me that you also need to get about," Joanna chided.

Her aunt blushed a rosy pink, then said, "Lord Osborn wishes to walk with me. Do you know, his first name is Henry? I heard Sir Lucas call him that yesterday. Henry is a good English name," she ended contentedly, picking up her work again to resume her lace-making.

"Indeed," Joanna observed with a smile.

Mrs. Hawkins bustled to the front door, and minutes later Sir Lucas entered the room with a faint frown. "I am continually amazed how that woman manages to open the door before I knock."

"She likes to look out of the window from time to time. Little goes on down the lane that she misses," Aunt Caroline said.

"Yet she did not see the man who set the fire," Sir Lucas said, with a look at Joanna.

"I asked her about that. She was busy with a cake in the

oven and could not have seen anything. Cakes are quite delicate and require watching."

"Where is your bonnet?" he asked, not commenting on cakes, delicate or otherwise. "You promised to go for a drive with me this afternoon, should the rain stop. It stopped. The time is here. Shall we?" He stood close to the door, waiting for Joanna.

"The rain has indeed abated. I will join you, if you will but wait a few moments." Without expecting an answer, Joanna whisked herself around the corner. She tiptoed into her room and gathered her prettiest bonnet, her gloves, and the nicest shawl she owned. It promised to be a lovely day outside, but the breeze could be cool following a rain.

The gig awaited them. Sir Lucas took the reins from his man after helping Joanna up into the carriage. He joined her in the little vehicle and they were off down the lane.

"Oh, my," she exclaimed, as they whisked along, the breeze proving to be quite as cool as expected. It was pleasant, though, and Joanna enjoyed the treat.

"Ah, I see a bit of pink in those pale cheeks again," Sir Lucas said approvingly. At which Joanna felt said cheeks grow a bit warmer.

She gazed up at the sky, then sighed with delight. "Look, a rainbow. 'My heart leaps up when I behold a rainbow in the sky,'" she quoted from Wordsworth. She had been reading a few of his poems to Mary. The child had been surprised to learn that man who had once lived at the far end of the lane from her had published poems.

Joanna shared that little bit with Sir Lucas. "She is of the opinion that if something is in print, it must be important," Joanna concluded. "I think he would be amused to know that."

"Rydal Mount, where he lives now, is but a short distance away. Shall we pay him a call? Many do, you know," he said with a quick glance at his companion.

"I should not wish to intrude," Joanna protested, fiddling uneasily with the reticule in her lap.

"It would mean driving past Rydal Water," he admitted.

"I am silly regarding Rydal Water, you know. I should not feel so apprehensive about the place. After all, what can anyone do if we but drive past there?" she said with a serious look at Sir Lucas. "If you think it would not be objectionable, I would enjoy meeting the famous poet and his family."

"To Rydal Mount we go," Sir Lucas responded with a jaunty air. With a flick of the reins the horse picked up his pace.

Joanna tore her gaze from Sir Lucas with difficulty. When she had decided to take a trip to the Lake District, she'd never imagined that she would encounter him, nor that she could be so strongly attracted to him. He put other gentlemen quite in the shade. That turned her thoughts to her future. What in the world would she do when it came time to return to London?

It seemed Aunt Caroline was in a fair way to becoming the next Lady Osborn, which suited Joanna very well. However, it also brought a problem. If Aunt Caroline married, what would become of Joanna and little Mary? For Joanna was determined to take her little heroine with her.

They *must* find another place to live. Neither her father, who was soon to marry, nor Aunt Caroline, if she married, would likely welcome Joanna and Mary into their new arrangements

"Look," Sir Lucas exclaimed, jogging Joanna from her musing. "The rainbow goes completely across the sky."

Joanna set aside her problems to gaze at the sight with appreciation. "It *is* lovely," she said with wonder.

Sir Lucas had paused at the top of the rise of the road from Grasmere. The rainbow spanned the sky with brilliant color. It was an unusually complete and distinct arc.

"Do you believe in omens?" he asked absently.

"What sort?" She gave him a startled look.

"That rainbows are bad luck."

"You mean like placing sticks on the ground to cross out the rainbow so as to make it go away? My cousin used to do that," she said. "I think them pretty, and the rain will come regardless, won't it?" She shared an amused look with Sir Lucas, then turned to look skyward again.

"Well, we most likely will have rain again, for as you said before, all this green grass must have water."

They set off anew, although at a quicker pace.

Joanna breathed deeply, inhaling the fresh air scented with wildflowers. "I am glad you persuaded me to go for a drive with you this afternoon. It is quite what I needed."

Sir Lucas did not have an opportunity to answer her, for a large, black bird suddenly flew out into their path, startling the horse. Sir Lucas had his hands full trying to control the animal, which seemed to take exception to everything Sir Lucas attempted. The horse reared, then began galloping along the road.

The little gig jounced along behind it, tilting now and again at a precarious angle. Joanna clung to the side for all she was worth.

They hit a sizable stone in the road. The gig bounced several times, then careened over the side of the road and down the embankment, ending on its side against a tree.

Sir Lucas found himself snarled in the reins. He lay perfectly still for a few moments, collecting his wits about him, then tested his limbs to see if they still functioned. It was then that he realized Joanna was no longer at his side.

"Joanna!" he cried, swearing at the black bird, the horse, the gig, and a few other things while he climbed from the wreckage. Then he saw his companion.

Joanna was crumpled in a heap below the tree and close to a jagged rock. Had she been thrown a greater distance, she most likely would have been badly cut or worse. He looked again and realized that had they been going faster or slower, that tree would not have been there to prevent the gig—and them—from plunging all the way into the lake. There was little doubt in his mind but that one or both of them might well have drowned.

He scrambled down the slope around rocks and over boulders. Once he reached her, he checked to see she was still breathing. "Joanna," he said urgently, hoping she might regain consciousness.

When she failed to respond, he gingerly picked her up, cradling her in his arms. He looked up the slope, wondering how he could make his—and Joanna's—way back.

Sweat trickled down his forehead as he staggered up the hill with his precious burden. Rocks shifted, sliding from beneath his feet. He fought to retain his balance.

"Joanna," he pleaded when he was forced to pause for a rest, "say something, anything. Scold me, cry, but please wake up." She remained limp and silent.

Once he attained the shade and protection of the tree, he placed Joanna gently on the ground, wishing he had a rug to put under her, something thicker than her shawl. He glanced about him, hoping to see a sign of an approaching vehicle and help. The only object in sight was enough to make him gnash his teeth.

Not far away the horse stood placidly gazing back at his driver, the traces dangling to either side.

Far more concerned for Joanna Winterton, Lucas turned back to her. First, he removed her bonnet—amazingly, all things considered, still on her head. Then he unbuttoned the two tiny buttons at the neck of her gown, checking her pulse. She was pale and made not the least movement. Lucas held her hand, willing her to awaken and make some scathing remark to him.

She did not move.

He debated a moment, then ran his hands over her arms, her torso, then her legs, testing. As far as he could tell there was nothing broken or bleeding. Unless, could there be some internal injury? Lord, he hoped not.

Lucas stared at the face he had once termed passingly pretty. She was all of that, true. But there was more than mere prettiness in that face. Strength of character and integrity could be found. She also possessed a compassion and humor that were rare indeed.

He could think of no other woman who would have worried about little Mary, much less personally nursed her, then insisted the orphan return with her to London. But Joanna had done all these things without a thought of receiving a thing in return.

And she had not once flirted with him.

Why? He stared at her, wondering. She seemed to enjoy his company. She had turned to him for advice. She had even called him wonderful and kissed his cheek when he had come up with the reading cards for Mary. But she did not flirt. She did not even seem to care if he came to call on her or not.

It was certainly not the attention he was accustomed to receiving from a lady. Perhaps that was it. Joanna was truly a lady in all aspects. Could she be holding her feelings in reserve?

She stirred and Lucas called to her again. "Joanna? Speak to me," he demanded.

Her lashes fluttered, her eyes opening wide. "Sir Lucas?" Her eyes locked with his in wordless communication. "What happened?" she queried in a faint voice.

"Accident." He could hear the relief in his voice as he spoke. "Plunged off the road. Stupid bird frightened the horse, who bolted. It could have been worse, but I fancy you doubt that at the moment. Do you hurt very badly?" He brushed an errant curl off her forehead.

"No," she assured him. That she winced slightly when he eased her up caused him some alarm.

"Where does it hurt? Are your legs all right? Your arms?" He had never felt quite so helpless in his entire life.

"Just a twinge," she said, her voice growing stronger. "The ground is rocky."

"Perhaps we should try to reach the road, in case someone chances by. I could carry you," he said, trying to gauge whether she was trying to hide her pain.

"I suppose that's best," she agreed. "I believe I'd be a trifle wobbly." Her attempt at humor made him shake his head. How brave she was. He thought he would rather have her scold him than jest in that gentle, fragile wisp of a voice, so unlike her usual musical tone.

Gathering her into his arms, Lucas struggled up the rest of the slope to the road, gingerly working his way around another boulder, avoiding a cut that permitted the rainwater to flow to the lake.

He rather liked the way she clung to him. Not that she was a clinging woman, not at all. She was far too independent to his way of thinking. But now she nestled so trustingly, clinging to his shoulders without the coyness that another might have adopted.

He glanced at her face as he trudged upward. It would have been, he decided, a great and tragic loss had she been killed. The world was a better place for having Joanna Winterton around.

"We are here. You may put me down again." She gave him a reproving look when he hesitated, holding her close for a trifle longer.

Back to normality. He grinned at her. "How like you to scold me."

"I did not scold, sir, merely suggested."

Sir Lucas looked up to the heavens and laughed. "I believe you are not seriously injured after all. And for that I am most grateful." He sat down at her side and continued to study her in a way that truly disconcerted her.

Joanna wondered at the expression on his face. Had Sir Lucas really been so worried about her? She faulted the man; of course he had been worried. Why, most anyone would have been anxious in such an instance.

She hesitantly flexed her arms, then her legs, pleased when she found no indication of injury other than a few aches. She supposed she would have a dozen black and blue areas by tomorrow, but, fortunately, she had no broken bones.

"I am fine." She wondered about him, yet hesitated to ask. It was rather personal, after all.

"Good," he replied. He looked down the road in either direction. On a route that was usually busy, it was remarkably quiet this day. Not a horse nor a vehicle could be seen either north or south.

"I believe we shall be here for a time," she said, attempting to be practical. How she longed for a nice soft bed and a feather pillow upon which to put her aching head.

"Possibly."

"You were not injured?" she asked at last, giving voice to her concern.

"Minor, I suspect." He held up a bloodied and bruised hand.

"How dreadful. I believe you ought to wash it off." Then she looked down at Rydal Water and could not repress a shudder. For it suddenly came to her just how fortunate she and Sir Lucas were.

"Indeed. I would, but the very thought of climbing down there again is beyond me at the moment." He bestowed a grimace at the crystal waters below them.

"And you carried me up, I suspect, for there is my reticule." She pointed to the little purse that had been dropped when he picked her up. "I am far more in your debt than I realized."

"Any gentleman would have done the same."

"And you are most assuredly a gentleman."

Lucas looked at her and wondered at the inflection in her voice. Could she be chiding him? Impossible. And yet . . .

"What did you say caused the accident?" she asked, turning his mind in another direction.

Lucas rose and stared down the road toward Grasmere. "A bird," he murmured. "A black bird." He rose and limped down the road until he found what he sought. Dead. Not surprising in the least—except this bird had been dead for some time, if he was any judge. He did not like the conclusion that leaped into his mind.

He nudged the dead bird with the toe of his boot. Indeed, it had not been an accident.

Looking back down the road he could make out Joanna's white, anxious face. She would only become frightened if he told her what he suspected—yet, could he keep this from her? He doubted it.

"You are limping," she accused when he returned.

"The gig. I was tangled in the reins," he said tersely.

"You found something in the road. Usually, if a bird darts out, it flies away. Doesn't it?" When he failed to answer her, Joanna spoke again. "Does it not, sir?"

"Joanna," he said with great reluctance, "I believe that someone tossed a dead bird onto the road with the hope that we would be killed or at least injured."

"I do not like this in the least." She thought a few moments, then said, "I am very frightened. And I wish that you and I were in London, safe from this madman. Can we ever know peace again?"

"I do not know." He met her gaze for long moments before both looked away.

"What a pity we do not have a deck of cards, sir," she said

in a sprightly, if somewhat forced, voice. "You might teach me how to gamble. I should wager impossible sums I do not have on the probability of our being found. How long do you think it might be?"

He admired her attempt to be nonchalant about their predicament.

"Oh, any moment now there ought to be a carriage along here. Surely there is someone in Grasmere who wants something in Ambleside. Or is perhaps on their way home again?"

"It is growing late," she said, studying the sky.

"And it looks to coming on rain again."

"My favorite bonnet," she wailed, then laughed, albeit weakly, when she viewed her once pretty headgear. "It is sadly crushed, I fear."

"It might keep a bit of rain off your head and face."

"And you have your hat," she agreed.

He joined her, glanced at the sky, and prepared to wait through the rain, hoping it might be a light one.

"I have not always been agreeable to you, I fear," she confessed. "I thought you vain and egotistical."

"And I have felt you mourned Mr. Underhill quite foolishly," he admitted. "I did not understand the background of your betrothal."

"I suspect that is often the way it is," she began, then stopped when he stiffened and half rose. Joanna turned toward Grasmere to see a coach approaching them.

By leaning on Sir Lucas she was able to stand and walk along at his side. He waved at the coach, which stopped when Joanna called out.

"Aunt Caroline, can that really be you?"

"I had this feeling in my bones, you see," her aunt began, then cried out in horror when she saw Joanna's tattered appearance. "Goodness, something truly *did* happen to you." She looked about to have the vapors, but before Joanna might reassure her, Lord Osborn moved to her side.

"Now, now, dear lady. Your niece seems well enough. Why do we not gather her and Sir Lucas up before the rain begins. Explanations can come later."

"How practical you are, to be sure."

Sir Lucas and Joanna were nicely settled in the coach, Tom Coachman had turned them about and was briskly returning to Grasmere, when the heavens opened up and the rain poured down again.

"The rainbow," Sir Lucas murmured.

Joanna nodded. "It must be green, remember?"

"Now will you two please explain?" Aunt Caroline demanded politely.

"It was all because of a black bird," Joanna began.

"The horse bolted," Sir Lucas commenced.

They both stopped, then Joanna said, "I believe Sir Lucas had best explain, for I doubt I should make much sense."

In a surprisingly brief time, Sir Lucas outlined what had happened. Even to Joanna it sounded rather bizarre.

"I do not wish to be rude," Aunt Caroline said, "but it sounds rather far-fetched."

"Face it, Lucas, it is difficult to believe that at the precise moment that your horse passed, someone could manage to toss out a conveniently dead bird." Lord Osborn gave his younger friend a dubious look, then settled back against the squabs to see what defense might be given.

"I know that," Lucas said. "I am inclined to agree with you. It is not logical in the least."

"We feel the person involved is not sane, you see," Joanna added softly.

Her words were followed by a long stretch of silence during which all that could be heard above the creaking of the coach was the rain pounding on the roof.

"I see," Aunt Caroline said finally.

When they drew up before Rose Cottage, the gentlemen scrambled out, then assisted the women from the coach. There was nothing to do but dash through the rain as best they could, none having brought an umbrella along.

Once inside, they sought the sitting room and the pleasant fire gently burning there. Lucas limped over to stir the fire and add more coal. The flames shot up and he held out his hands to the warmth.

"You are hurt," Aunt Caroline cried. "I had not realized it. I wish I might wring that wretch's neck for the grief he has caused the two of you."

"Why, Aunt Caroline," Joanna exclaimed, "I had no idea you were so fierce."

"A mother tiger defending her own," Lord Osborn declared. "Quite natural, I believe. But I agree with Miss Staunton. Would that we could summon Bow Street or even the local constable. We have nothing but suspicions to offer."

"I cannot say it is very agreeable," Joanna admitted.

"As usual you make light of it," Lucas said. "While admirable, you also must confess you are frightened. But how to trap someone we can neither see nor hear? We have no idea when he will pop up to attempt some deviltry."

"We had best try to set some manner of trap," Lord Osborn said.

Lucas frowned at the open door, then limped across to close it. With the tightly shut door behind him he turned to face the others. "No matter how excellent Mrs. Hawkins might seem, I trust no one other than ourselves. You said she usually sees everyone who comes up the lane. It's remarkable that she did not see the man who started the fire."

"He must not have come up the lane," Joanna reasoned.

"Did she see Mary?" Lucas inquired softly.

"I do not know. I confess I did not ask her."

Caroline Staunton rose from the chair near the fire, where she had attempted to dry her skirts, and began to limp back and forth. "I find it impossible to accept that Mrs. Hawkins has the least to do with this matter."

"How does this fellow know our every action, our every plan?" Lucas countered.

"I suppose that is not so very difficult. If we send someone to fetch the gig or the coach, he is bound to know one or two of us intends to travel somewhere," Lord Osborn said. "And I suppose he manages to keep a close watch on the houses."

"From where?" Lucas demanded.

"Right you are. I see what you mean." Lord Osborn strolled across the room to sidle up to the window. He eased over to peer out into the gloom. "I see nothing now—I suppose because of the rain—but before we leave the houses again, we had best beware," his lordship concluded. "Could your coachman be trusted to mouse around a bit, check the area, as it were?"

"He has been in my employ for several years," Aunt Caroline said. "I should think we might trust him."

"Tomorrow we shall set a watch. Anyone walking in this immediate area will be a suspect. Agreed?" Sir Lucas asked.

Aunt Caroline exchanged an uneasy look with her niece. "Agreed."

"Let us hope a speedy end to this . . . this nonsense," Joanna said, clasping her hands before her. That it was far from nonsense was clear to all.

Chapter Thirteen

Mary scampered into the sitting room wearing a new white dress. She ran to give Aunt Caroline a hug. "I am much better, dear Auntie," she said in her piping voice.

It had proved far simpler for the child to call Miss Staunton Auntie and Joanna cousin than anything more complicated. Joanna thought that once in London, Mary's presence might cause less comment if it were believed that the girl was a distant relative.

Aunt Caroline returned the embrace, then gently examined Mary's hands and nodded her approval. To Joanna she said, "Those herbs you used have done wonders."

"We are fortunate that she used those little hands on our behalf. Only the next time she sees a fire, I hope she will find some dirt or a rug to throw over it." Joanna gave Mary an admonishing look that quickly changed to a fond smile.

"It is not raining today, or at least it is not more than a slight drizzle at best," Aunt Caroline said. "Do you plan to go for a walk?"

Joanna wandered over to the window, gazed up at the sky, then looked to the cottage across the lane. There was no sign of life there.

"I believe it is time for us to return to London," Joanna murmured to her aunt. "I know you have found this holiday enjoyable for the most part, but I must go ahead with my plans for the future. I understand that Lord Osborn was on his way to the City when Sir Lucas persuaded him to stay on for a bit. I fancy he is anxious to continue with his plans as well."

"What about Sir Lucas?" Miss Staunton queried. She did

not mention Lord Osborn or possible intentions he might harbor.

"Well, Sir Lucas will wish to find the villain—as do I, but I suspect he is not ready to face Society again. That is a pity. I wonder if he and his jilting have not been relegated to the past by now. There is usually something new and surely scandalous to discuss over teacups every week."

"I had a letter from a friend in London—in fact, it was the day we went to find you on the road to Rydal Water. She wrote that Captain and Mrs. Fortesque are returned to London and set up in a pretty little house in Mayfair. No doubt her father is coming around most handsomely."

"Surely Sir Lucas is not going to permit that to bother him." Joanna crossed her arms before her and tapped her foot. Then, observing the puzzled expression on Mary's face, she put aside the question of Sir Lucas and what he might do. "Come, let us walk down to the shop. I am certain that they must have a new supply of sweets."

Once properly attired in pattens and a rain cape and carrying a large umbrella Joanna and Mary gaily marched from Rose Cottage and down the lane. Rex trotted between them, then ran ahead, circling about and barking at everything in their path.

Caroline Staunton watched them skirt puddles and smiled when their happy song drifted back to her. So, Joanna wanted to leave just when things were coming to a point. How odd.

Shortly after the girls had gone, Lord Osborn crossed to pay a morning call on Miss Staunton.

"She is talking about returning to London and I believe it has as much to do with distancing herself from Sir Lucas as it has her fear of the villain," Miss Staunton said, leading her guest over to sit before the pleasant fire, offering him wine and biscuits along with their conversation.

"I sense her regard for Sir Lucas has grown. She seems most comfortable around him, although she never fawns on him as so many do. I suspect this intrigues him." Lord Osborn sipped the wine she handed him, then leaned back to enjoy her excellent company.

"No, Joanna is not the sort," she admitted, clasping her

hands before her. "I expect she awaits her father's plans for her future, and most likely with more than a little trepidation. His new wife may have influence there. Perhaps Joanna seeks to gain her support for whatever scheme she has in mind. I'm sure I do not know what it might be," she added in answer to his raised brows.

"So she is concerned for her future?"

"Yes," Miss Staunton confirmed with a sad shake of her head, exchanging a look with the man she admired.

"Would you marry me, Miss Staunton? I believe we could enjoy our remaining years together," he said, placing his glass aside and appearing most hopeful.

"Marry you, sir? I had not thought . . . that is . . ." Caroline stuttered. "At my age? To wed? I scarce know what to say." One hand fluttered to her throat in a gesture revealing her surprise. There was a hint of apprehension in her eyes, quite as though she could not believe this was actually happening to her.

"It would please me greatly, my dear lady," he said, placing a courtly kiss on her hand. "We agree on most everything, and you must confess we suit one another well."

"That is true," she admitted with a tender smile.

"Then agree to be my wife," he said with a persuasive manner and look that Caroline found impossible to resist.

"Yes, I will," Caroline Staunton said simply, savoring her only offer, one she'd never expected to receive. "I find you excellent company, sir."

"And Joanna?"

"I do not know how she will accept our plans, dear sir."

"She is a good gel. I foresee no problems there. Assure her that there will always be room for her in my home. It is quite a sizeable place. Could swallow up a dozen young people with not the least trouble."

Caroline eagerly questioned her intended about his home at great length.

When Joanna, Mary, and Rex returned his genial lordship was just departing. Joanna smiled a cheery greeting at him.

Shortly after Joanna sat down with Mary to give her the morning lessons in reading and writing.

"She wishes to make her 'mark' like we do," Joanna had explained to her aunt.

Caroline gave her niece a dreamy smile and drifted along to the back of the house where she spent a time inspecting the roses.

Sir Lucas soon came to the house to report on what he had managed to discover about the supposed accident—which, unfortunately, was very little.

"We have no proof of anything other than a dead bird," he said as he absently strolled about the sitting room.

Joanna sat in her chair regarding him with a wary gaze.

"I have ordered the gig brought to the village. It will be repaired. I doubt if anything good can be done with that wretched horse. He is well, but hopeless."

"I am sorry about the gig. Your gracious offer to take me out for a bit of fresh air ended in near tragedy."

"There is one itinerant around here who seems to answer our needs, as it were. Most come and go. This chap has hung around ever since we arrived. No one knows his name, nor where he is from, indeed, any details of his life. He wears the garb of a soldier, such as it is after all this time."

"I suppose it is something like that man I met while on my walk to Butter Crags—tattered and faded," Joanna said.

"It might be the same fellow," Sir Lucas replied, walking over to survey the lane from the window. "Amazing all you can see from here." He slowly turned around to fix his gaze on Mary.

"Child, did the man you saw trying to set the cottage afire wear the clothing of a soldier?"

"He might have," she said, "He had shiny buttons, I saw that. But he wore an old hat pulled down over his face. I could see nothin' there."

"Nothing," Joanna corrected automatically.

"Nothing," Mary said, following her correction with a grimace.

"Go out to the kitchen and see how Mrs. Hawkins does," Joanna said by way of dismissal.

"There goes your little chaperone," Sir Lucas said wryly. "Are you so certain you do the right thing?"

"Who can say, truly? I must do what I can, however." Joanna placed the teaching aids on a small table, ready for the next session. Mary had so much to learn.

"What will your father say to this?" He watched her clasp the back of a Windsor chair, a determined look crossing her face.

"My father will say nothing, for neither my aunt nor I shall say a word about it until it is an accomplished fact. You would not spoil it for me, would you?" she suddenly asked.

Lucas stared at her, wondering anew what it was that drew him to her. "No, I might not approve of what you contemplate, but I'd not spoil it for you."

"But then," Joanna said with relief, "you are in no hurry to return to London, are you? Did you know Captain and Mrs. Fortesque are returned to the City and are happily settling into a new home? At least, I assume they are happy. Aunt had a letter from a friend in London who passed the news along. *You* were not mentioned."

Lucas drew himself up, looking down his nose at this utterly impossible young woman who simply did not understand his position. "How kind you are to pass the news along to me."

"Well, I thought you might wish to know that current scandal omits any reference to you. Aunt wrote to find out if my so-called bereavement has ceased to be of interest. It seems my father's remarriage has replaced me as gossip. The prattle boxes are about evenly divided in opinions, but lean slightly to the conviction that he ought to try to provide his name with an heir, and they approve his marriage to a younger woman."

"You do not mind in the least, do you?" Lucas said musingly.

"My father must live his own life," she replied softly. "I would that he do me the same courtesy."

"You have reason to believe he will foist another such as Underhill on you?" Lucas was incredulous. Surely one such betrothal was sufficient for any young woman.

"His new wife has numerous relations. There are a few second sons who are in need of an heiress. I doubt if I err in saying that it would not be unlikely for one of them to be presented to me as my future husband."

Lucas, for perhaps the first time in his life, could truly see the dilemma a young woman of marriageable age faced, particularly were she possessed of an even modest fortune.

"I see," he said, suspecting he saw even more than she guessed.

"And you, sir, you must do your duty by your name, surely," she said. "Do you return to London to find a proper wife, perhaps?" She clung to the top of the chair, the only clue that she felt uneasy at quizzing him about his personal life or future.

"Not for a while," Lucas replied easily. "I have no desire to face the tabbies yet."

"What? You are reluctant to allow another damsel the hope of becoming your wife? Of succeeding where Miss Thorpe failed? Of course, she did not truly fail—she merely lost heart and ran away. Rakes tend to daunt young girls. You would do better to select someone with a bit of seasoning." She referred to those girls who had come to London on the husband-hunt for more than one year. Suddenly, she covered her mouth in a horrified gasp. It seemed that pretty Miss Winterton realized she had gone too far.

Lucas crossed the room in a few steps, then gazed down at the intrepid miss who disturbed his thoughts far too often. "You deem me a rake? I suppose some do. I do not actually consider myself one of their ranks. Merely a member of Society," he admonished in a soft voice intended to sound intimidating. It seemed he achieved success. She looked terrified.

"You might well look apprehensive, my girl," he said, tilting up her chin so he could see the expression in her eyes. More often than not, she tended to look down when addressing him. Perhaps she knew how much she revealed in those beautiful eyes.

"No," she whispered. "You'd not harm me, I know that."

"Never harm, my dear. Rather a bit of dalliance. Is that not what you expected of me when you called me a rake?"

"Abandoned, assuredly, by Miss Thorpe, but not lost to all that is proper, surely." Joanna's eyes were wide and they revealed surprising emotions in them.

"Think anew," he murmured before he closed the gap between them and captured her lips in the sweetest of kisses. It pleased Lucas to think that she had secretly desired his kiss. Although he did not know for certain, he had read something in those eyes and it was not revulsion nor dislike.

She felt soft and her curves nestled against him just perfectly. He'd noticed that before. Her scent drifted up and around him. He could not tell what she wore, other than she reminded him of a bouquet of spring flowers—fresh and fragrant. Her skin, when he touched her cheek, felt as smooth as the petals of a rose. And, oh, he did enjoy the taste of her.

She wrested free in a twist of her body, glaring at him with accusing eyes. "How dare you, sirrah? You are most improper. Yet I must accept some blame," she admitted in a subdued voice, turning away from him. "I ought not have remained here alone with you, nor should I have teased you about your future. What you do with your life is none of my business."

"Agreed," Lucas said coldly, wishing that he might have chilly rain rather than her rejection.

Then she turned her head to look back at him, holding her hands clasped tightly before her. "I still say you frighten young girls just from the schoolroom. Look elsewhere for a bride and you'll not risk a repetition of what happened."

"When I marry," he declared suddenly, "I shall do so with a special license and without any fanfare whatsoever. It shall be an accomplished deed before a single tabby has wind of my intentions."

She chuckled. "I wish you well."

"And nothing more?"

She turned away again to look out of the window. "You may have all you wish, I imagine. I should think you could point a finger and the chosen girl will do your bidding without question. Her parents will see to that. Good day, Sir Lucas. I hope you find the soldier before he finds you."

Lucas hesitated. Something told him that he ought to go to her side and crush her in his arms as he wished to do. Yet she had clearly dismissed him, even now was staring out of the window, not so much as giving him a glance. But then, she never did flirt with him.

"As you wish. Good day, Miss Winterton." He bowed in

irony to her back, then marched from the room and toward the front door. Behind him he could hear soft slippers running along the hall. No doubt the child, coming to see if her adored Joanna was safe from the dragon.

What a remarkable conversation they'd had. He could not recall one remotely like it in his entire life. Had a woman ever been so direct, so open in her feelings? And with that subtle hint of fire, that banked passion? For in spite of her name that prompted one to think of the cold, Miss Winterton fairly seethed with passion.

He slowly walked along, savoring the brisk air that followed the end of a rain. He was so engrossed in the amazing confrontation he'd had with Joanna that he almost failed to catch sight of the shadow off to one side of him. Masculine, somewhat bent.

Lucas wondered what he ought to do. Should he draw the fellow toward the village? Or ought he confront him? With no weapon at hand, Lucas felt uncomfortably vulnerable. What to do?

Joanna stared out at the lane where Sir Lucas slowly strolled along quite as though he had not a care in the world.

She had been a fool to yield to his passionate expertise for even a moment. Yet, she had to admit to herself that she was unlikely to know such again, if her new stepmother had her way. From all Joanna had heard, those arranged marriages might be ordered, but could not often produce passion—seldom even liking, for that matter. It was a civilized arrangement, polite, cold, filled with duty and little else. The best she might hope for was children to love and cherish.

"Cousin Joanna, be you all right?" Mary asked.

"Are, my dear. The word is *are* you all right," Joanna said absently, watching as Sir Lucas slowed his steps to a near halt. She sharpened her gaze. He had seen something to his left— she could tell by the faint inclination of his head.

She also looked that way and could see the shadowy figure of a man slipping from tree to shrub to tree again.

"Oh, goodness me," she cried. While she might not marry the gentleman, she did not wish him dead or harmed in any way. He had already suffered enough.

"Wait here," she cried to Mary, then dashed from the room and out the front door, pausing only to grab a stout cane from the umbrella holder in the hall. She ran down the lane after Sir Lucas, trying not to make any noise.

She stumbled and scratched her arm on a wild rosebush. Since she tried to be ever so quiet, she dare not so much as utter an "ouch" as she longed to do.

When she deemed she was close enough, she veered off the road and crept up behind the man who tailed Sir Lucas. Raising the cane with the intent of creasing his head, she was aghast when the man turned to face her.

He said not a word, but wrested the cane from her hands, raised it, and brought it down over her skull with a crack, then ran off into the woods on the edge of the village.

Joanna slumped to the ground without a whimper, the cane by her side.

Lucas had been aware of the man who followed him at a distance. When he suddenly realized something had changed, he whirled about, crying out in alarm.

He was too late to prevent the casualty. Joanna was crumpled on the ground, no doubt the victim of the man who was after him. Again.

Why did it seem that he was continually rescuing this woman who had not the least use for him? And what was she doing here in the first place? Never say she had watched him, kept an eye on him while he strolled toward the village.

He ran through the woods until he reached her. It was almost like a repeat of the carriage accident. Only this time her bonnet had not protected her head. She was out, quite out and he feared for her life now.

"Joanna," he murmured, then more insistently he demanded, "Joanna, please!" White and utterly still, there was an angry red lump with a jagged gash atop her head. Nasty-looking wound, he thought, grimacing when he gently brushed her hair aside.

There was nothing for it but that he again pick her up, which he did. Thankful that his slight limp had healed, he carried her up the lane. It was a wonder with all the homes in the area that no one ever seemed to be around when needed. Would that the London ladies practice the same reticence.

"Joanna, my little riddle, what shall I do with you? Not what I please, obviously. But you are going to drive me around the bend one of these fine days," he muttered to his unconscious girl, knowing that he was forcing himself to believe she would be fine.

She desperately needed medical attention of the best sort and he wondered if they'd find the doctor at home.

Mary met him at the door, holding it wide while watching him carry Joanna down the hall to the room he surmised was hers.

"Why is Cousin Joanna hurt?"

"The man who started the fire hit her over the head when she chased after him." It sounded odd when he put it like that, but there was no time for precise explanations. "Go find Miss Staunton, please. And hurry."

The girl rushed off without a whisper.

Lucas thought it ironic that not many minutes ago he had been dismissed from this house by this very woman. And now he sat on her bed holding one of her hands. Actually, he chaffed each of her hands in turn, then looked about to see if there might be such a thing as an astringent that would help her regain consciousness. Nothing was in sight.

"What has happened now, Sir Lucas? And what are you doing with Joanna on the bed?" Caroline Staunton cried, coming quickly into the room.

"Not what I please," he murmured to himself. More loudly he said, "She was going to crown that chap who's been bedeviling my life and I suspect he turned on her. Hit her over the head and left a nasty wound. Would you be so kind as to fetch me a basin of water and a bottle of whiskey?, Oh, and see if the doctor can be found." Privately, he had little confidence of this.

He had observed while on the Peninsula that when he'd cleansed wounds with the only liquid readily available—that potent brew the Scots produced—there had been no infection, and little fever. He did not understand why, but he would take no chances now. Joanna was not going to die if he had anything to say about it.

Miss Staunton produced his requests with a disapproving murmur, "Mrs. Hawkins keeps this for her brother."

He set about cleaning the wound, then poured the whiskey over the open slit, wincing as he did so. It was as well that Joanna remained unconscious. He then requested a length of black silk thread and a needle.

Miss Staunton produced those even faster, then took Mary from the room.

It did not take long to repair the damage to the scalp. He sewed with fine, even stitches that he hoped would disappear before long. He was forced to clip away a few of her curls. They would grow again.

When he was finished, a neat bandage covered not only the wound but also a great deal of her pretty head. "Joanna," he said insistently, gently shaking her shoulder in an attempt to awaken her.

"I hurt," she murmured finally, slowly opening her eyes. "You are alive."

"Which is about all I can say for you," he snapped back, his patience evaporating at that look of innocent joy that had flashed in her eyes so briefly before it was replaced with a guarded expression he could not interpret.

She reached up to touch the bandage and frowned. "Why is this thing on my head? What have you done to me?"

"Probably saved your life," he muttered, removing her hand from the white linen and placing it on the counterpane. "Do you recall anything at all of what happened?"

"I remember telling you to leave. And here you are again, and sitting on my bed," she said, but not as spiritedly as she would have had she been herself.

"You left the cottage and ran after me,"

"Oh, no," she interrupted softly, "I'd not have done such a wicked thing, surely."

"And," he doggedly continued, "you had a cane in hand, obviously intending to beat someone over the head with it."

"I might not like you, but I'd not beat you," she murmured sleepily.

"The chap who has been making my life hell saw you. He hit you over the head with the bloody cane," Lucas said in utter frustration.

"I do not remember," she said drowsily, then closed her eyes. They snapped open a minute later to focus on Lucas with an accusing gaze. "You are still here."

"I shall leave with pleasure, just as soon as your aunt returns." He sat back in the chair, slouching against the cushioned back and wondering if he could ever be the same again once he left here.

"Fine," she murmured and closed her eyes again. She appeared to sleep, but it seemed to be natural and not a prelude to something worse that Lucas preferred not to consider. He sat staring at her pale face until he heard Miss Staunton's footsteps in the hall.

"I sent for the doctor. He's away," she said quietly as she slipped onto the chair where Lucas had sat while mending Joanna.

"I cannot believe this happened," he stated, half to himself.

"The two of you do seem to have a penchant for trouble," she replied, inspecting the bandaging Lucas had done. "You have had some experience at this, I see. You did an excellent job of it."

"Thank you, ma'am. Let me know when she wakes up again. No matter what time it might be, I wish to know. You see, she *saw* the fellow I want to nab, but she insists she cannot recall what he looks like. Says the last thing she remembers is telling me to leave."

"And did you?" Miss Staunton inquired with obvious interest.

"I did. Walked down the lane until I noticed that someone was off to my left, shadowing me. Joanna—that is, Miss Winterton apparently saw him as well and attempted to knock him over the head with a cane."

"I believe that after all you two have gone through together you might be given leave to call her Joanna. All the time."

So Miss Staunton had caught his slips, had she? She'd not said a word, which gave him an odd sort of encouragement— for what, he wasn't sure.

"I gather she intended to spare my life. Thought to knock the chap out. It never occurred to her that her own well-being might be in danger."

"That is quite like Joanna, you know. She rushes in to defend those she cares for without regard to the consequences. Foolish darling," her aunt said softly.

Lucas doubted he had heard right and left the room after making certain that Miss Staunton had all she needed.

He came upon Lord Osborn standing in the hallway, holding Mary in his arms. "Well, what is going on over here?" his good friend asked quietly.

The little girl's head rested contentedly against his shoulder and Lucas wondered if she would have come to his arms as readily.

"Mary, would you ask Mrs. Hawkins if we might have a pot of strong tea? In the sitting room, perhaps?" While the child disappeared down the hall, Lucas guided his friend into the front room and sought a comfortable chair. He collapsed onto it with a sigh.

"Explain, if you please." His lordship arranged himself by the mantel, watching his young friend through narrowed eyes and with a penetrating gaze.

Lucas repeated his tale again, embellishing it with a few harsher words for the villain.

"What will you do now? To be so close and then have this happen," Lord Osborn said.

"It was not a pretty sight, I can tell you," Lucas said with a shudder. "She has a hard skull, else she would most likely be an angel at this point, I suspect."

"That bad, eh?" Lord Osborn left the support of the mantel and walked slowly across the room to gaze out of the window, hands clasped behind his back. He rocked to and fro, deep in thought. Then he turned to face Lucas.

"Any ideas?" Lucas asked as Mrs. Hawkins entered the room, bearing a tray with not only a pot of tea, but little sandwiches and a plum cake as well.

They remained silent until the housekeeper had left, closing the door behind her.

"As I understand it, the fellow bashed Miss Winterton over the head, then ran. He does not know what happened to her."

"Correct," Lucas replied. "He ran so fast, I doubt he even saw me run after him. I might have caught him had I not stopped to care for Joanna."

Lucas poured out both teas, helped himself to a large slice of plum cake, and eased back on the chair again. He had swallowed his bite of cake, relishing the flavor, when Osborn dropped his bomb.

"I believe we shall give it out that the lady recalls the appearance of the man. *She* shall be our trap."

Chapter Fourteen

"Out of the question!" Lucas leaped to his feet, plum cake crumbs flying everywhere and his teacup tipping over so that tea puddled on the floor. "That poor girl has been through quite enough. I'll not have her life endangered by that madman again."

"Now, now," his lordship soothed. "She shall be most carefully guarded."

"Then you do not know her very well," Lucas muttered. "That young woman attracts danger like flowers attract bees. No, I'll not have it," he said with a fierce look at his worthy friend. "Not even to save my own life."

"I see," Lord Osborn murmured. "Perhaps Miss Staunton has an idea. I shall have to ask her."

"She ought to know what her niece is like," Lucas said, relief in her voice.

"Shall we abide by her advice?" his lordship said mildly.

"Very well," Lucas said, sinking back on the chair and rescuing his teacup just in time.

Miss Staunton opened the door and bustled into the room, glancing at Lucas, then his lordship. She eyed the puddle of tea on the floor and hurried over to mop it up with a cloth. She straightened and placed the cloth aside to give her report.

"She is sleeping well now, I believe. That was a remarkable bit of mending you did, Sir Lucas," Miss Staunton said approvingly. "Wherever did you learn a skill most surgeons hope to master?"

"I helped the medics for a brief time on the Peninsula, before my mother called me home to assume the family cares. I cannot say I was grieved to leave that hellhole," Lucas said, rubbing his chin in reflection of some less than pleasant moments in his life.

"I vow, her head will be almost as good as new once she is better. I do wish she could remember all that happened." Miss Staunton turned to his lordship and said, "Do you think that might occur? Or will this always be a blank for her?"

"Hard to say. Lucas? Any experience with this sort of reaction to a hit on the head?" his lordship inquired.

"She might regain her memory. Then again, she might not. The mind is a curious thing. I cannot predict how it will be with her. Sorry." Lucas picked up another piece of plum cake and idly nibbled at it.

"Well, I daresay she will not mind forgetting the pain of it all. But if she could only remember what that villain looked like." Miss Staunton looked distressed and clasped her hands before her in a worried gesture.

"I wish to ask you about that, in a way," his lordship began hesitantly. "You see I thought that if we gave it out that she *did* recall the face of this chap, that he might come snooping around and we could snabble him. What do you think?" Lord Osborn gave Lucas a warning look, but he had been prepared this time. Now he merely sat and waited, munching on the plum cake and wondering what she might say.

"Oh, dear," Miss Staunton murmured. "That would place her in jeopardy again, would it not?"

"True," his lordship agreed. "However, when you think of how she so bravely dashed out in the hope of thwarting an attack on Sir Lucas, would Joanna not wish to help? We would protect her most carefully."

"Hah," Lucas muttered. "Protect, my foot and Aunt Fanny."

"Well, if one of us were with her at all times, would that not be sufficient? And when dear Miss Staunton is with Joanna, Susan could attend as well, thus offering additional assistance if need be," his lordship said most persuasively.

"I believe that would be acceptable," Miss Staunton declared. "I feel sure that Joanna would wish to repay Sir Lucas for his skill in mending her head."

"Which would not have been needed had she remained where she ought, instead of haring off after a chap I was keeping an eye on," Lucas reminded them. "You may think her sensible and practical and all that sort of rot, but I think her an utter madcap."

"How fascinating," Miss Staunton said with a considering look at Lucas that quite made him feel like an insect. "I shall confide that to Joanna when she is better. She has always believed herself rather dull, you see."

"Anyone *less* dull, I cannot fathom," Lucas murmured.

"Well then," his lordship said, "I believe we can go along with our plan. You shall inform the baker and butcher and such. I shall pass along the news at the inn and the hotel. If we chatter enough, the information we wish to pass along is bound to reach his ears."

"Oh, dear, but I dread the coming days," Miss Staunton said, looking as worried as she sounded.

Lucas, thinking of hours spent at Joanna's bedside, keeping an eye on her so she wouldn't be killed, felt like groaning. "I hope we will not rue this decision," he said with a firm look at his friend and advisor.

When Joanna gained consciousness she found Lucas at her bedside, watching her while slouched in a chair, his chin propped on his hand.

"Hello again," she murmured. "Water, please. My head aches dreadfully."

"I'm sorry about that, Joanna," Lucas said in an attempt to soothe her. "I did the best I could for you, the doctor having been off in Ambleside tending some woman giving birth to twins."

"Twins? I am impressed," she said with a faint smile. "What did you do that makes me feel so wretched?" She obediently drank the water he offered, then grimaced, disliking the willow bark decoction that had been added to it.

"You suffered a wound on your head. I sewed up the scalp—a mere few stitches. I do not wish to disturb it now, but will look at it later on. You will do well enough," he concluded.

"Mercy," she said in alarm. Then after a time she said, "How did this happen?"

"You still do not recall? You were chasing a man and he turned and hit you over the head with a cane."

"I would never do such a thing," she protested. "You make a sorry jest, Sir Lucas."

" 'Tis true," he said with a shrug.

"Mercy," she murmured. Then she studied Lucas with an intensity he found uncomfortable. "You are worried about me," she concluded.

"Why should I be?" he challenged. "You are the veriest cabbage-head. You do not have the sense God gave a flea, no matter how your aunt claims you to be sensible and practical and prudent—all those commonsensical things."

"Well," she said in an affronted manner that Lucas found vastly amusing.

They sat for a time while she seemed to drowse, then, just before Lucas was about to leave, her eyes snapped open and she said, "You think me so dreadful, do you? Well, I think you a coward, sirrah. You creep away to the Lake District rather than toss off the jilting of a foolish girl. Did you not think your reputation could tolerate this little affair? Perhaps you had best look to your past and mend your ways should that be the case."

Lucas stared at her, transfixed. Could he have heard right? She could not possibly understand what he had gone through.

"You are nursing your fancied wounds, sir. What you need to do is return, face Society, and certainly not allow that silly group of arbiters to dictate your life." She looked up at him with clear eyes, her demeanor calm.

"Is that so?" Lucas said in a menacing voice, intent upon battle before he recalled the circumstances. The poor woman was most likely out of her head. She would never have uttered such sentiments had she been rational.

But, he realized, she would have thought them.

"I have given it all a great deal of thought and when I am mended I intend to return to London as well. If anyone dares to reproach me for not mourning so worthless a man, I shall tell them to mind their own business." An unspoken "so there" could as well have been added.

Miss Staunton entered the room just then, effectively ending the discussion. She fluttered about her niece, fluffing her pillow, offering her a soothing potion to drink.

"Good day, Sir Lucas," Joanna said in dulcet tones of dismissal.

"The best to you, Miss Winterton," he replied, then informed her aunt he would return later for his next watch and to tend the wound.

Lucas left the room so deeply in thought that he nearly bumped into Lord Osborn.

"Well," his friend said heartily, "Joanna is on the mend and I believe our planted words are going to bear fruit. Several former soldiers were standing just by the door to the inn when I loudly related the tale of Joanna's daring dash to save your life. I made it clear that she recalls his appearance and intends to seek justice. If that doesn't bring the chap on the run, I do not know what will."

"Me," Lucas said gloomily. "All I have to do is stand out in the lane and he will rub me out. I should like to know why, however. What notion crept into his worthless skull that prompts him to seek my death? For he does not seek to injure. He wants my demise," Lucas said while leading his friend from Rose Cottage.

"Indeed, it would be most interesting to learn."

"Mark this well, I intend to find it out." Lucas kept alert, his gaze flickering around him while the two men sauntered down the lane to the hotel.

"I think this tedious," Joanna complained. "I should like to get up, if you please. There is nothing seriously wrong with me." Then, wondering if her aunt was keeping something from her, Joanna said, "Is there?"

"Nothing so terrible physically wrong. There is a nasty gash on your head that Sir Lucas sewed up very well. However . . ." Her aunt looked decidedly uncomfortable as she hesitated. "You do not remember what happened."

"And?" Joanna demanded to know. She suspected there was a great deal more going on about her than she had been told so far. With luck, if Joanna pressed her, her aunt would open her budget.

"You are better off not knowing, dear," Aunt Caroline said, suddenly deciding that a number of things needed folding and books shelving and clothes put away.

"Pooh bah," Joanna said quietly. Then she whispered, "I want to know all."

Alarmed at Joanna's whisper even more than her demand, Aunt Caroline dropped the clothes on the bed and walked around to feel Joanna's forehead.

"You do not have a fever, no doubt thanks to Sir Lucas and whatever he poured over it. I must say," Aunt murmured, "He seemed remarkably competent."

Joanna would look into that later. Right now she wanted to know what was going on, particularly what involved her that her aunt did not want her to know.

She quickly clasped her aunt's hand, tugging her down on the bed. "I think it would be best if you tell me what is planned." The four of them had talked about the necessity for a plan some time back. Had they at last thought of one?

"Very well, dear. If you wish. They have put it about, and I have helped, that you do recall the man's face and intend to seek justice." Aunt Caroline sat back as though awaiting an explosion, or at the very least a scolding.

"Is that all?" Joanna asked, then winced when she turned her head. "I fancy the man is strong, for my head does pain me," she admitted.

"Take this potion of willow bark. It will help the bleeding stop," Aunt Caroline said, smoothing the counterpane with nervous fingers. "I promised I would make an infusion of violet leaves to cleanse the wound when Sir Lucas returns to inspect it."

She rose and crossed to a tray where a carafe of water and various bottles of herbal potions were arranged. After mixing the willow bark distillation with water, she brought it to Joanna, who obediently swallowed the bitter liquid.

Aunt Caroline left the room to prepare the violet infusion after telling Joanna that Susan would join her in a few moments.

Joanna stared at the ceiling, studying the cracks which ran every which way. Then the truth struck her. She was a sitting

duck, as her cousin might phrase it. It would be a simple matter for that man to gain entrance to the house when Lord Osborn and Sir Lucas were elsewhere and just do away with
Joanna, thinking she knew more than she did.

"Susan! Aunt Caroline!" she called.

The maid rushed into the room, her arms full of fragrant
linen, fresh from the clothesline and interlined with costmary.

"Goodness, miss, you frightened me, that you did."

"Not half as much as I would like," Joanna replied. If only
her head didn't hurt her so much.

"Your aunt is in the kitchen, stirring up a pot of something
green," the maid said with respect for Miss Staunton's skill
with herbs.

"Violet leaves," Joanna murmured. "Just in case I am still
bleeding when Sir Lucas removes this bandage." She debated
a while, then with a smile she hoped was convincing she said,
"I truly feel much better and I think I should like to sit up."

"Not yet," a voice said from the doorway.

"Sir Lucas," Joanna said, resigned to remaining flat on her
back a little longer.

"Determined creature, aren't you?" he said, strolling across
the room to stare down at her.

Joanna glared at him, thinking he was the root of every
trouble she had. "I know what you are about," she announced.

"Wormed it out of your aunt, did you? Feel better now?"
That gleam had returned to his eyes again.

"No. I mean, yes, I feel better, but no, I am not pleased with
your plan. How could you?"

"I tried, I truly did. I was outvoted by your aunt and Lord
Osborn. You see," and he pulled up the chair to sit close to
her, leaning over in a confiding manner, "they think you are
wonderful. That you would want to do this to save my worthless hide after I saved you, more or less."

"You are not a nice man," Joanna said softly. "Did you pull
wings from butterflies when you were a boy?"

"Never," he declared in an equally soft voice. "And I have
no intention of being *nice* where you are concerned. You
wanted the truth, you shall have it." He leaned back in the
chair to observe her.

They stared at each other, sizing up their opponent.

"I wish to get up. If I am to be a target, I want to face the man, not be reclining in bed."

He did not answer. Rather, he reached over to check her face, then unwound the bandage, his touch as gentle as the brush of a butterfly's wings.

Then he leaned over her and she could smell his skin, his clothing. Spice and fresh air were a potent combination, she concluded.

"Well?" Joanna held her breath. Her head ached frightfully, although she refused to admit it. If that wound showed signs of infection, she could be in for serious trouble.

"Doing nicely," he murmured. He turned when Aunt Caroline entered the room with a small amount of the violet infusion. "Ah, just the thing. There is a tiny bit of bleeding."

He busied himself over her head, ever so gently dabbing a bit of the infusion on the wound.

Joanna studied his crisp white shirt, his elegantly tied cravat, the strong column of his neck, then his jawline. Then she shut her eyes, for her inventory had reached his mouth. The memories of his three kisses flooded her mind.

"She is flushed, Sir Lucas. Do you think she is developing a fever? I was so certain the decoction would reduce any chance of fever," Aunt Caroline murmured from close by.

Joanna felt a strong, surprisingly warm touch on her forehead and cheek. She opened her eyes to find him looking down at her, a damp cloth in one hand.

"You do not have a fever." His eyes gleamed with private thoughts, then he added, "I suggest you think of mountain streams or cold lakes."

"That will not help in the least," Joanna retorted, forgetting her aunt listened. Joanna vividly recalled that kiss while wading in the lake water.

"Hmm," Aunt Caroline said. "I believe I need to prepare another potion." With this vague remark, she drifted from the room. Unfortunately, she was not missed by either Joanna or Sir Lucas.

On the far side of the room, Susan busily folded clean linen strips for bandages. She was not the least interested in such a dull conversation.

"You are serious about wanting to leave this bed?" He placed the damp cloth on a tray, then wound fresh bandages about her head again.

"Indeed," she replied hastily.

"You will obey my dictates—in regard to your health, of course," he said, that gleam returning to his eyes once again. He fastened the bandage, tucking under the end, then sat back. She was surprised that he did not rise, but remained leaning slightly over her. "Promise?"

"I promise," Joanna said breathlessly.

"Very well." He rose then and turned to the maid. "Your mistress wishes to get out of bed. Please help her into a robe and slippers."

Joanna watched him stride to the door, then saw him pause and turn to face her again.

"I shall be here. Should he try to enter through the window, do call out. When Susan has you ready, let me know and I shall transport you to the sitting room."

Joanna nearly lost heart. Transport? To her mind that meant in his arms.

And so it did.

Once Susan had tenderly helped her into a lavender wrapper and put soft slippers on surprisingly weak feet—after all it was her head injured, not her feet—he came.

Sir Lucas scooped Joanna into his arms and slowly made his way along the hall and into the sitting room. "Here you are. The sofa, my dear girl."

His touch was all she had feared and, it must be confessed, hoped for. Why was it that she was so affected by this dratted man's touch? Why, she could nestle in his arms forever, so strong and comforting did she find them.

And then he set her down, gently, to be sure, but in a way that made it clear to Joanna that he was glad to be rid of her. What a lowering thing, indeed. There was no danger that she might attach his affections.

Joanna could not help but smile. She had exchanged the four walls of her bedroom for the four walls of the sitting room—both with ceiling cracks, she supposed. The bed was marginally more comfortable than the sofa. But here she might see more and chat with the others. And she could see if that man came.

"She looks well enough," Aunt Caroline said, coming into the sitting room at their heels. "Now if only she does not take ill. I fear, my dearest, that you are not well advised to leave the safety of your bed."

"I will not be a sitting duck," Joanna muttered, leaning back against her pillow—tucked behind her by a solicitous Sir Lucas.

"And what do you know of ducks, sitting or otherwise?" Sir Lucas said with a smile.

"My cousin . . ." she began when she noticed someone in the shrubbery outside the window. "There," she whispered and gestured toward the window. "A stranger. I suspect he might be the man we saw while on the walk to Butter Crags."

"What man? And why did you not mention this before?" Aunt Caroline sputtered.

"Shh," Joanna murmured.

She grew alarmed when Sir Lucas swiftly left the room, disappearing in the direction of the kitchen, pulling Aunt Caroline behind him.

Joanna was alone and this time she had no cane or umbrella, nothing with which to defend herself. She glanced about her, not assured that Sir Lucas or Lord Osborn would reach the man in time to help. A vase. The teapot. It was full of hot tea, so that might help. Nothing else.

The front door opened so quietly that had she not been straining for the sound, she'd not have heard it. The floor squeaked. Nothing else.

Outside, Joanna glimpsed Sir Lucas whisking himself around the cottage, so he would be right behind the intruder. All she could do was sit still and wonder if the madman had a gun or a club or a knife.

"There you be," he said.

Joanna remembered the voice from the trail, its gruff tones as he'd told her about the kissing gate. She also remembered how his expression had altered when Sir Lucas came.

"What are you doing here? This is a private home, sirrah," Joanna bravely declared, tilting her chin up and glaring at him with undisguised loathing. If she guessed rightly, this man had attempted to kill Sir Lucas many times, and herself as well, although accidentally. She just happened to be in his way. Only now, it seemed that she was his intended victim.

"Why do you seek me out?" she demanded. "And why do you wish ill to Sir Lucas? What could he possibly have done to you?"

"You know me, do you? They said you had lived. I thought you dead. You'll wish yourself dead," he said while slowly crossing the room, glancing about him to make certain no one was hiding in corners.

"You did not answer my question," Joanna said, fighting for calm and trying not to tremble or cry. She very much longed for strong arms about her again.

"The man what was with you? Why d'you call him Sir Lucas? That ain't his name, milady," he mocked. "It be Captain Frazer. Him what sent me into the line of fire. Becuz of him I lost me hand. Ain't good for nuthin' now. No job, no food but what I can beg or steal. Me fam'ly throwed me out. And then I saw him as fine as fivepence. Made me boil, it did. I means to make him as miserable as I am."

"You are wrong, this man is not Captain Frazer. I doubt he even knows a Captain Frazer."

"In this you err, Joanna," Sir Lucas said as he rounded the corner, a pistol trained on the former soldier. "I knew the captain. I tended his wounds on the battlefield. He died, most likely after the same battle where you lost your hand, my fellow. Wouldn't wonder if that is where you saw me. And I bear a vague resemblance to Frazer. I treated a goodly number of wounds after battles. Hands, legs, feet—never mind, it was a grisly affair."

Joanna made no sound. She stared at the two who confronted each other, the gun giving one man the edge. Never had she felt such tension. It was thick in the air, a palpable thing.

"Dead? He be dead?" The man seemed to shrink into himself. He fixed his gaze on the floor and kept murmuring, "Dead. He's dead."

Then Lord Osborn came from behind the draperies on the far side of the room. He took the poor fellow by the scruff of the neck and pushed him from the room.

Not quite able to believe the danger was finally over, Joanna buried her face in her hands and gave in to her desire to cry. Tears of relief trickled down her cheeks and into her fingers, her shoulders shaking slightly.

"I hope you are not shedding tears for that vile wretch," Sir Lucas said to her in amazement. "He deserves to hang."

Her tears ceased and she glared at him. "You are the most odious creature. That man's life has been utter misery."

"How like a woman. One moment she trembles in fear for her life—and mine as well. The next she has pity for the criminal. Make no mistake, I will prosecute that man. He would have killed me—and you—had he the chance. How do we know but what he will not take it into his mind to kill someone else he thinks is to blame for his misfortune. Others lost an arm and they did not become such as this knave."

"You think of Lord Somerset, I suppose," she said soberly, referring to the Wellington aide who had lost his arm at Waterloo. "He had the support of his family, no doubt."

"That is no excuse for this wretch."

"You do as you think best," Joanna said, exhausted by the ordeal.

Sir Lucas left the room and Joanna sank back against the pillows, a few tears creeping down her cheeks as she contemplated her return to London, for go she would.

There was no hope for her in regard to Sir Lucas, never mind that she had developed a partiality for him. It was quite plain that he detested her.

"I shall refuse to see him again," she said to the ceiling cracks.

"Are you all right, dear?" Aunt Caroline said when she quietly entered the room to check on her niece. "They took that dreadful man away. He threatened to kill Sir Lucas again, claiming he lied and was indeed this Captain Frazer. I believe the fellow must be all about in his head, quite, quite mad."

"So Sir Lucas said," Joanna replied just as quietly. "I intend to leave for London as soon as may be. I do not wish to see Sir Lucas again, if you please. We have nothing to say to each other. Not anymore." Her voice trailed off while she studied the pattern of the ceiling cracks.

"Your wound . . ." Aunt Caroline began, then stopped at Joanna's expression.

"You do very well at injuries with your herbal potions. I trust you more than anyone. Will it upset your plans if we go now?"

"Plans?" Aunt Caroline tried to look innocent and failed miserably. "What plans?"

"To marry Lord Osborn. *Those* plans," Joanna said, a smile creeping out. "I am not blind."

"Well," her aunt said, darting a glance at Joanna, "he said we would wed when we return to the City. He intends to obtain a special license. And he insists that you and dear little Mary come to live with us."

"Mary! Where is the child? She must be frightened half to death!" Joanna tried to rise, then realized she was far too dizzy.

"She took Rex for a long walk. I expect she is home by now, sitting in the kitchen with some bread and jam," Aunt Caroline said.

"Bread and jam," Joanna mused. "That sounds welcome. I should like that with a pot of tea, if you please. And then, I believe you may tell Susan and Bodkin that they may begin packing for London. It will take a few days, and by that time my head will be much better."

Aunt Caroline took one look at the determined girl on the sofa and nodded. "London. I hope you will not be sorry, my dear."

"I intend to find a husband," Joanna whispered, with a sparkle entering her eyes. "And I believe I know just the way to find the one I wish."

Chapter Fifteen

"How good of you to stay with me while Aunt Caroline is off on her wedding trip," Joanna said to her backgammon partner, Cousin Emma.

"Never let it be said that Emma Staunton does not know where her duty lies," the older woman replied with a tipsy smile. Cousin Emma was inclined to indulge in ratafia made to her own secret recipe. She patted her cambric cap trimmed with rows and rows of lace and hiccuped very faintly. She giggled, then gave Joanna an apologetic look.

"I will do well enough for a few months longer," Joanna assured her. "You ought to be able to return to the country by autumn, perhaps. I have little patience to wait much longer," Joanna said, while fiddling with one of her pieces and staring off to the opposite wall. She had never liked that painting—it should be replaced and soon.

"Wait for what? I confess I do not understand what you are planning." Cousin Emma gave Joanna a confused look, then moved her piece on the board.

"My plan. You shall see. When we go out today, I believe we shall go to a gallery where I may look for a new painting. Then you shall see what I am about. My hair has grown out, my scar has almost disappeared, and this morning I learned that *he* has returned to Town again."

"*He* being?" Cousin Emma inquired in her loud, rather carrying voice, after a sip of her ratafia.

"Why the man who saved my life, of course. And," Joanna mused, "I believe there will be a number of others in the soup."

"Do you know, you confuse me at times." Emma gave her

cousin a bewildered look, blinked her eyes several times, and rose from the game table. "I believe I am not cut out to be a backgammon player. Cards are more my thing," she said after a turn about the room.

Joanna privately agreed and wondered if Emma's card playing skills weren't just as erratic, given that she was usually a faint bit tipsy. However, one never knew about Emma. At times she could be amazingly sharp-witted.

When the two ladies left the London town house where Joanna had resided most of her years with Aunt Caroline, they were garbed in the very latest of gowns and possessed clever parasols of the most recent design. Joanna's was like a pagoda with delicate little fringe along the edge. Cousin Emma called it flirting fringe. Joanna laughed at that and gave the parasol an experimental twirl.

"I believe it will do," she said with a delighted giggle.

They drove along in the landau left for their use by Lord Osborn looking the picture of *a la modality*.

The gallery that proved to be their destination was also close to a print shop frequented by the young bucks and dandies of London.

Joanna gave demure looks and shy nods to one or two gentlemen she recognized. "Cousin Emma, you ought not say a word about my inheriting a fortune," Joanna said while they crossed the walk to enter the gallery shop.

"Not tell anyone you inherited a fortune?" Cousin Emma cried, her voice even louder than usual.

"Hush," Joanna said. "We would not wish any gentlemen to overhear you." She guided her confused cousin into the gallery and led her around to various paintings until Joanna found one that would do. It was a magnificent rendering of Windermere Lake.

"Joanna," Cousin Emma whispered when the delighted clerk was busily arranging for the painting to be billed to Joanna's bank and to be delivered to the lady that afternoon. "Joanna," Emma demanded with a tug on Joanna's sleeve, "I did not know you inherited a fortune."

"It is only modest, I suppose, but nothing to be sneezed at, my dear." Joanna tapped the floor with the furled parasol, idly watching the fringe jiggle.

"Really?" Cousin Emma elected to assume a wise look and nodded absently to the two gentlemen who entered the gallery.

"Miss Winterton, is it not?" said the first of the dandies after he had hastened to their side. His bow was elegant. He smiled at her as though she represented all the angels of heaven.

Joanna gave a delighted smile, for she had hoped he might nibble her lure. "Why Lord Atherton, how lovely to see you after this long time. I trust you are well?" Her curtsy was precisely correct, not too deep, yet enough to show she held the gentlemen in respect—and not a little interest.

"Well enough. May I present Sir Wilfred Dunmoll," he said with some reluctance after his friend gave him a subtle nudge.

"I believe we were introduced at a party given by Lady Jersey last spring. Lovely to see you again, Sir Wilfred."

The clerk bustled importantly to the front of the gallery shop with the papers for Joanna regarding the painting. She gave the two gentlemen a polite and dismissive smile, then turned her attention to the papers.

The gentlemen waited.

When Joanna and Cousin Emma were satisfied all was correct, they turned to leave only to find the two gentlemen at their side, opening the door with a flourish and escorting them to the landau with fond regard.

"May we have the pleasure of calling soon?" Lord Atherton said as he bent over Joanna's beautifully and expensively gloved hand.

"Oh, indeed, Lord Atherton, it would be charming. London is a trifle dull this time of year, although the heat of summer has fortunately abated. Do come by." She murmured her address, in the event he had not the connections to find it out, then requested their driver leave.

"London is a mite different from living in Wiltshire," Cousin Emma observed with one backward look at the two dandies watching their departure.

"It is blessedly different from a holiday in the Lake District as well," Joanna said with a reminiscent smile. "Do you know,

I have not been hit on the head, half drowned, nor tumbled from a carriage since I returned?"

"From what you have told me, you had a dreadful time up there. I believe I shall stay in the south," Cousin Emma declared. Since she was well-enough looking and possessed of a decent portion, Joanna suspected that Emma would most likely marry the widower who sought her hand once she decided to settle down. Emma was very independent, having a great number of relatives she loved to visit.

When they returned to the house, Mary and Rex came down the stairs to greet them.

"I am learning my numbers ever so well, Cousin Joanna," the girl reported. Rex barked, then wagged his tail when Joanna bent to scratch behind his ears.

"I do not recall anyone in the family with a daughter that age," Emma murmured.

"The connection is on my father's side and somewhat distant. But I quite enjoy having my little love here with me. You do like your new governess, do you not?" Joanna asked anxiously. "I thought her to be charming and pleasantly young."

"She is, and I understand why you had to stop teaching me. You are a very important lady," Mary said gravely.

"Well," Joanna said, laughing, "I did well with letters, but I confess that I am a trifle rusty at numbers." She ruffled Mary's curls, then drew her along with them into the drawing room. Shawe entered the room with a tray of tea and ratafia plus a plate of biscuits.

"We shall have nursery tea here, if you please," Joanna said while removing her bonnet.

What followed was a delightful hour of chatter and tea, with all the biscuits consumed by Mary and Rex, who had tagged along with them.

About three of the clock, Shawe ushered in another of the gentlemen Joanna had espied outside the print shop.

"Mr. Grace, how charming to see you again." Joanna rose to politely greet him, personally ushering him to a comfortable chair.

"London is happy to see that you are back and nicely out of mourning, if I may say so." He bowed over her hand, and joined them for a pleasant chat, quite obviously pleased at the attention shown him.

Shawe impassively showed in two of the other men from the print shop at about the time Mr. Grace was due to leave. They bestowed narrow and excruciatingly polite looks on one another.

Joanna exchanged a glance with Cousin Emma and smiled delightedly. Mary tugged Rex off to the nursery when the dog took exception to one of the men.

"Heard about your Aunt. Dashed nice she could marry after all this time," Reginald Ireton said smoothly once Mr. Grace had departed. "Fine chap, Osborn."

"Indeed he is," Joanna agreed. "He has been uncommonly kind to me."

"Is he the one who gave you the fortune?" Cousin Emma chimed in, her eyes a bewildered daze. She had consumed three glasses of her ratafia and was not thinking too clearly at the moment.

"No, dear, and we ought not speak of it," Joanna chided gently with an apologetic look at Mr. Ireton. He was a second son, she knew, and highly in need of a wealthy wife.

"Jolly good things, fortunes," his companion, the plump and also second son, Harry Letheby, declared.

"To be sure," Joanna agreed with a demure smile. The conversation turned to other matters and the gentlemen learned that the lovely and still unwed heiress would be attending Lady Smeeton's party the next evening.

When they were again alone, Cousin Emma leaned back in her chair and sighed. "My, Joanna, you do confuse a person. I did not recall an invitation from Lady Smeeton. But then, I did not know you were an heiress, either." She gently fanned herself while Joanna instructed the footman on hanging the painting that just arrived from the gallery.

"Not to worry, Cousin Emma. I shall take care of the details. All you have to do is sit and look pretty."

Since this required no effort at all, Emma continued fanning herself and looking enormously pleased with the world.

The Smeeton party overflowed with young and attractive guests the following evening, particularly gentlemen. The hostess looked a trifle dazed at her wonderful success at a time when London was usually thin of company.

"Lady Smeeton, how charming of you to entertain so beautifully when we were simply perishing from the doldrums," Joanna said with sincerity. "After my injury I could not go about for such a dreadfully long time, and now that I am in the swim of things again, your lovely party is just the thing," she vowed.

"Just how did it happen? Your accident, I mean," Lady Smeeton dared to inquire. Society had been abuzz when Miss Winterton returned with news of a mysterious accident while on holiday.

"Well, I was hit on the head quite badly. Sir Lucas Montfort sewed up my wound, you know. Of course the villain was after *him*, so I suppose he felt a bit guilty about *me* being injured, you see. It was a difficult time for me," Joanna concluded with a heartfelt sigh.

"Really," an enthralled Lady Smeeton said. "Do tell me more, my dear. Your Aunt Caroline?"

"Met and married that excellent Lord Osborn. He has been wondrously kind to me," Joanna beamed a smile at her hostess, one that was full of meaning. "He insisted that Cousin Emma and I have the use of his elegant landau—fitted in the latest fashion, to be sure. Is that not nice?"

"Oh, very nice, indeed," Lady Smeeton agreed. "And what about Sir Lucas Montfort?"

"Well," Joanna said with proper dignity and a touch of wistfulness, "he was required to remain in the Lake District for some time. I believe he handled the case against the madman who tried to take his—and my—life. You know how it is with the assizes. I fancy he comes to London to conclude matters in the superior courts here. I heard that he is come to Town lately."

"And he did not come to call to see how you are?" Lady Smeeton asked, overstepping the bounds of propriety in her eagerness to hear the entire story. What wonderful gossip, and she was the first to know, for Miss Winterton had just begun to go about Town.

"I am certain he is an exceedingly busy man," Joanna said with a regretful smile and a brave demeanor.

At that moment, Mr. Grace approached to ask Joanna for her hand in the coming country dance.

Happy she was now free to dance and enjoy the party as she wished—had wished for months and months—Joanna gave him a soft smile and instant assent.

Lady Smeeton watched the young woman who had endured so much go off to enjoy a country dance and sighed with delight that she could offer such pleasure to a young and brave heiress.

She swiftly crossed the room to chat with Sally Jersey, a woman after her own gossipy heart. "Sally, you will never guess what I just this minute learned."

Sally, never one to turn aside a bit of gossip, and now glad that she had come into Town from her nearby country house, drew closer. "What, my dear?"

The two huddled together for some minutes, glancing in Joanna's direction several times.

Mr. Grace brought Joanna back to Cousin Emma with perfect propriety, but handed her over to Lord Atherton with evident reluctance.

Lord Atherton drew Joanna into a lively reel where she revealed a decided talent for the dance. They were laughing with pleasure when he returned her to her chaperone. His smile faded when he saw Harry Letheby waiting, posy in hand.

"Hoped I would see you here this evening. Picked this up when I saw it, for it reminded me of you," he said with a bow to Joanna.

Truly pleased, for she had not been given flowers by either Mr. Underhill or Sir Lucas, Joanna dazzled Harry with her smile and accepted his hand for the next country dance with obvious delight.

"Dashed fellow has a consumptive brother who's a viscount," Lord Atherton grumbled. "Pots of money, to boot. Thought old Harry needed the blunt. Can't as badly as I do," his lordship complained to his good friend Sir Wilfred.

"He don't cut as good a figure as you, and that cravat is a disaster," Sir Wilfred replied, holding his quizzing glass to examine the competition. "And I need money more than either of you two, so do not cry on my shoulder."

"She's a lively creature—pretty, too," Lord Atherton murmured to his friend so no one else could overhear.

"Nice of her to come out of mourning without waiting for the Season to begin."

"By that time, I might be well and truly in the hatches," his lordship said gloomily.

"I told you not to bet on that horse," Sir Wilfred chided.

"Shh. Here she comes again. Dare I try for the waltz?"

"No. You are a trifle awkward at waltzing. I shall have the honor." And Sir Wilfred strolled off to claim the belle of the party for the highlight of the evening, the waltz.

Joanna was tired and almost breathless when she was deposited with her cousin at the conclusion of the dancing. But she was happy. Her cousin had been content to chat with such luminaries as Lady Jersey, who had shown a flattering interest in dear Cousin Joanna.

Emma revealed the conversation while she and Joanna were driven home in the landau. "I want you to know that I let her hear about your travails, my dear. You must be the bravest woman in London to have given chase to that madman."

"Or the most foolish," Joanna murmured. "What was her reaction?"

"She said she intends to have a little party while in Town and insists that we attend. Is that not kind of her?"

"Indeed," Joanna said with a gleam in her eyes that promised mischief.

The following day brought floral tributes to delight any girl's heart and Joanna was no exception.

"Look at all these flowers!" she cried to Emma. "I vow there must be a dozen bouquets here. And that nice Mr. Grace sent you a posy as well! How thoughtful of him."

While Joanna sniffed her flowers, Emma looked more dazed than usual when handed her posy.

"Oh, my, it has been many years since I was given a posy. The year of my come-out, I expect. I did not take, you know," Emma concluded sadly. "But I have a very agreeable life. And I am so pleased to be able to assist you, dear cousin."

Joanna persuaded Emma they ought to take a drive in the landau, Emma being afraid of horses and not willing to actually ride on one.

"With the carriage and a driver up front, it is not so dangerous," she explained. "We shall be quite safe from harm's way."

Joanna recalled her perilous carriage drive to Rydal Mount, the goal she had never reached, and did not reveal how dangerous a carriage might be, given a dead bird or two

But Emma remembered once they were bowling along in the park. "Oh, my! Dear Joanna. I ought not have agreed to this. Are you not yet frightened of a carriage drive? I would be forever," Emma concluded with a shiver at the thought of what Joanna had endured.

"I trust some gentleman would come to our rescue." Then she tilted her parasol to look another direction and quietly said, "Look, there is Mr. Grace and Mr. Ireton. And I believe that is Harry Letheby trotting up behind them. How odd," Joanna reflected aloud, "neither of those men look pleased to see him."

"Well, I am pleased to see how well you are taking—and it is not even the Season! Perhaps my mama ought to have taken me to London when there were not so many other girls making their come-out at the same time?" Cousin Emma wondered aloud.

"And bruited about word of a fortune," Joanna murmured, but was turned away so Cousin Emma did not hear this last comment.

"Miss Winterton," A familiar voice exclaimed. "You appear to be healed and back in fine form again."

"Sir Lucas? What a surprise. I thought you miles away in some musty old court."

He frowned, then cleared his brow and said, "I am pleased to know you thought of me in any way, my dear."

Joanna gave him the most demure of smiles, then turned her head to greet Mr. Grace, Mr. Ireton, and Mr. Harry Letheby. She smiled and offered her hand. "You are all most wonderful, you know. I cannot recall when I have seen such lovely flowers. You quite turn my head." She blushed and looked adorable.

Lucas stared at the scene before him. Could this actually be his Joanna behaving like a simpering schoolgirl? His brave girl with the direct speech, who said precisely what was on her mind and no mincing of words in the least? He listened to the trio of fawning, flattering fools dumping a dozen butterboats over Joanna's head and wondered why she didn't send them off with a flea in their collective ears.

"Joanna," he said, interrupting the flow of adulation, "I shall stop by to see you later."

"La, Sir Lucas," she said sadly, "I shall do my best to accommodate you. We have so many callers nowadays." She fluttered her eyelashes at him and gave her pagoda parasol a twirl. Then she ordered the driver on and disappeared into the distance with the trio riding along at her side of the carriage.

All of which served to render Lucas speechless.

What had happened? He was determined to find out. In one of those fortuitous occurrences that so rarely occur, Lady Jersey chanced to drive in the park that afternoon and when she saw him, beckoned him to her side.

"Sir Lucas, I am so pleased to see you again. You have been gone far too long. I trust you have put that little incident of last spring from your mind by now?" she inquired in a brisk manner.

Lucas grimly wondered if one truly described being jilted at the altar a little incident. He revealed none of his thoughts, however. He bowed from his saddle, and smiled at her. "Indeed, ma'am."

Lady Jersey was just as susceptible as any other female when it came to one of those famous smiles Sir Lucas was so accomplished at bestowing. "Ah, good," she managed to say. "I wish you would call on me later. And I am having a little party Friday next. 'Tis not the Season, but London is amazingly busy this year, in spite of the month. You promise to come?"

"I shall call on you later and you may be certain I will be at your little party."

She passed along, and Lucas laughed to himself. Sally did

not know how to give a *little* party. He'd wager that all of Society present now in London would attend. And that meant that Joanna would be there as well. Then he could get to the bottom of what was going on.

He turned his attention to two young girls, most likely in London to gain a bit of polish and become accustomed to *ton* manners and life before the Season began. He rode over to greet them as he knew their mother slightly.

They were nice; nice clothing and nice manners and nice faces. They were also a trifle lacking in sparkle. Perhaps that was an acquired accomplishment. Somehow he doubted it. Joanna most likely sparkled from birth. The thought put him into the dismals and he rode home.

He needed a bride, he knew that. Joanna was impossible, too independent, too outspoken, and, it seemed, too courted by others to be considered for the position. He could ask her opinion, then decided that might not be wise. Women could be the oddest creatures at times. As practical as Joanna had shown herself to be, he wondered—most uneasily—if she did not have her moments as well. Witness her performance in the park.

Once home, he changed and then marched along to where Joanna lived with that addlepated Emma Staunton as chaperone. Why anyone had the idea that she made an adequate sponsor was beyond Lucas. He had met her last year and wondered if she was quite right in the head. But, he admitted, she seemed a kindly soul.

The butler looked Lucas over and condescended to usher him into the drawing room with dispatch. Lucas wondered what manner of reception he would receive, given the performance he'd witnessed in the park.

"Sir Lucas," Joanna said quietly, rising to greet him with an outstretched hand. "You see I am quite healed now, and able to return to Society." She drew him along with her to the sofa. "And now I must find a husband, as you will recall, before my father remembers I am unwed and finds one for me." She grimaced, then laughed.

She had reached the heart of the matter without his having to query her, quite like the Joanna he recalled from Grasmere.

"As to that, I suppose I am in much the same position. My aunt reminds me in frequent letters that my duty is to find a bride to carry on the name. I suppose relatives are ever the same," he said reflectively.

She gestured for him to sit down. Lucas noticed that her cousin dozed in a comfortable chair over in the corner of the room, her feet propped on a little stool.

Joanna smiled fondly and said, "As it is you come to call, I shall allow her to nap. I fear her life with me is more active than she is accustomed to living."

Lucas was not sure if he was pleased with the idea that he was so harmless that he did not require a chaperone to protect Joanna's virtue. Then, again, perhaps Joanna was merely being kind. She had been most considerate of her aunt Caroline, as he recalled. In fact, she had been compassionate toward everyone but him. For the moment he quite forgot her chase after the madman, at which time she was hit on the head for her pains.

"Let me see that scar. You have suffered no ill effects? No headaches?" Lucas leaned over to examine the obediently bowed head. In among the soft curls he found the thin line that showed where he had taken the stitches that day not so very long ago.

"I have had a few headaches, but," she assured him when she saw how worried he became, "they are trifling. And they become fewer and fewer as days go by."

An enormous bouquet of flowers was brought into the drawing room and placed on a table. The card was offered to Joanna.

She begged leave to read it, then smiled when she saw who it was from. "Mr. Grace," she informed Lucas.

"He is naught but a fortune hunter," Lucas said quickly, although normally he would have kept his tongue between his teeth rather than gossip.

"I suppose we all are when it comes to that," she said mildly.

Lucas had expected her to round on him and was surprised at the meekness of her reply. He gave her a questioning look and was rewarded with a sweet smile.

"Can you think of one person who does not look to gain by a marriage? Even our good prince married for money, and I wager his daughter will as well," Joanna observed quietly. "I cannot blame Mr. Grace if he seeks an heiress."

"And are you one?" Lucas asked, for he'd not heard of her wealth before, merely that she was comfortable.

"Passably well to do," she admitted. Then she gazed at him with an impish look and said, "And you? You are well? No accidents, no sinking boats or overturning carriages? I suppose you have not had one incident to mar your serene existence."

He forgot about fortune hunters in the force of her charm. "I am fine, and I look forward to seeing you from time to time while in the City. I have to finish up the business of that chap who tried so hard to kill us off. He cannot be allowed to be free to murder some innocent soul."

"Indeed. Do promise to consult me on a bride. I know all manner of little secrets. And I," she confided innocently, "I shall seek your advice on the matter of a husband. You know the sort of husband I should seek. I want a man who is strong yet loving, kind and courteous. Surely you could assist me should I need help? Lady Jersey has also vowed to see me wed before long, so I have hopes."

Somehow Lucas found himself at her side, walking down the stairs to the front door. He held his hat in hand and felt as awkward as a schoolboy. "Please be careful," he said, then realized that he truly did care for her future. What an odd position to be in.

Sally Jersey welcomed him into a scented room with a delighted embrace that was at once feminine and distancing. She never forgot that she was Lady Jersey. Perhaps she was also conscious of her mother-in-law's reputation.

"And now, dear boy, you simply must tell me what happened this summer up at Grasmere. I had no idea that a holiday in the country could be so full of excitement."

Lucas smiled wryly and said, "Then you obviously have not spent much time in Miss Winterton's company. She has a knack of attracting trouble." Lucas remembered likening

Joanna to a flower who attracted bees. Like sweet honey. He thought of her kisses, and sighed slightly.

"Well, this is what happened," he began and continued with a highly edited version of what had occurred while he was in Grasmere with Joanna. Although they were not precisely *with* each other, it was as like to it. He had almost lived at Rose Cottage, having his dinner there and spending hours enjoying the dry sitting room and cozy fire when it rained.

"My," Lady Jersey murmured, wide-eyed and visibly impressed at the conclusion of his tale. "You do realize that I simply cannot keep this to myself!"

Lucas nodded, smiled, and wondered how this would affect his marriage prospects. He said as much and Lady Jersey laughed. "I know just the woman for you."

Chapter Sixteen

Lucas left the Earl of Jersey's home without being any the wiser in regard to Sally's choice for a bride.

"I must see for myself if you will do, Sir Lucas," she had said with a flirtatious lift of a brow.

Heaven protect the bachelor from matchmaking women, he thought later on while sauntering along Bond Street. He nodded to various acquaintances who, like himself, had come to London for a variety of reasons—although he doubted any of them came to prosecute a man who had tried, and bloody well near succeeded, to kill him.

Bored with what he saw to view in various windows, he took a hackney home, then ordered his horse. Perhaps a ride in the park would calm his nerves before he was required at court. He did not like what he had to do.

He rode past the house where Joanna Winterton resided with her batty cousin. What could he expect next from that quarter?

Upon reaching the park, he headed down along Rotten Row at the customary pace. He'd prefer a wild gallop, but knew better than to flout convention.

Then he saw a young woman coming toward him wearing a rich blue habit, a jaunty jocky hat perched atop her head, and accompanied by Lord Atherton and Sir Wilfred Dunmoll. He'd recognize their hacks anywhere.

He spurred his horse forward, whether to pass her quickly or meet her, he wasn't sure. He did know that his call to her only yesterday seemed ages ago.

"Good day, Miss Winterton. Out for a bit of fresh air?" he inquired, after a glance at her escorts.

"Indeed, sir. I must confess the park seems mild after the wilds of the Lake District. Do you find it so?"

"It is more peaceful," he admitted. "Yet there is an untamed beauty about the area," he said with a slow smile, the sort he knew disconcerted her. "I found that most enjoyable."

Her cheeks grew pink and her eyes flashed with that familiar sparkle. She tilted up her chin and smiled. "Why, Sir Lucas, one might think the City bores you. Can that be? The premier rake of the City is bored? Perhaps you grow old?"

He bowed, acknowledging her hit. Rather than continue their sparring, he said, "Perhaps." He tipped his hat and murmured the names of the two men, who had sat silently through the encounter.

He rode off, knowing he would like to banter with her longer. But, he confessed, he would far rather kiss those sweet lips than talk, and those were dangerous thoughts for a bachelor. Especially one who had promised his aunt that he would marry soon. He wondered who Miss Winterton would select among all the beaux who courted her.

None of the chaps was good enough for her, of course. He couldn't think of one of them who would take the time to really know her and all her interesting turns of mind. Perhaps someday down the road . . .

His thoughts were halted when a chicken dashed across the road followed by an irate lad who chased the bird as though his life depended upon it. Lucas laughed as he had not in ages. His mood lightened, he completed his ride, and headed for his house. Once changed, he was to attend the court session. He hoped the matter could soon be resolved.

Joanna glanced at Sir Lucas as he rode past them. Oh, she had not mistaken that gleam in his eyes. Wicked man, to remind her of the "untamed beauty" of the hills. She had no doubt but that he recalled a kiss he had stolen from her. She grimaced a moment, then smiled at Lord Atherton.

"Do you attend the party that Lady Jersey gives?"

"Indeed," he responded quickly. "I fancy your entire court will be there and you can reign queen supreme." He looked over to Sir Wilfred for confirmation.

"He is right. Lady Jersey has invited us all. London is a bit thin of company at the moment. Lady Jersey always likes to have a goodly crowd attend one of her affairs."

"But, dear sirs, I have no wish to reign as a queen. I am content to see my friends and enjoy a few dances." Joanna chuckled when she thought of the dance she had enjoyed with Sir Lucas while in Grasmere. Yes, he was most likely correct when he spoke of the "untamed beauty" in Grasmere—even if she would never admit to it.

"If it please you to think in that manner, we shall not argue. But who is this?" The two men slowed as they viewed the stranger who approached most purposefully toward Joanna. They placed their mounts slightly ahead of hers in an instinctively protective move.

Since she had taken the trouble to quiz her cousin and her aunt about any young or otherwise unmarried male relatives of her new stepmother, Joanna had not the least difficulty in recognizing the gentleman. She stifled a groan with effort.

"Cousin Joanna, I presume. Cousin Emma said you'd be dressed like a peacock. I had not the least trouble finding you." He bowed as well as he could, given his girth.

"Cousin Bertram Rolleston," Joanna explained to the two gentlemen at her side. She introduced them, all the while assessing her new cousin.

He was not precisely fat, Joanna decided charitably. There was simply more weight than his height could attractively accommodate. His voice was not truly displeasing; he most likely had a cold, and therefore sounded like a sick frog for that reason.

She could not like his eyes, however. They were cold and hard, a stone gray color that seemed to have no life in them even if he were trying to please her with his polite speech. She had heard that Bertram Rolleston was not a kind person. She was prepared to believe it.

The four rode back to Joanna's house, an uneasy silence punctuated only by her infrequent queries.

"Your aunt, my new stepmama, is well?"

"She is," he said disinterestedly.

"And my dear papa?" Joanna was prompted to ask several minutes later.

"Your father is a most generous man," Cousin Bertram said with a smile that most definitely did not reach those cold gray eyes.

Lord Atherton and Sir Wilfred, being finely attuned to certain nuances in accent—as fortune hunters were apt to be— looked at each other in dismay.

"I know," Joanna said demurely. "I have enjoyed living with Aunt Caroline these many years. Dear Papa has generously footed our bills. And now dear Cousin Emma is a great comfort to me."

This reference to the Staunton family shatter-brain brought a frown of awesome proportions to Cousin Bertram's brow. "I trust the arrangement is only temporary."

"Not that you need concern yourself with my problems, Cousin, but indeed, the arrangement is quite temporary. I believe all will be in train in a month or so," she murmured with hope clear in her tone.

"You are not betrothed, are you?" Alarm rang in his voice and manner.

The other two men first looked at her, then her cousin, with equal amounts of apprehension.

"No, although a young lady must always nurture expectations, must she not?" she said serenely.

The men agreed in varying degrees. Lord Atherton and Sir Wilfred left Joanna and her new relative in front of her house. Mr. Rolleston dismounted and handed over his horse to the groom who ran up to tend to Joanna's mount.

"You are coming in now, Cousin Bertram?" Joanna asked in affronted surprise.

"I do not have much time to spend in London this time of year. Country matters to tend to, you know." He followed Joanna up the stairs to the drawing room, entering as though he were an occupant rather than a caller.

Joanna very much feared that he meant to force a brief courtship on her, then—with the blessing of her father—compel her to marry him. It was not an agreeable thought.

"It would be a shame were you to travel to London and not

sample what delights are to be found here. Although the major theaters are closed now, there are other offerings to be found."

"I do not approve of the theater, nor of most of the other frivolous entertainments to be found in the City," he declared, quite as though Joanna had invited him to attend wicked and abandoned affairs.

"Well, I am to attend a little party given by Lord and Lady Jersey Friday next. Perhaps you might like to attend?" Joanna said with forced courtesy. "Since you are by way of being a relative and new to London, I should be pleased to request you join me."

He thawed slightly at the mention of members of the peerage. He might not have heard of the Jerseys, living on a secluded farm as he did, but he did recognize a title. "If it is no trouble."

Joanna suspected that even if it were a great deal of trouble, he would expect her to do her utmost for him.

"What is this, Cousin Joanna! I did not know you had returned so soon. And to be entertaining a gentleman in the drawing room is not at all the thing," Cousin Emma exclaimed.

Joanna was thankful that Emma did not carry on with that theme. Rather, she had taken a second look at the guest and frowned.

"Bertram Rolleston, I believe, is it not? I never forget a face." It was evident that the memory was not a pleasing one.

"Quite, Miss Staunton." Emma, being the eldest of the unmarried Staunton girls, could lay claim to the distinction of being called *Miss* Staunton over the others. When she was about, Aunt Caroline had been reduced to Miss Caroline.

"Mr. Rolleston is visiting in London for a brief time," Joanna explained.

"Why?" Cousin Emma inquired with improper curiosity.

Since Joanna needed to know this she made no rebuke, subtle or otherwise, to her outspoken cousin.

Bertram looked disconcerted, even uncomfortable. Joanna suspected that Emma had forced his hand. It was almost laughable, were it not for the frightful truth she feared he might speak.

"I have received permission from Lord Winterton to pay my addresses to Joanna," he said with an unrefined haste. He stood in his countrified glory, hands behind his back, feet well apart, looking apprehensive—as he well might. He also had the look of a stubborn mule, a very rustic mule to be sure.

"I see," Joanna replied, slowing walking over to stand by the window so that her face would be in shadow. She did not wish Bertram to be able to detect her thoughts. She turned to face him.

"Joanna is much in demand here in London," Cousin Emma said with a spiteful glance at Bertram.

"I do enjoy the company of a great many friends, it is true," Joanna amended. She was afraid that if Bertram thought she was in a fair way to developing a partiality for a particular gentleman, he might act. And what nature that act might take was enough to make Joanna very careful when selecting her words.

"You are perhaps skilled in the art of conversation?"

"La, Joanna can chat about anything under the sun," Emma declared with misplaced enthusiasm.

"I like exchanging views with interesting people," Joanna said with caution. "There is much to learn if one listens."

"As is only proper with a female," Bertram said pompously. "She needs to know her place."

"Where will you be staying while in the City?" Cousin Emma said with her usual directness.

Bertram looked pained, then said, "I do not suppose . . ."

"I believe that Ibbetson's is the most proper and economical place to stay. Our vicar was used to stay there when he came up to Town," Joanna said swiftly before Emma might plunge them into duck soup. It seemed to Joanna that Bertram was about to most improperly request lodging with them. She also feared that the inquisitive Emma might allow it, just so to keep him beneath her nose.

He squirmed, but allowed that he would take a room at that establishment.

Once the door had closed behind him, Joanna let out a sigh of vexation. "As if I did not have enough worries—now this."

"If that is a sample of your newly acquired cousins, you

have a problem," Emma murmured in one of her rare moments of astute observation.

"Indeed, you are correct. Well, I had best change into a gown, then perhaps I had best pay a call on Lady Jersey. I believe I need some help."

Thus it was an exquisitely garbed Joanna, dressed in delicate white muslin adorned with rows of tucking and discreet bits of lace, ventured to call on Lady Jersey.

She was admitted at once and only had to wait for ten minutes before her ladyship appeared.

"My dear girl, what a lovely surprise. I trust all is well?" the clever Lady Jersey inquired, suspecting that something had happened to put her caller in a bother. "Or has a problem popped up?"

"Indeed, my lady. I do not know what to do or where to turn for advice," Joanna said, twisting her handkerchief between her fingers. "My new cousin Bertram Rolleston is come to London. He is nephew to my new stepmama. My father has given him permission to pay his addresses to me," Joanna blurted out in her distress.

"I see," the intelligent lady replied thoughtfully. She might not be so very much older than Joanna, but she knew everyone, had heard every scandal worth repeating and a few that weren't, and had acquired a certain social power that few attained.

"I gather this match is not to your liking?"

"If I may be candid, the first match my father arranged for me was most repugnant. This is worse, if possible."

Surprise at this revelation raised Sally's brows. "Indeed? You must have wished us all to perdition."

"Your words, not mine," Joanna said with a wan smile.

"Well, then, the thing to do is to arrange matters to your own liking. Dare I assume you have a partiality for a certain gentleman?"

"I do," Joanna confessed out loud for the first time.

"How does he feel about you, not that it matters particularly?" her ladyship probed.

"Well," Joanna hedged, unwilling to reveal those stolen

kisses, "he has cared for me most tenderly, risked his life for me, and in general seemed to enjoy my company."

"That is more than most women enjoy," Lady Jersey said with a pleased nod. "I shall help you all I can, dear girl. I think I know your inamorato. I have invited him to attend my little party Friday next."

Joanna blushed. "All of London attends, I suspect," she said with a smile. "I have even promised my Cousin Bertram to ask on his behalf. I suspect I cannot come without him."

"But I think we shall arrange it so that you do not have to leave *with* him. I shall see to his disposal, never worry." Lady Jersey brushed off her hands as though eliminating a bit of dust.

Since Joanna wished the man to the ends of the earth, that would be a relief.

"What does your plan involve?"

"Let me see . . . I wish you to be quite prepared, my dear girl. What do you think of this?" And she proceeded to develop the plan that had this instant presented itself to her clever mind.

Joanna was at first aghast, then amused, and finally laughed with joy. "You truly are an inventive lady and, I fancy, quite resourceful as well. I shall do just as you suggest. I will be prepared and hope that all goes well." She saluted her ladyship as her superior.

They both rose, gave each other appraising looks and smiled. "I believe we make an excellent pair of conspirators. Oh, I am so pleased I elected to come into London just now," Lady Jersey crowed.

"I am, too, my lady. I am, too." Joanna curtsied nicely, and left the house full of plans. There was much to do for her part, and she was not quite certain just how to go about it all.

"Miss Winterton," said a familiar male voice, interrupting her musings, "surely nothing can be so dire."

"Sir Lucas," Joanna said with a startled jump, "how you surprised me. I fear I was deep in contemplation." She failed to look about for her carriage, intent upon the man at her side.

"All is well?" he asked, showing concern in his manner.

"Well? Just as I feared, my papa sent one of his new wife's

nephews to London with express permission to pay his addresses," she confided in a burst of ire. Sir Lucas was one of the very few with whom she had felt this perfect accord.

"No! And who is this presumptuous puppy, may I inquire?" Sir Lucas revealed polite interest, making Joanna feel as though she was perhaps imposing by her revelation.

"Mr. Bertram Rolleston. But you cannot be concerned about my little difficulties, can you? I vow, women tend to worry about every little thing," she said in apology, backing away from him. "Excuse me, I ought not have troubled you with my problems. I shall come about, I assure you."

He stepped forward, placing a light hand on her arm. "Joanna, surely we know each other better than most? And I do know Rolleston. Met him when I was in the country. Had to go with my agent to look over some sheep. Mr. Rolleston is not the most honest of dealers," he said in what Joanna guessed to be gross understatement. Cousin Emma had related a few things that indicated that Bertram was a trifle on the shady side.

"I suspected as such from what Emma said. I have no intention of marrying Mr. Rolleston," she declared with a tilt of her chin.

"You most assuredly deserve better than that puff-guts. May I be of any assistance?"

Joanna studied him, then asked, "How does one go about ordering a post chaise? I require one, and for obvious reasons would not ask my cousin to help me." She withstood the keen look Sir Lucas gave her quite well.

"When do you wish this coach?" He toyed with the quizzing glass that dangled over his elegant waistcoat. It was a silvery hue to compliment his silvery hair and Joanna thought it striking under his coat of deep green.

"I must have it the night of the Jersey party," she dared to confide in him.

"You are not going to do something you will regret, are you?"

"Oh, I hope not," she said with great sincerity.

"I shall make the necessary arrangements. You intend to

travel far?" She sensed he wanted to know all, but she had no intention of revealing that much to *him*, of all people.

"To the north," she admitted.

"The Lake District?" he inquired with a gleam creeping into his fine, dark eyes.

"That would be telling, would it not? Suffice to say that my plans are well thought out and I intend to follow through with them. I shall evade my odious cousin Bertram and find my heart's desire all in one effort."

She beamed a dazzling smile on him, then climbed into her waiting landau, and was off.

Lucas watched her carriage disappear into the hubbub of London traffic. What on earth was she up to? he wondered. Then he noticed that Joanna had evidently come from the Jersey house. What had those two been plotting? That they were doing precisely that he had no doubt.

Well, he would do as promised. He had no intention of thwarting her in an attempt to avoid marriage to that corkbrained fool Rolleston. But, he decided he would linger in the area to see who it was that she had claimed as her heart's desire.

He suddenly decided it was a fine day for a few rounds at "Gentleman" Jackson's Boxing Establishment at 13 Bond Street. A fine teacher, the former champion could be counted on to provide a bit of sparring. Not that Lucas would actually box with the gentleman, but there would be someone there who would oblige.

With a grim set to his mouth, Lucas set off for Bond Street and his sport. He felt an urge to practice his punishing right.

Meanwhile, Joanna debated on what to take along with her when she fled London. Never having contemplated such a thing before, she sensibly made a mental list of practical needs and packed the minimum in a large valise. This would go to the Jersey house, to be kept in waiting for the exact moment of departure.

Once this had been sent off, with Cousin Emma none the wiser, Joanna restlessly paced the drawing room, pausing to gaze out of the window from time to time.

"La, Cousin, you have a case of the fidgets. Do you worry so about your Cousin Bertram?" Emma inquired gently.

Seizing upon a likely reason for her uneasiness, Joanna swiftly agreed. "Indeed so, Emma. He is not the sort of man one easily trusts."

"And whom do you think trustworthy?"

Not about to be trapped into revealing her partiality, Joanna shrugged and replied, "Oh, about any of the gentlemen I have met here could fill that bill, I suppose."

"Lord Atherton is pleasant. But then, I fancy Sir Wilfred would make an excellent husband," Emma said, cautiously probing.

"True. And Mr. Grace or Mr. Ireton or even Harry Letheby would be a good spouse as well, I imagine," Joanna added, wishing to confuse matters as much as possible. With the unfortunate habit of blurting out precisely what one did not wish known, Emma could not be confided in at all. This was a pity, for Joanna had come to like her scatter-brained cousin very much. While a bit totty in the head, she was nevertheless a good friend.

Come Friday evening Joanna felt as though an entire troup of fairies were performing pirouettes in her stomach. She tried to conceal her nervousness from Emma, although that dear lady might well attribute the nerves to going among such exalted company.

"Joanna," Emma said earnestly, "I am so pleased you invited me to stay with you. I have never so enjoyed myself, not at any of my relatives."

"You are welcome to remain in this house as long as you wish," Joanna vowed. One way or another she would repay her good-hearted cousin.

The Jersey home was overflowing as might be expected of one of Sally's *little* affairs. Anything less *little* Joanna couldn't imagine. Since Emma and she had arrived early at Sally's suggestion, she went immediately to her hostess.

"All is in readiness," she whispered. "Your valise is in the closet near the foot of the stairs. The footman is instructed to place it into the coach as soon as it arrives. He will let me know as well. I dared not tell him your name, for servants are wont to gossip, you know."

Emma had been so captivated by the decor of the house that she had paid not the least attention to the whispered conversation. When Joanna tugged at her sleeve, Emma obediently drifted along at her side. Before the dancing the two women wandered through the rooms open to view and marveled at all they saw.

"I shall just sit here and watch you," Emma declared when the dancing was to begin.

Joanna had different ideas. As soon as she spotted Cousin Bertram—for she had insisted he use his own transportation—she suggested that he squire her dear Emma in a country dance.

Once that was en train, Joanna turned her hand to her own plans. She searched the room until she found her quarry.

"Lord Atherton," she cooed, "how lovely to see you here."

Not proof against such a reception from a lady he hoped to interest, his lordship begged Joanna's hand for the country dance and she accepted with delight.

After that Sir Wilfred appeared pleading for a dance.

Since Emma was still in a daze from the energetic country dance—and having Bertram step on her toes no less than a dozen times—Joanna had no one to consult. She went along with him and seemed to enjoy his company hugely.

Mr. Grace and Mr. Ireton, along with Harry Letheby, popped up the moment that dance concluded and Harry demanded the next reel.

Joanna smiled bravely and hoped she would survive the evening in sufficient form to complete her plan.

It was during the reel that she spotted Sir Lucas. He paused to chat with Lady Jersey for some moments before coming into the room. She peered over a gentleman's head, then around a lady's evening hat to see where he went.

The card room. Double drat. She chanced to catch Sally's eye and relaxed when that lady smiled and nodded ever so slightly. It would be all right. Sally was not one to mislead.

A country dance with Mr. Grace was followed by a

quadrille with Reginald Ireton. After this taxing dance Joanna longed for a respite.

A minuet was to be next and Joanna wondered if she would have a partner.

"Joanna," a low, familiar voice said softly in her ear, "would you do me the honor of this next dance? I do not see Cousin Emma anywhere about. She is not ill, is she?" Sir Lucas inquired.

"She is with Cousin Bertram," Joanna managed to say in her surprise. "He stepped on her toes so much that she demanded he help her to a seat in the garden where she might be restored."

"What a pity for her."

He took Joanna's hand in his strong clasp and led her through the first of the elegant movements. After the strenuous quadrille, a minuet was utterly delightful.

"You are enjoying yourself this evening?"

"I have escaped Cousin Bertram and found pleasant company," she admitted with a mischievous smile.

"Your post chaise awaits you outside. I would like to know who goes with you. I doubt it is Emma, somehow," he said with an inquisitive look.

"No. It is not Emma," Joanna said, relishing the perplexed look on his face.

"Then who?" he demanded softly.

"I suppose you would not come to say goodbye to me, would you, my friend?" Joanna said with what she hoped was a properly wistful manner.

"Your friend?" he said, somewhat startled. Then he frowned and nodded. "You meet someone and wish me to approve the chap. Very well, I will come."

Joanna took his hand and slipped from the room with scarcely anyone the wiser. They skimmed down the main stairs to the front door, where a footman stood at attention.

"I believe my post chaise awaits me?" she said with a significant look at the fellow.

"Indeed, miss. All is in readiness for your departure."

"But there is no one here," Lucas objected.

"In the carriage," Joanna said with a tug at his hand.

"I see," Lucas said, clearly in a fog. He followed Joanna to the chaise and helped her inside, unable to see the identity of her chosen mate in the darkness. Then, when he would release her hand, Lucas found himself pulled urgently within.

He scrambled to the seat even as the chaise took off at a fast pace along the street. "What in the world is going on?" he demanded once he had gained the seat and turned to face Joanna.

"I am eloping with you to Gretna Green, sir. You are my captive and I'll not let you go." She smiled merrily into his dark eyes, hoping she had guessed rightly.

He shook his head, scarcely believing what he had heard. "Now, Joanna, I know you are a madcap, but this is going a trifle far, you must admit."

"If I must wed, it will be to no other. For in spite of your sometimes less than winning ways, I have come to love you dearly, Sir Lucas Montfort." She gave him a hesitant smile. "Will you please be my loving husband?"

He discovered there was nothing in the world that he wished for more than this. Lucas drew her into his arms and gave her a simple answer. "Yes, indeed. Particularly the loving part."

And following that pledge, there was precious little to be heard for some time. The post chaise sped along the Great North Road as ordered.